EVERYTHING I AM

JENNY BOND

A catalogue record for this book is available from the National Library of Australia

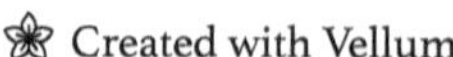
Created with Vellum

$$1$$

THE FIRST QUESTION RATTLED HER. It gave her the feeling of stepping on a step that wasn't there. But Eva had told her when they first began their sessions that she liked to ask the hard questions and Rebecca had to be prepared.

'Like George Negus,' Eva had joked, releasing a throaty chuckle.

Rebecca soon came to realise that this woman spoke the truth, always. Often that was hard to bear.

Today, she had only just sat down on the faded sofa in Eva's office when she was hit with it.

'How did you love your brother?'

She wasn't expecting Luke to be the focus of her therapy just yet. Rebecca had hoped there would be more time before she was forced to go there. Surely Joe would be the logical person to begin with, she thought.

'How?' she asked.

Eva nodded.

The word ricocheted off the surfaces of Rebecca's mind, but she couldn't focus; she could only gasp. There were just some things she'd never been able to articulate. Trying to answer Eva's question was like trying to describe waiting for a set – that potent mix of trepidation and excitement. In the past, she'd attempted to put the experience into words, but nothing she'd ever written had measured up. Nothing had ever truly captured that sensation. Her feelings for Luke fell into the same category. They were indescribable.

'Unconditionally?' she replied, her voice rising, the response a question in itself.

'This isn't a test, Rebecca. There is no right or wrong answer, just the truth.' She paused a moment before repeating the question.

'How did you love him?'

She didn't have an answer. Rebecca didn't know how she had loved Luke ... or how she loved him still. She tried again to think of a way to say it, but nothing came. She shook her head, defeated.

Eva looked at her for a moment then jotted down an unreadable sentence – her handwriting was a scrawl – underlining the words three times. Her pen left blue grooves in the paper.

'This will be a good point of reference,' she said.

Eva's second question was simpler.

'Why are you here?'

Even though Rebecca knew exactly how she was going to respond – in fact, she had already played this particular scenario out in her imagination – she took a deep breath before answering.

'I truly believe I'm losing my mind. Losing myself.'

Her psychiatrist smiled gently and tapped the point of her biro lightly on the notepad.

'That's an excellent place to begin.'

'MY BROTHER and I showered together until we were thirteen or so, until my mother found us examining each other's "bibs and bobs", as she liked to say. We weren't regular siblings. Twins aren't regular. We bathed together, slept together and played together long after regular brothers and sisters would have stopped because, well ... we always had. It was painful when Mum forced us to stop, a little like trying to pull apart two pieces of paper after the glue has dried. It's never neat. There's always damage. We had an unusual family dynamic, I realise now, although Mum and Dad did a good job of keeping everything as normal as they could. It must have been extremely difficult for my parents at times.'

Eva looked over her bifocals at Rebecca.

'Do you realise you always refer to Luke as "my brother"?'

'No,' replied Rebecca, shivering, suddenly aware of the boxy portable air cooler whirring in the corner blowing cold air on her naked arms.

But she did. It was a conscious choice she made, a way of distancing herself from Luke.

'I grew up extremely close to my sister,' Eva said. 'She was only a year older than me and we were very close. We still are. But your experience must be different. What was it like being a twin to Luke?' she asked, pen poised.

Turning to the misted, rain-splattered window, Rebecca scoured her mind, attempting to express plainly the nature of existing as her brother's twin. Her hands began to shake. She pressed them under her thighs, breathed deeply, taking in the pungency of Eva's coffee brewing in the kitchen.

'Luke was more than a brother. He was my best friend, my protector and my sounding board. It was freeing, I suppose, to have that person always within reach. But for me, that security brought with it an overwhelming sense of responsibility. It tethered me to him.'

Eva hastily scrawled notes in her untamed cursive, four words to a line. As her pen scratched the paper, Rebecca caught sight of the tattoo on the soft, loose underside of Eva's forearm. Six numbers faded with time but still present.

'Describe your most powerful memory of him,' Eva said.

Rebecca crossed her legs and repositioned the cushions behind her back. The psychiatrist sat in a cracked leather armchair and looked at her from the other side of the vintage steamer trunk that served as a coffee table. Eva was short and round-faced with tight silver curls. In her seventies, Rebecca guessed, but perhaps older if she'd been in a camp during World War II. Her hazel eyes were sharp though, like cut crystal.

'There's not just one memory in particular that stands out,' she lied, running her fingers through the altered texture of her shorn hair, the sensation still a novelty. 'It's been almost thirty years. All the memories have blurred together.'

Eva sensed Rebecca's reluctance to elaborate. She smiled and rose.

'I'll get the coffee.'

Making coffee was what Eva did when Rebecca hedged. Heimo had warned Rebecca of the doctor's eccentricities – this was one of them. Breaking the doctor-patient seal by exiting the room defied current practice. Eva used it as a pause to allow her patient to frame their responses. Heimo had said that her methods were somewhat unorthodox but highly effective.

While Rebecca waited, her eyes moved around the office. Despite the cobwebs in the corners of the ceiling and the peeling paint, she was comfortable in this stuffy room overlooking a laneway lined with wheelie bins. The walls weren't hung with the degrees and inspirational quotes she'd expected to find in a psychiatrist's office. The furnishings didn't match and there was a thick, dull varnish of dust on the windowsill. Rebecca appreciated the unconcealed decay, thinking that if a different, younger, more Bondi owner had their way, they would restore and remodel the apartment at once, thereby stripping it of its charm.

Eva returned with a tray holding a moka pot and two small cups.

'I much prefer moka to the espresso they make in the cafes around here. It's so grainy, like molten mud.'

Rebecca nodded. Eva always said this as she poured the coffee, although sometimes she likened it to 'hot lava' or 'warm sludge'.

'I was thinking when I was in the kitchen,' Eva continued. Rebecca leaned closer. After almost forty years in Australia the doctor's accent remained thick and gritty, much like the coffee they were drinking.

'The 1980s weren't so long ago. You must remember songs from that time, outfits you wore. I remember my daughter seemed to wear a lot of ruffles and frills back then.' She glanced at Rebecca and laughed, then took up her notepad and pen again. She scribbled in the corner of a page, testing the ink.

'Why have the memories of Luke become blurred?'

Rebecca shrugged. Sipped her espresso. Her heart now beat so frantically, she was certain it was visible through the fine cotton of her shirt. Rebecca shook her head.

'The hallucinations you're experiencing suggest to me,' Eva said, taking a different tack, 'that you're suffering from post-traumatic stress.'

She paused, staring gravely at the print above her

patient's head. Rebecca swivelled on the cushion and examined it too. During her previous sessions, she hadn't looked closely at the artwork. It was comprised of boldly coloured geometric shapes and a big red number five.

'I believe the cause of your trauma has something to do with Luke,' said Eva.

Rebecca turned, startled. Eva pushed her bifocals along the bridge of her nose then held her pen at the ready. Outside, the weather was beginning to clear and the sun winked off the silver wedding band on her right hand.

'What do *you* believe is at the root of your problem?'

Rebecca straightened, gathering herself as she ran her eyes over Eva's bookcase in an effort to avoid her doctor's gaze. *Crime and Punishment, Heart of Darkness, Wuthering Heights, Atonement, Ordinary People, Girl with No Past, Room.* There were no medical texts in the office, just as there were no degrees on the wall. On her first visit, Rebecca had wondered whether if, in fact, Eva Lakatos was actually a registered psychiatrist. Did reading the occasional psychological thriller qualify her to practice?

'My partner, I suppose,' Rebecca finally answered.

'His death?'

'And the aftermath.'

Eva licked the tip of her pen and held it to the page.

'Where would you like to begin?'

2

THE WOODEN PEW WAS HARD. Although the church was cool, Rebecca felt the damp of nervous perspiration rising in her armpits. She was glad the occasion required her to wear black. Rebecca had wanted to enter the church first and be seated before anyone else. But it was customary, she had been informed, for the family to enter last.

But it's Joe who will enter last, she thought, as she walked down the aisle. He was still waiting in the hearse.

Rebecca didn't recognise many of the mournful faces in the congregation as she made her way to the front row. Most looked her way, except one woman seated by the aisle who kept her head lowered. She was sobbing. Rebecca noticed the woman's shoulders heaving silently; she appeared small and wounded. Rebecca wondered who she was. A colleague? A cousin from Belfast? Joe had collected hundreds of friends and admirers over the years. Rebecca couldn't see the woman's face, but she envied the freedom of her release.

Finally, she slid into her seat.

Rebecca studied the Order of Service clutched in her hands. *The Funeral of Joseph Eirnin O'Neill*, the cover read. She ran her finger delicately across his name, feeling nothing but the paper.

She hadn't attended a funeral since Luke's. But that had been an informal gathering of 'pot heads and dole bludgers', as her father had grumbled in his grief, on Werri Beach at sunrise. Although his board had been washed up at Boat Harbour two days after he disappeared, Luke's body was never found. There had not been a coffin, just the board – a smooth JS Forget Me Not – strewn with branches of water gum and bull bay magnolia that was paddled out beyond the waves and set alight. She had thought it was poignant. Poignant and tragic. She couldn't have written the scene better herself.

She lowered her head. The hat, the one Meredith told her to buy, joggled forward. Stupid hat, she thought. She was certain it made her look like a cockatoo or a peacock ... some kind of bird. A strange black bird.

The choir took their seats and Rebecca raised her head, roused by their muted shuffling. Trying hard not to disturb the precarious tilt of her headpiece, she pushed a lock of hair behind her ear, twisting it gently around her finger, feeling its substance. Her mind began to drift. Anywhere but here, she thought, as Meredith clutched her hand, squeezing it uncomfortably tightly.

'I don't like being led,' Rebecca called. The cold air numbed her throat. When the pub closed and the others had drifted away, they found themselves alone on the street. Joe had snatched at her hand and ran with her trailing behind.

Joe didn't reply, didn't even look back. Their path was lit only occasionally by the headlights of a cab.

The truth was, she didn't consider resisting. Rebecca allowed herself to enjoy the sensation – being towed through the streets and into the unknown.

'St George's Gardens,' she panted when they reached a pair of high, locked iron gates.

'Up and over,' he said, interlocking his fingers waiting for her foot. She was just drunk enough to allow herself to be hoisted over the fence. He clambered over after her then led her into the belly of the green space. They rested, leaning against a headstone.

In the dark, standing so close to Joe O'Neill – so close she could feel his breath against her cheek – Rebecca suddenly became shy. He gripped her shoulders and moved her slightly to the left so a shaft of light from a neighbouring flat's window caught her face.

'You are a beauty, mo ghrá, aren't you?' He pushed the hair from her face and clutched the thick, honey-coloured mess in his hands, making her chin rise. He leant in and kissed her on the mouth. His body, his lips, his tongue, his entire presence entered and engulfed her and she gave in to him completely. When their lips eventually parted, he drew her close and she rubbed her cheek against the soft, worn leather of his jacket.

'Mo ghrá,' she repeated in a whisper.

'My love.'

In that instant, she became so proud. Proud of Joe and proud of herself for being there, being kissed by him. How far she was from where she'd started out. It's here and now in this graveyard that I'm reborn, she'd thought; or, if not reborn, then refashioned, redefined.

Startled by the cathedral's bells beginning to ring, Rebecca shivered slightly. The memory of that evening was still so vivid – the mist stinging her cheeks, the distant hiss and lurch of buses, and the tobacco smell of Joe's jacket. Meredith squeezed her hand more tightly.

Her friend relished a drama, a spectacle, and Joe's

funeral definitely qualified. Rebecca eased her fingers from Meredith's grasp and glanced curiously at the less conspicuous headwear her friend had chosen for herself. The tasteful beret was nestled among her glossy blonde locks.

Rebecca looked further along the pew to Angus, Joe's agent and best friend. His noble profile would sit quite happily on a coin, Rebecca thought. His narrow, anxious gaze was fixed on the dome of the cathedral and his hands, knotted into fists, rested formally on his knees. Sensing Rebecca's gaze, he turned and offered her a comforting smile. Sweet, kind, patient Angus. How'd you ever wind up with Meredith? she wondered.

There was no low murmur or hum of voices. The only sound came from the organ playing a Bach Chorale. Rebecca had chosen the piece. Bach was the only composer she was familiar with and Joe had no favourite hymns, no requests for the funeral, apart from 'No Fun'.

'The Sex Pistols at St Paul's?' Rebecca laughed for the first time in weeks.

Joe scribbled hastily in the same notepad in which he scribbled ideas and rhymes, or images that came into his mind as dreams. He thrust the page into her face.

Apt, don't you think? it read.

'Very. But the idea of those sweet young choir boys singing ...'

Smiling, he watched her for a few moments then wrote again.

You haven't laughed like that in ... thank you.

Halted, her face returned to stone.

'Why do you even want a funeral at St Paul's? You're Catholic.'

LAPSED.

'Don't worry. I'll organise it.' She took his hand and kissed the palm. The truth was that Rebecca didn't want to begin arrange-

ments for a funeral. It would make his death real, imminent. Joe scrawled on, uneasy.

After a moment he turned his notepad in her direction.

It has to be St Paul's. I want the last laugh on that BITCH Thatcher.

Rebecca smiled and nodded gently. Once throat cancer had stolen Joe's voice, Rebecca took to saying very little. She lay down next to him and stared at his profile as he wrote. Sallow and drawn, his knife-edge nose had blunted. He was barely recognisable as the man she had so easily fallen in love with when she was nineteen. His emerald eyes had dulled in illness and what hair remained was wispy white. His lips, his perfectly formed lips that were made more exquisite by the words that poured from them, had dried and withered. Joe had seduced her with those lips and those words. That's how she would remember him — as the eloquent, passionate, dark-haired poet she met at City University when she was still a teenager.

He tapped the pad with his pen. She read.

DO IT or I'll haunt you!

Rebecca pressed her face into his neck. 'I wouldn't mind.'

<hr>

REBECCA STARED at the casket for the duration of the service. The knowledge that Joe's body lay within the mahogany box only metres away was terrifying. She wasn't certain whether she was frightened for herself or for Joe.

His friend, the writer and media presenter David Cook, read a eulogy he had penned himself.

'Joe faced death with the same directness with which he faced life,' Cook began, then paused. He gazed at the mourners over his spectacles.

I'd have thought he could have come up with a better opening, Rebecca imagined Joe remarking.

'He was a voice of protest. A dissident. A peacemaker. The poet of his people,' Cook continued.

It's nothing more than a succession of banal tweets ... Rebecca knew Joe would groan if he could be present in a living, breathing state. An abbreviated laugh escaped her lips. Meredith took her hand again, mistaking the sound for a sob.

'*Maireann na daoine ar scáil a chéile,*' Cook then said in Irish before translating. 'People live in one another's shadows.'

'Joe O'Neill was *larger than life,*' Cook said, emphasising the phrase, leaning over the pulpit towards the congregation.

And you are as boring as bat shit, Joe would respond ... if he could have. Rebecca lowered her head to conceal her amusement. It was an expression she had used once and Joe had been so struck by the absurd weight of the phrase that he had adopted it as his own.

'You asked him to deliver your eulogy.' Rebecca's lips moved instinctively, as though in prayer. 'To be fair, you weren't meant to hear it.'

Meredith turned and spoke softly into Rebecca's ear. 'Pardon?'

Rebecca shook her head.

She was sure the rest of Cook's tribute must have been moving, humorous and esoteric, but she didn't hear a word of it. Rebecca was certain Joe was correct: the eulogy was banal.

Hugh, Rebecca and Joe's godson, read *HMS Maidstone,* which Joe had written about his brother Brendan's 1973 internment on the English prison ship. It was Joe's most renowned poem. Rebecca forced her eyes closed and attempted to recite the lines in her mind. She had transcribed the first draft of the poem herself in 1991. She had deciphered Joe's crude shorthand and attentively followed his annotations. They'd splayed out like dreadlocks from each line. When she offered suggestions she was ignored and rebuffed.

'Don't ask me to read the bloody thing,' she screamed, 'if you don't want me to suggest changes!' She threw the pages at him then stormed out of the tiny glassed-in sunroom of their Camden apartment they called his study.

He rose from his desk quickly and caught her in the doorway. He gripped her tightly around her slim hips. Turning her to face him, he pressed his forehead against hers.

'I'm sorry, mo ghrá,' he whispered. 'It's hard for me to consider changes when the words are still so raw.'

She calmed and accepted his soft lips against her own.

'You're most beautiful when you're incensed.' He kissed her again.

At not quite twenty-one, Rebecca was struggling to understand the man she was in love with, attempting to know him more completely through his writing. In the fifteen years that separated them, Joe had lived an entire lifetime of tyranny, pain and loss. Her experience was so meagre in comparison.

Rebecca opened her eyes and pictured Joe's thin, frail body inside the coffin.

When the ceremony concluded, Rebecca followed the casket at a sedate walk towards the exit. It was as though she could reach out and touch him if she chose, as though the glossy walls of the wooden box were transparent. Then he slid easily and without complaint into the back of the hearse.

The prime minister offered his condolences on the steps

of the cathedral, as did Irish poets Jackie Boyle, Breffni O'Callaghan and Paul Meehan. Together, the trio was hailed in *The Guardian* that morning as 'Joe O'Neill's likely successors'. One person was simply not enough to take the place of 'Ireland's leading poet'.

They voiced their commiserations – 'such an enormous loss to literature', 'he changed the face of poetry in the UK', 'Joe was one of the great modern elegists' – then moved away. If Joe had heard, he would have criticised their use of cliché and questioned their dedication to the craft.

Angus touched Rebecca's elbow. 'The car's waiting down here ...' He indicated a black Bentley parked behind Joe's hearse.

Rebecca shook her head. 'I'm not going. I can't watch him burn.'

Angus gazed at her gently and Meredith flashed a look of displeasure at her husband.

'But you must, Rebecca,' Meredith cautioned, stepping closer. 'How will it look?'

'I don't care how it looks,' Rebecca replied. 'It wasn't one of Joe's stipulations.'

'This isn't about you,' Meredith retaliated.

'When has it ever been about me?'

Affronted, Meredith drew her husband away to discuss the matter. Hugh stood uncomfortably at Rebecca's side. After a minute, she removed her hat.

'Have you ever seen anything as big?' she asked him.

The teenager eyed her uncertainly, loosening the knot of his tie as though it was strangling him.

'It's okay,' she said. 'You can laugh ... or not. I don't care. I just don't want to see him burn.'

Hugh nodded thoughtfully.

'The fire ... it's so final.'

'Yeah,' he answered. 'I don't want to see it either but I'm not brave enough to take on Mum.' The young man smiled, running his fingers through his thick ginger hair.

'I'm going to miss him so much. Joe was like a father to me sometimes. He was always honest. Most people aren't.'

Rebecca brushed Hugh's cheek lightly with her hand.

'Joe loved you like a son. We both do ... did.' She winced. Rebecca wasn't sure which tense to use. That was the problem when death was still so fresh.

'You know that, don't you?'

'I know.' Hugh's voice broke. Rebecca pulled him to her, hugging him tightly, perhaps more tightly than she should.

When they parted, Rebecca noticed a woman's eyes on her. It was the sobbing woman, the one who had been seated on the aisle, absorbed in her own grief. She was standing at the base of the steps with two adolescent children. When she met Rebecca's eyes, the woman looked away clumsily towards the road, as though in search of a cab. She was attractive. European-looking.

'Hold this, please.' Rebecca handed the hat to Hugh and walked quickly towards her, bounding down the steps two at a time. She was instantly glad she hadn't given in to Meredith and worn heels. The woman craned her neck, now desperate for an exit. A cab stopped.

'Wait!' Rebecca called, waving, as she approached.

The woman turned to Rebecca as she bustled her children into the back of the car. Her brown eyes were red and swollen.

'I'm Rebecca Collins.' Remembering the woman's tears, Rebecca reached out and touched her arm. 'Thank you for coming. Did you know Joe?'

'Yes ... a little,' she responded. She was extremely pretty, Rebecca thought, but she seemed rumpled. Her fine chestnut-coloured hair hung over her shoulders and face in limp strands.

'I enjoy his poetry.'

Rebecca winced. *Enjoyed* ...

She was French, Rebecca guessed from her accent, an accent so different from her own. Although the rough edges of her Aussie twang had been smoothed out during her twenty-eight years in London, it was still brutal to her ear.

'What's your name?' Rebecca said as the woman placed a foot into the cab. 'Joe probably mentioned you ...'

The woman's black silk blouse had come untucked from her skirt in her effort to get into the vehicle. She was a bird too, Rebecca thought, a panicked bird.

'I doubt it. I'm no one,' said the bird, scrutinising Rebecca's face. 'Just an admirer.'

'A friend?'

She nodded. 'We must go.' The woman stepped into the cab. Rebecca drew closer and, before the stranger could shut the door, leant in and peered into the interior of the cab.

'Thank you for coming,' she said to the children.

They raised their faces to her. The girl, about thirteen, was the woman's mirror. She smiled politely and moved along the seat to be closer to her mother. The boy was older. He shot Rebecca a hard look.

Even in the dimness of the cab's interior, his fierce green eyes were unmistakable.

'We must go,' the woman piped. 'Will you close the door, please?'

Rebecca didn't hear the request.

'Please ...' The bird began to thrash, moving closer to the door and grabbing the handle. 'I'm sorry. I had to come.'

'When?' Rebecca's entire body felt boneless. She wasn't certain how she was still upright.

'Please!' the bird cried.

Rebecca stepped away, allowing the door to shut.

3
______

WITHOUT SAYING goodbye to Angus and Meredith, or thanking the prime minister or any other mourner for that matter, Rebecca followed the cab. It was instinctual; she wanted the answers to questions that hadn't yet formed in her mind. Cannon Street was congested and, at a fast walk, Rebecca was able to keep sight of the vehicle for a long time. Then the traffic cleared and the cab was lost.

Finding herself at Monument, Rebecca stopped and checked her phone. Four missed calls from Angus. She slid the phone back into her bag and began to cross the river. Struck by a scent in the air, an odd feeling of déjà vu came over her. She stopped as she tried to place it, choking the flow of pedestrians on the bridge. She breathed in more deeply.

'Petrichor,' Luke said.

'Who?' Rebecca replied, hoisting her schoolbag onto her back.

'Not a who, it's a what. P-E-T-R-I-C-H-O-R,' he repeated slowly, loudly, leading the way home. 'It's the name for the smell of rain, retard.'

'How do you know that?' Thunder grumbled a menacing warning. Rebecca lifted her eyes. The sky was gunmetal grey.

Luke shrugged.

'Read it somewhere, I s'pose.'

They had been eleven, maybe twelve. The word had dropped out of her vocabulary years ago. Why had she thought of that now? Disturbed, Rebecca looked into the sky. Clouds gathered in brooding clusters but she kept walking, across the Thames, across Hyde Park. It began to drizzle, but she didn't notice. She was disoriented, as though wedged uncomfortably into another person's reality. Nothing seemed familiar – not the maple trees pushing up the footpath at the corner of her street, nor the mossy cobblestones outside her home that were slippery in the rain. Even the front door, the one she had painted emerald green when she and Joe had moved in, seemed foreign. She didn't know what time it was when she eventually opened it and walked in on a stranger's life.

By the time some feeling returned to her mind and body it was almost six o'clock. The rain had passed and the sun, now low in the sky, fell upon her face and startled her from her torpor. There wasn't much in London that reminded Rebecca of Australia any more, except for the early evening of a summer's day. It immediately brought to mind memories of sand and spinifex and the sting of her taut skin as she walked home from a day in the waves. Nothing compared. Sheened in salt and splendid weariness, she and Luke would dump their boards against the back fence then make their way to the table on the veranda where their mother had dinner waiting. Rebecca could still recall the peach-like scent of the frangipani that dominated their backyard. It mingled with the smoky odour of sausages and chops from the barbecue.

She glanced around the sitting room of her mews house, at the pictures, books, furnishings and knick-knacks. Nearly twenty-nine-years worth of accruements. A pullover that had belonged to Joe lay over the back of the lounge. It had been there for weeks. Superstitious she wasn't, but during Joe's illness, Rebecca had felt that if she folded the sweater and put it in a drawer it would be a sign that Joe would never wear it again.

Then her eyes lit upon the mantel and the flowers Angus had sent her the day after Joe's death. The card, still attached, read 'Angus x'. It was written in his hand.

She rose, removed her stockings and threw them into the fireplace. She did the same with her skirt, blouse and shoes. Hugh must still have the hat, she thought. I'll burn that another day. Then she clutched at Joe's pullover and threw that onto the hearth as well.

Rebecca took the stairs two at a time, to Joe's study. The room was cold. She hadn't opened the door in weeks. She scanned the space for a moment before yanking open drawers, frantically scattering sheaves of paper and books on the floor. She began searching. For what, she wasn't certain. By the look of the boy in the cab, the relationship had gone on for at least fifteen or sixteen years.

Joe didn't own a mobile phone. He didn't have an email account and he wrote everything in longhand. Rebecca managed his emails and typed up his work. There were no Facebook accounts she could scour, no text messages to scroll through. He didn't even own a computer. Joe's resistance of technology and social media in the name of 'clarity' now just seemed like duplicity. It was all a lie, she decided.

Joe was a fraud. He just didn't want to leave any clues. How could she have been so blind?

Sitting on the floor in her underwear, with files, books and papers spread about her, she remembered the telephone bill. The only IT Joe abided was the landline telephone. Crawling over to the filing cabinet, she wrenched opened the bottom drawer and rifled among papers until she found a bill. She scrutinised each number. Most of them were international. She could ring each one, she thought ... then what would she say? She'd sound like a lunatic. Throwing the bill on the floor, she screamed, a loud angry 'fuck you' to the world. Then she caught sight of her reflection in the glass doors of a book cabinet – hair wild, make-up smudged, face streaked with tears. She *was* a lunatic. Joe would have called her a 'banshee'. Rebecca rose and left the room, slamming the door behind her.

Making her way to her bedroom, she opened her dresser and stared into the tangle of bras, socks and underpants for some time before remembering her purpose and beginning to dress. She walked into the bathroom, opened the medicine cabinet and produced a pair of scissors, a sterling silver pair she'd bought from an antique dealer on Portobello Road. They were over-priced, Joe had warned, but she had liked the confident *schlick* they produced when metal met metal.

Holding the cold blades against her cheek, she stared at her reflection for a moment and glimpsed someone standing in the doorway behind her. It was Joe, she was certain, and she turned quickly.

He was gone.

'Fuck you,' she said, unperturbed.

She remembered Charlie the ghost cat. She and Luke had been about twelve when Charlie died, but for years afterwards they would see his shadow out of the corner of their eye, either asleep on Luke's pillow as they passed down the hall or walking into the kitchen when someone opened the fridge.

Joe was just a ghost cat.

She turned back to the mirror. Clumping a handful of hair together in her fist, she began cutting it off as close to the scalp as possible. Glancing at the curls lying on the bathroom floor, Rebecca waited. Regret, panic, sadness ... but nothing struck her. She kept on cutting. When she finished, she placed the scissors on the edge of the sink and lifted her face to the mirror. The sight of her new reflection took her breath away.

Twenty minutes later she had laced her running shoes and left the house.

4

'Where's your accent from?'

Eva finished pouring the coffee. She dropped three sugar cubes into her cup – tiny black drops flew millimetres into the air – then she stirred. The doctor had so many rituals. All were performed in a graceful, meditative style. Even the pushing of her glasses along the bridge of her nose was done smoothly, as though her skin was polished marble.

'Hungary. I was born there. Have you visited?'

'Yes, once. A few years ago. But I was only in Budapest, at a writers' festival with Joe.'

Eva tilted her right arm sideways revealing the tattoo on her wrist.

'The Nazis took me away when I was six.'

Rebecca had never spoken to a Holocaust survivor about their experience, but she had prepared herself. She had been prepared since she had noticed the tattoo when they first shook hands on meeting. Rebecca had appreciated the soothing coolness of the psychiatrist's fingers as they confidently wrapped around her hand in welcome and acceptance.

'I'm so sorry. I can't even imagine what that must have been like.' It was a stock response. Prepared. Rebecca wanted to say more but she wasn't certain what to say. Supportive remarks and reflections might be read as offensive, patronising or feeble. So she went with a platitude instead.

Eva raised her cup and drew the liquid between pursed lips.

'It wasn't so bad at first because I didn't know what was happening. My parents were calm. They didn't fight. They were teachers. Educated people. They thought there had been some mistake. I had my mother and sister with me and my father and brothers were sent to another camp. A few of the guards were kind. They gave my sister and me sweets and made us laugh. It wasn't until my sister and I were separated from my mother that we realised the gravity of it all.'

'Did they take your mother to another camp?'

'No. The Germans killed her,' Eva said with startling matter-of-factness. 'She caught pneumonia and couldn't work. She was useless to them after that so they shot her. We weren't allowed to say goodbye.'

Rebecca swallowed.

'Oh.'

'That's very important, you know – saying goodbye.' The doctor paused. 'She was thirty-six. Of our family, only myself and my sister survived.'

Rebecca's issues seemed meagre by comparison.

'I'm only telling you this to illustrate that humans are remarkably resilient and possess the ability to overcome great tragedies.'

Tragedy. Was her relationship with Joe a tragedy? If so, who was the tragic hero? Herself, surely. Complacent, comfortable, she hadn't seen the signs. Or was it Joe, blinded by renown and ego?

'You seem at peace. I can't imagine ever being at peace after that.' Another stock response. Measured, despite her fermenting emotions.

'I was troubled for many years. It destroyed my first marriage. When my husband would ask me about those years I'd freeze, turn numb. The memories were there but I couldn't voice them,' Eva explained. 'I didn't return to Hungary for thirty years. I was terrified. Sometimes memories are like an exhumation. It can be very slow. Painful, too.'

Eva paused and waited, gazing at Rebecca thoughtfully.

Rebecca had a sense of where Eva was heading, but made no comment.

'I turned to God, then I sought the help of doctors, then I became a doctor. It has taken forty years of hard work to confront my past. Let's hope it's quicker for you.'

The women locked eyes. After a moment, Eva smiled.

'Is that how you met Heimo?' Rebecca asked, breaking the impasse.

'Yes, he interviewed me as part of his doctorate thesis.'

Rebecca bit her lip, opened her mouth to speak then quickly closed it again. Heimo's background was German. His parents were immigrants. His connection with his heritage is strong. Like Eva, Heimo is a doctor. Scientific minds, they would argue, allowed for an objectivity that someone like Rebecca, with a creative mind, could not grasp. But sinew and muscle, heart and soul had their origins thousands of years ago and everything that has happened since, through each subsequent generation, has cultivated their development. How was Eva able to reconcile Heimo's backstory with her own?

'What is it?'

'Nothing.' Eva drained her cup and slid it back onto its saucer. She picked up her notepad and pen once more.

'My patients often groan when I ask them about their histories, their family background, but it's vital. Everything we are stems from our parents. They are our first and our most profound connection. The severing of that connection, no matter what the age of the child, is also profound. Would I have become a psychiatrist if not for the loss of my parents?' She shrugged.

'But when we consider the loss of a sibling, the grief can be just as overwhelming as the loss of a parent; perhaps even more so if that sibling is a twin.'

Rebecca nodded warily.

'You told me, Rebecca, that you and your brother had an emotional connection.'

'That's right.'

'Was it environmental or intuitive do you think?'

'Innate. Cognitive. I never fully understood it until I was at university studying psychology myself. I read journal articles about twins and their connection.'

She paused and licked her lips.

'Luke and I always thought the same, liked the same colours and music and food. But it was deeper than that.'

'When did you first become aware of it being different?'

Rebecca stared at the doctor for a minute, a cache of memories shuffling this way and that in her mind like cards in a deck.

'We were young, very young, five or six. We'd try to read each other's minds. We were pretty good at it, too. But we really didn't grasp the power of what was between us until a few years later.'

'Can you recall what happened?'

'Vividly.'

'Do you live in a tent?' Mum asked. The children stared at her blankly.

'Close the door, you'll let flies in.

The screen door banged shut.

'Sand?'

The kids examined their bare feet for a second.

'Nup,' they answered in unison.

Luke and Rebecca mounted the stools at the breakfast bar. Charlie the Wonder Cat jumped onto Luke's lap, purring as his back was stroked. Their mother was icing a three-tiered cake for Julie Merriman's wedding on the weekend. She was wearing her favourite apron. 'What's cookin' good lookin'?' read the slogan. Dad had given it to her for Christmas.

'How's the water?' she asked, her eyes not leaving the cake.

'Good,' the kids replied, again in unison.

Joyce Collins pinched the corner of her lip between her teeth as she piped five-petalled flowers the size of two-cent coins onto the side of the middle tier. In summer, she liked to ice her cakes early before the heat made the icing too soft to work with.

'Mum,' Rebecca said.

'Shush.'

'Mum ...' the girl went on. Luke began rolling a stray piece of fondant icing between his fingers.

'Luke!'

'Now you see it ...' The boy popped the ball into his mouth and swallowed quickly.

'Now you don't.'

He gazed at his mother innocuously. Charlie nuzzled against his chest.

'For goodness sake!' Joyce tossed the piping bag into the sink

and wiped her forehead with the back of her hand. The cat leapt to the floor, out through the cat flap and into the yard.

'What do you two want?' She placed her hands on her hips and waited. They were always 'you two' or 'you pair'. Their father liked to call them 'the Dynamic Duo.'

The twins looked at each other, trying to feel out who should begin. The song of the cicadas was deafening.

'What have you done?' Joyce asked, looking directly at her son.

'Nothin',' Luke said and began to toy with another piece of icing. His mother slapped his hand away.

'It's just that sometimes ... well, sometimes ...'

'One of you spit it out.' Joyce glanced back and forth at her children's almost identical faces.

'Sometimes,' Rebecca continued. 'It's like Luke and me can read each other's minds.'

Their mother sighed but her skepticism spurred Rebecca on.

'No, really! A few weeks ago, at school, it was just before recess, I was in the library with my class and I got this weird feeling in my tummy, like ... I just didn't feel like me. It was like a nervous feeling, but I was also scared and I didn't have anything to be nervous or scared about. Then the bell rang and when I saw Luke in the playground he told me ...'

'I'd just gotten in trouble, gotten the cane, from Beardsley,' Luke said.

'You got the cane! What for?'

'Nothin',' Luke answered. 'But Bec felt it all.'

Joyce turned to her daughter.

'You felt the cane hit your hand?'

The girl shook her head and frowned.

'I felt what was inside him, his feelings.'

'It's probably just a coincidence.' Joyce said, sliding the cake to one side of the bench. 'Sometimes I get a funny nervous feeling in my tummy that I can't explain either.'

'But it happened yesterday as well,' Rebecca said, jumping off the stool and going to her mother.

'It was in my piano lesson. Mrs Beck was making me play this piece and I just couldn't do it. It was too hard and I started to cry.'

'Why don't you two tell me any of this stuff?' she asked. Joyce brushed her daughter's tangled hair away from her face and gripped her tanned cheeks in her hands. 'One of you gets the cane while the other is in tears at a piano lesson!'

Luke interrupted.

'But Mum, I wanted to cry too … I didn't, but I really wanted to. I felt what Rebecca did. And she can feel what I can.'

Joyce looked at her children, her mouth slowly puckering in thought.

'For seven-year-olds, you two really throw some curly ones my way, you know.'

She leant her elbows on the breakfast bar and examined her fingernails for a moment. Digging out the fondant buried beneath them, she contemplated the problem. Joyce liked to paint them pink in summer, a colour called 'Guilty Pleasure'.

'Look, it's probably just that you're twins. You know how each other tick, that's all.' She straightened her arms. 'Now, go. I have to get this cake done before it gets too hot.'

But Rebecca knew their bond wasn't a coincidence or just because they were twins. They weren't two, they were one. They had been aware of what one another felt, really felt, about things for as long as they could remember. It had been a special secret.

It was just that now they had a way to talk about it.

WHEN REBECCA LEFT Eva's office it was almost midday. The humidity had settled into a miserable pall and steam rose from the bitumen, creating an eeriness unexpected in Bondi in the middle of summer. Rebecca stood underneath Eva's office with her back against the Thai takeaway's shopfront and considered her options. She didn't have any close friends in Sydney. All her ties were far away. Returning to the small apartment she'd rented just wasn't palatable. She was lonely, she supposed, hungry for life.

A bus stopped in front of her, its brakes emitting an offensive hiss and she immediately darted between the pedestrians and traffic of Campbell Parade. Drizzle had turned the outlook sombre and disappointment was apparent on the faces of tourists holding hastily purchased umbrellas. A few wandered across the sand, taking photographs regardless, and built sandcastles that quickly became pocked by the rain.

Rebecca couldn't see the horizon. She kicked off her thongs and buried her toes in the damp sand. Apart from a few surfers taking advantage of the swell, it was empty out there. Rebecca sat and hugged her knees to her chest. She watched them snap and turn, shooting grey spray into the grey sky, their limber young bodies mastering the board and surrendering to the wave. Humility, Luke had told her, was the key to surfing. But she had always wanted control, always tried to read the waves, analyse and predict, wondering where in the world the original swell had begun. What had been its journey? she'd think. Luke had simply accepted.

Eva was certain the root of her problems was Luke. Rebecca was growing certain of it, too, but she wasn't sure why, or why she couldn't tell Eva. Luke would come to her in dreams some nights – most nights – wanting her to follow him. Rebecca always lost him in the shadows. He was too fast. Then again, she thought as she watched a surfer paddle out beyond the break, perhaps I'm too slow and hesitant. Too untrusting.

A group of Japanese tourists, barefoot and wrapped in identical clear plastic ponchos, headed to the shoreline. When a petering wave reached their feet they laughed and turned to one another, amazement brightening their faces. Phones were magically produced from the pockets of lurid-coloured board shorts. A childhood dream recognised: pilgrims blessed by the sacred waters of Bondi.

Rebecca stared past the kids on boards and into the murky distance. She could see heavier rain dropping in angled sheets kilometres away, heading to shore. She decided to wait until it reached her, until she could feel the sting of it on her bare shoulders.

5

REBECCA CROSSED Holland Park at a sprint then navigated the warren of lanes and roads to the High Street. She ran even faster now, dodging the summer masses as she went, the summer frocks and sandals, the couples with shopping bags laden with picnic supplies from Marks and Spencer and Whole Foods Market. Rebecca carved through the wave until she reached Round Pond in Kensington Gardens.

She stopped, breathless. Doubled over.

Rebecca struggled to draw in air. A swell of nausea threatened and then subsided. Sweat stung her eyes and she winced as she wiped her face with the hem of her shirt. Once recovered, she continued at a more relaxed pace. When she reached Angus and Meredith's home in Lowndes Square, her hand hovered over the gleaming brass knocker. Did she want to know?

She hammered the door slowly, three times. Angus's form became visible behind the stained-glass panels.

'Bloody fuck, Rebecca. What in the name of …' Angus stopped. He stepped onto the landing, quietly drawing the front door shut behind him. His hazel eyes combed her head like a doctor examining a terminal patient. He ran his fingers through his own curls and looked at the ground. He still wore the same black trousers and custom-made shirt he'd worn to the funeral.

'Did you know?' Rebecca asked.

Angus shook his head.

'Not until Joe was diagnosed.'

'Meredith?'

'I had to tell her this afternoon. She saw everything that happened. She watched as you ran after the cab.'

Angus stepped back from the doorway.

'Come in.'

Rebecca didn't want to. She wanted to keep running until she ran out, until she was so far away that the funeral wasn't even a memory. Until it was a blip so small that she could no longer recall the betrayal and the pain and the false bedrock of her life. False and unsteady, it was still crumbling as she stood there. She could feel the tremor. Everything was giving way. Angus was speaking. His lips were moving. A surreal dumb show had begun. He was close but she could barely feel the press of his hands against her arms. Aware of her quick shallow breaths, she tried to draw air deeper into her lungs. Despite the run, her skin became cold. She stared at her quivering hands, tried to stop shaking; tried to lock her knees, stand straight and let air into her lungs, but she was at the mercy of a fury that was big and wild and rampant.

'Rebecca,' Angus's voice sounded muffled. 'You're having a panic attack. Come inside.'

She shook him off.

Then, standing on the Redmeyer's tessellated-tile doorstep, immune to comfort and condolences, she screamed a loud, fierce, angry shriek, until her breath ran out. An exorcism. Breathing normally, she leant against the doorframe and looked at her friend. Angus gazed back calmly, took her elbow, then eased her over the threshold into his house, guided her to his impeccable sitting room, sat her on the sofa, and covered her shoulders with a cashmere throw rug.

'I've had a few of those myself,' Angus said gently. Sitting by her side, he instructed her to take slow, deep breaths, rubbing her back in gentle, wide arcs. Rebecca focused on the photographs standing on the mantel. They were mostly family shots. Others were of Hugh alone, taken throughout his infancy, childhood and adolescence. Meredith entered with a large glass of iced water and a towel. She ran her gaze over Rebecca's crumpled form then raised her eyebrows fleetingly.

'We'll be fortunate if the Spencers don't call the police,' she said, feigning lightness. But Rebecca noted the hysterical edge in her tone.

'That scream and ...' She gestured to Rebecca's hair. 'What *have* you done to yourself?'

Meredith asked this in an offhand way, as though she didn't care but she knew she should. The legs of her pants *swished* as she walked. She wore a belted jumpsuit in a light floral print with wide, blowsy legs. She looked cool, Rebecca thought, raising the towel to her face, aware of the heat trapped in her cheeks.

'Do you have anything to say, Rebecca?' Meredith asked, smiling. 'You scared us half to death.'

Rebecca drained the water then rose and rested the glass on the mantel. Since the funeral, there had been a seed, a tight, nasty, fiery nut of anger balling in her chest. Hacking madly at her hair had extinguished it for a moment. But that small retaliation had not been enough.

Now she wanted to vent it again, lay it all on Meredith's smooth, tanned shoulders. She envisaged it spewing from her mouth, flaming. A tight, red spitball of fury that would hit Meredith right in the middle of her botoxed forehead. Rebecca imagined reeling on her friend, screaming in her face, telling her that she had a right to howl if she wanted to. What did she care if she chopped off her hair? Wasn't spite better than feeling nothing at all? Hadn't she nursed Joe O'Neill through a terminal illness, wiped his arse, emptied his drains, cleaned his wounds, bathed him, pureed his food then struggled to spoon it into his tongueless mouth? Didn't that give her the right to be angry and vicious?

Meredith narrowed her eyes.

Angus cleared his throat.

'Meredith, dear, would you mind leaving us?

'Really?' she said.

Angus nodded.

Meredith looked at Rebecca and quickly decided it was the best course of action. She left – *swish, swish, swish* – squeezing Rebecca's forearm briefly as she passed and offering her a forgiving smile. Rebecca flinched. The nut in her chest flared.

'Cool down,' Angus murmured. He moved to her and cupped her cheek softly in his palm. 'She's gone now.'

Rebecca's shoulders and breathing relaxed and, as she stood with Angus's hand resting lightly on her cheek, she managed to compose herself.

'Thank you,' she said.

'Not at all.' He removed his hand hastily and pushed it into his pocket.

'I'll ring Meredith tomorrow and apologise.'

'I know you will.'

'Tell me everything, Angus,' she began calmly, examining a photograph of Hugh on his first day of school. Apart from the ginger hair, he had most resembled his mother then. Now he looked like the Angus she had first met in a frowsty tutorial at City University. Fathers and sons.

'Perhaps it should wait ... until a less emotional time?' Angus suggested.

Rebecca turned.

'No. I want to know now! Christ, my entire life's just fallen apart in one afternoon. I want to know why.'

Angus placed his hands on his hips and looked intently at her.

'Please.'

'Right then,' he said, finally.

Angus walked to the picture window and looked out at the gated garden opposite. He removed his cufflinks and placed them in his pocket. He rolled up his sleeves deliberately, taking great care with each fold. Rebecca's stomach tightened with impatience, but Angus was methodical and didn't like to be rushed. She knew he took his early morning constitutional in that private green space every day with Noodle, the family's yellow Labrador. Joe had aided a six-year-old Hugh with the name when they gifted the puppy to their godson. In doing so, Joe had given the child a rudimentary lesson in figurative language. Man and boy had been extremely pleased with themselves.

'He was like an older brother to me ...' Angus said, closing the curtains and turning to face her.

'And you feel like you're betraying him?'

'No, on the contrary ... I feel betrayed,' he answered. He switched on an Art Deco lamp.

'I had no inkling ... not the faintest idea.'

'We were both duped.'

Angus took her in for a moment. She felt embarrassed to

be standing in his finely furnished sitting room in her running gear, red-faced and sweaty. She couldn't even imagine what her hair must look like.

'Do sit down, Rebecca,' he said, rubbing his hand over his mouth. 'You're making me extremely uneasy, as though you're going to sprint out the door at any moment.'

She sat and grasped at a cushion, pressing it into her abdomen.

'Please, Angus. Just get on with it.'

He positioned himself on the edge of the sofa then stared at her for a moment, priming himself, preparing to leap off a high rock into deep water.

'Her name is Karina Bonnay. She's French. Lives in Geneva. She has two children.' The information seemed to surge from his mouth and Rebecca envied his relief.

She nodded.

'The boy is clearly Joe's child.'

'Yes. So is the girl.' He sat down heavily, slumping into the Chesterfield sofa.

'I'm so tired, Rebecca.'

She reached over and placed her hand lightly on his arm.

'I know.'

Angus examined her fingers silently.

'Keeping this information to myself. I wanted to ... I so wanted to ... it has been extremely difficult.'

Angus always spoke hesitantly. Rebecca noticed this idiosyncrasy as a student. It was as though something remained perpetually unsaid. It was a small quirk of character that she found endearing, even charming early on. She had mentioned it once, interested in its effect on her. He told her it was a consequence of a childhood stammer.

'I've so appreciated everything you've done while Joe

was ill and since his death,' Rebecca said. 'You've protected me from the media and the well-meaning.'

'I want to keep protecting you, Rebecca.'

'You can't protect me from this. I have to know.'

He looked at her soberly. He shook his head.

'I don't think I can tell you. I don't want to hurt you.'

But she was already hurt. Mortally wounded, it seemed to her. Nothing Angus disclosed could make it any worse.

'You were my friend before you were Joe's,' she said finally, in desperation. 'Before you were his confidante you were mine ... you were my best friend, Angus ...'

She moved closer and took his hand.

'Remember when you read my first manuscript? You were the first person I showed, before Joe even. You knew more about my life and Luke than anyone else. I asked you to be truthful and you were. Don't you remember?'

Then later, when the words stopped coming, he had taken her on as an employee, to proofread and edit manuscripts. It was his plan to get her writing again, although she never did.

He tried to blink away the moisture from his eyes.

'Of course I remember, Rebecca.'

He wiped his eyes quickly with a pressed handkerchief retrieved from his trouser pocket.

'You told me to rip the manuscript to pieces if I wanted to, tear it to shreds, but you needed to know if you could write.'

'Yes.'

'And you could.'

'Then please Angus ...'

He clutched at her hand.

'Joe told me everything about six months ago, when the doctors told him ... told him the score. Oh, I'm sorry.' He rubbed his forehead. 'That's a terrible way of putting it. He asked me to see to having his will altered.'

'Go on,' she said. Her bank balance was the least of her concern.

'He met Karina in the early 2000s – just after *Crumlin Road* was published. I think he was on a book tour, or perhaps it was when he was interviewed by France 3 ...' Angus began vaguely, '... or something.'

'It doesn't matter,' Rebecca said, attempting to hurry him. 'Joe travelled a lot. I never questioned his movements. As far as I was concerned, his travel abroad was all in the name of literature and world peace.'

'Anyway, they had a fling. Well, more than a fling. They hit it off quite well, in fact. When Karina became pregnant, he bought her an apartment in Geneva – and agreed to support her and his ... the boy.'

'Then the girl was born,' Rebecca added. 'They were ... a family.'

'Yes, of sorts. I don't know how Joe worked it ... logistically, I mean. I'm rather flummoxed, to be honest, as to just when and how he saw them.'

'That's not the point, Angus,' Rebecca explained, struggling to take in the fill of his revelations. 'They were a family.'

She'd never suspected, never doubted. Knowing this now was worse that losing him, she realised. She pressed the cushion hard into her belly. The morning he had closed his eyes for the final time and drifted towards death Rebecca had believed she was the unluckiest person alive. To experience such an intense hurt a second time just wasn't fair. But here it was again. Joe had made a fool of her and the life they had shared.

'He never wanted you to know,' Angus said, placing an arm around her shoulder.

'Obviously,' Joe's voice replied. 'Rebecca's never been equipped to deal with grief.'

Rebecca raised her head. Her eyes darted about the room. His voice was so lucid ... Be it spoken or written, it had been ever-present in her life for over twenty-eight years; it stood to reason, she thought, that despite everything, her mind would still crave it.

'She wasn't meant to be at the funeral,' Angus added after a minute. 'Swore to him she wouldn't attend.'

'I saw her in the church when we were walking down the aisle. She was sobbing her heart out and I wondered who she was. Christ, she was devastated ...'

'He left them the property in Geneva and established trusts for the children,' Angus said quietly, almost ashamed. 'You've been very well looked after, of course.'

'Of course,' she echoed, vaguely.

'I think that's all.'

'I think that's enough,' Rebecca said.

He laughed shyly.

Rebecca stood and handed Angus the cushion, the towel and the throw rug, each dampened by her perspiration. She had to get out. Her skin itched, as though minuscule invisible insects crawling beneath it were forcing their way out.

'Thank you for telling me. I have to go now. I'll be in touch in a few days. Don't worry. I need to do some thinking. And I should probably see a hairdresser.'

He smiled at this and touched her head gingerly.

'It doesn't look too bad. I'm sure it could be neatened up ...' He stopped.

'I think I know why you did it.'

'It helps that you understand.'

'Can I drive you home? You seem too calm ... are you sure you're –'

'It's okay,' she interrupted. 'I need to be by myself.'

He rose and led her from the sitting room.

'I'll be fine. It's all just a little unreal. I'm sure I'll be a basket case once it all sinks in.'

At the door, Angus pressed his fists tightly into the pockets of his trousers. Noodle emerged from upstairs and padded softly down to Rebecca. She scratched his neck fondly.

'Tell me, Angus,' Rebecca asked before she departed. 'What does she do for a living?' Rebecca couldn't call her by name.

'She's in insurance, I believe.' Angus opened the front door.

'Insurance. Really?' Rebecca queried, disbelieving, as she stepped over the threshold.

Angus thought he had misheard. 'Insurance, did you say? Really?'

Joe nodded then sat opposite his friend, silent, waiting for Angus to respond.

'Cat got your tongue?' Joe finally said.

'Insurance?'

'Yes. In-sur-ance.'

Angus wanted to be angry for Joe's deception of himself and of Rebecca but instead he was simply flummoxed. Totally confounded. Completely baffled that Joe O'Neill – poet, peacemaker, political activist – could be in love with someone who worked in insurance. Joe had fervently berated insurance companies around the dinner table and in the media for not compensating the victims of terror in Ireland, or their families. Angus recalled adjectives such as 'parasitic' and 'venal' being used.

But love wasn't necessarily logical, Angus had thought. Most of the time, he realised, it simply didn't make sense.

Rebecca stared at Angus, wide-eyed with disbelief.

He shrugged.

'I know. I had the same reaction.'

Outside, the sunset had begun to manifest as a glowing coal, smouldering behind the houses. Her shadow reached long and black along the footpath. She turned and embraced her friend. Angus placed his arms uncomfortably around her waist for a moment then gently allowed his chin to nestle into her hair.

6

REBECCA WALKED HOME SLOWLY. Not wanting to return to the empty house, she stopped outside Tina Hardy's on Kensington Church Street. It was 'the best millinery in London', Meredith had informed her a week ago.

'Rebecca, you must wear a hat to the funeral. Surely', Meredith had jibed, 'you antipodeans are used to wearing hats.'

Meredith might as well have used the term 'colonials'.

Although she hadn't told Meredith, Rebecca was familiar with Tina Hardy Millinery. She and Joe had strolled by on occasion, as they headed out to a restaurant or pub. They had often mocked the window display.

'Go way outta that!' Joe had exclaimed, pointing in genuine astonishment to a tiny hat, no bigger than a saucer, adorned with feathers. While Rebecca understood what he meant, that particular Irish idiom made no sense to her at all.

'The pink one ... is it a chief's headdress? Is it a cocktail? *Scrios Fia!*'

Rebecca always grinned when she heard him say that. She had picked up some Irish in the years she'd been with Joe and she could recognise certain words and phrases. The invective *'scrios Fia'*, or bloody hell, sounded far more obscene in Irish than English.

'If the Irish don't speak Gaelic, the language will die,' he had told her early on. 'Just like so many other languages that are on their last legs – Wukchumni, Kusunda, Hupa, Amurdag, Selk'nam.'

She had accepted Joe's knowledge like food from a god and was humbled and nourished.

'Twenty-five years from now,' he had said, 'as many as fifty per cent of the world's languages will only exist in archives and on recordings. One language dies every four months and on every continent people have forsaken their mother tongue for English.'

'Then why won't you teach Gaelic to me?' Rebecca had demanded. She often wondered why, if having people speak the language was so vital to its survival, her requests to be taught it were constantly snubbed.

Tussling her shaggy hair affectionately he'd stated, 'You might be descended from convict stock, *mo ghrá*, but that doesn't make you Irish. It's just not in your blood.'

Rebecca stared through the window now, at an array of summer hats perched on pedestals surrounded by flowers, great marble vases of large bold blooms. Lilies and irises. The flowers and the hats flowed into each other, vibrant and vivid. Arranged to persuade, the display told a simple tale of beauty and pleasure – explicit and splendorous. Unmoved, Rebecca wanted to melt into the pavement, into her darkness; a murky puddle of DNA for pedestrians to step over distastefully.

'Ms Collins?' a young woman said, exiting the shop.

Rebecca turned to her. It was the round-faced girl – 'the one from Essex' Meredith had called her – who had assisted Rebecca in the purchase of the £650 headpiece she was sure her godson was keeping safe for her. She cast her eyes over Rebecca's head quickly but her expression remained cheery. 'Can I help you with something?'

Rebecca shook her head. 'I was just admiring your display. It's lovely.'

'Did the hat work out for you?' the round-faced girl asked. 'The Swan Darla?'

'Is that what my hat is called, the Swan Darla?' The name struck Rebecca as tragic.

'Yes. Were you happy with it?'

'Yes,' Rebecca laughed. The girl from Essex tilted her head. 'I looked the part.'

***

WHEN SHE REACHED Holland Park she sat by the playground. Children still played in the dwindling sunlight, their nannies hovering close by.

Angus wanted to be her saviour. Did she need one? she wondered. Luke had been her saviour once and she had been his. When they were younger, they'd depended on one another entirely. Even later, when they hadn't spoken in months, the assurance remained they would be there for each other, no matter what.

A brown-haired boy jumped into the sandpit, a sheaf of papers clutched under one arm. Rebecca looked more closely. It was sheet music. Discarded in the sand, the pages were quickly being buried. Violin or piano? Rebecca wondered. There were only two choices for kids of that age.

Luke had been gifted at everything he attempted – surfing, guitar, football, skateboarding – and he hadn't required lessons. Rebecca, on the other hand, had always had to work hard. Apart from the ability to analyse literature and place words on a page so they formed meaning, Rebecca possessed no gifts. Apart from writing, nothing came naturally to her. She recognised this from an early age. Her mother did not. Ballet, gymnastics then finally piano, were all attempted and failed. But it had never bothered Rebecca that Luke had been blessed with talent enough for two.

She wanted to speak to the young musician and ask him whether he enjoyed his music lessons. She never had. Piano lessons with Mrs Beck were torturous. Besides the opportunity of eating German biscuits and drinking sweet tea (a beverage her own mother would not allow) with Mrs Beck's son Heimo, Rebecca found no joy in her weekly ordeal.

The boy ripped off his coat and hurled it at his nanny. She gathered it from the ground with a disapproving scowl and hung it over her arm. There was a time in London when all nannies were Australian. Now they were Filipino. Had she been running past this playground for so long that she had witnessed an entire cultural shift?

'Freddie!' the nanny called as she searched the pockets of the boy's coat. 'Where is your music?'

The child ignored her.

'How will you play if you don't have your music?' she said, walking to the edge of the sandpit, unwilling to enter the grainy tract in her moccasins.

'I don't want to play!' He screamed in reply.

'I don't want to play,' Rebecca whispered urgently to Mrs Beck as they waited in the wings.

'You'll be superb, Rebecca. Just take your time and breathe deeply. Relax.'

Mrs Beck spoke without haste and pronounced every syllable faultlessly with a soft sibilance that curled around Rebecca like a blanket when she struggled during her lessons. The student did as instructed but the air was stale, smelling like old wood. Musty. It made her feel worse.

Rebecca peered at the audience. Her parents and Luke were seated in the second row. The auditorium was full. All of Gerringong had turned out for the Talent Showcase of 1983. Initially, when Mrs Beck had asked her to sign up, Rebecca had refused. But over the ensuing weeks her mother had nagged, Mrs Beck had encouraged and it seemed simpler to give in.

Why did she agree? she asked herself now.

She licked her lips. They tasted of the cherry lip gloss her mother had insisted she wear.

'It will make your lips shine under the lights,' she had said as she painted the cold pink gloop on Rebecca's mouth.

'I thought I wasn't allowed to wear lipstick until I was sixteen.' Rebecca's mouth was stretched taut into a narrow slit.

'This is lip gloss,' Joyce answered. 'Stop talking.'

Luke chuckled, leaning against the bedroom door. Mum had made him comb his hair, the matted curls forced unnaturally into submission, threatening to spring loose at any moment. Ray, their father, insisted he wear a collared shirt. Her twin seemed alien to her. Nothing seemed normal.

'Luke should be the one doing this,' Rebecca said as her mother stuck bobby pins through her hair. 'He's the one with the musical ability.'

He grinned. 'Yeah, but you're the geek.'

'Shoo,' her mother said, as though to a cat.

Rebecca was introduced. The audience applauded. Mrs Beck clutched Rebecca's shoulders. 'Good luck,' she said as she shoved her student gently towards the piano.

Rebecca moved swiftly to centre stage and sat on the stool, her eyes fixed on the dented and scratched floor rather than the aged keys of the town hall's upright. She didn't look out into the auditorium or smile, even though she had known every person there since birth. The legs scraped along the wooden floorboards when she pulled the stool into place beneath her and she heard a snigger from the audience. She took a deep breath but its passage seemed to be blocked at her chest.

Bach's Minuet in G Major. It was a simple piece, Mrs Beck had reassured her, one she had played a hundred times in her lessons. Everything would be fine.

She began.

Her fingers were stiff and they moved slowly. Hundred-pound weights were attached to her wrists. She instantly became aware of her shoulders, hunched up, close to her ears; the headache that had murmured in the shadows of her head on the way into town was now a blinding high-pitched shriek behind her eyes.

She attempted to relax, lower her shoulders. But she hit the wrong key.

Laughter.

Another deep breath as she waded through her swelling terror, searching for the right notes. They were lost to her. Her fingers seemed mechanised, playing the same part over and over. It was endless, like being stuck on a fast-spinning merry-go-round.

Nausea and dizziness clawed at her chest and head and she forgot how to end the piece. She searched for the right notes, but they simply weren't there. No longer hearing the music, Rebecca's attention was fixed on her fingers and the keys, both blurring into one. When the audience realised she was going in circles, there was more muffled laughter. Then the whispering began.

She stopped.

Her fingers ossified.

Within seconds she heard the clip-clop of her mother's heels on the stage and she was being led away by the elbow, like an invalid.

But before she had reached the wings, she heard clapping. She eased her elbow from her mother's grasp. It was a loud, thunderous round of applause delivered by one person.

She looked towards the audience. It was Luke standing on his chair. Her father was looking at his son in dismay, tugging at his trouser leg. Then her brother began to cheer and whistle wildly between two fingers, encouraging the rest of the audience to join in. Rebecca stared. Luke was grinning like a fool.

Soon everyone had been swept into the intensity of Luke's enthusiasm for his sister's dismal performance. Tears welled in her eyes. Then she giggled and blushed and, edging away from her mother towards centre stage, she curtsied demurely. The audience burst into laughter. Rebecca curtsied again then left the stage.

Later that night, when her father had turned out the lights, Rebecca got out of bed and tiptoed down the dark hallway and into Luke's room.

'Thanks,' she said, climbing into bed next to him.

'That's alright. You're my best mate.'

She couldn't see him. There was no moon. But she felt for his hand and gripped it.

'Can I sleep here tonight?'

'Mum won't like it.'

Rebecca didn't care. Luke had known what she was feeling and he'd saved her. Her heart ached with love and she needed to be close to him. Luke rolled away and she fixed herself against his back, breathing in his brackish scent. Sticking out her tongue, a shy rabbit from its burrow, she tasted his toasted skin, flaked with salt.

'I'll always look after you, Bec,' Luke whispered. 'Always. It's my job.'

They fitted together like puzzle pieces, she'd thought, as she drifted towards sleep.

When the sun began to set in earnest, she left the playground. Luke was still on her mind by the time she arrived home at ten. Memories she hadn't thought of in years had begun to bubble and surface, like treasures released from the depths of her mind.

APART FROM HER stop in the playground, she had run all the way home from Angus's front doorstep, but the feeling was still there – a virulent, clawing sensation that every aspect of her world was about to give way and there was no way to stop it.

After a shower where she tried to scrub the events of the day away, Rebecca stared at herself in the bathroom mirror for a long time, mesmerised by how shearing her hair had transformed her. The new look redefined her face. She looked like a kid again, but a different kid to the one she used to be. Luke was everywhere – in her jawline and cheekbones, even in the shape of her ears. They were almost without lobes. She resembled him now more than she ever had. Removing the veil had remade her into a ghost.

When she got into bed, she glanced quickly at the emptiness beside her then switched on her phone. Thirty-four new messages idled in her inbox. They all had subjects like 'Our deepest sympathies', 'I'm here for you' and 'Let's catch up'. Rebecca deleted them all. Reading them seemed an exhausting prospect. Then she noticed the text message.

I know that you recognised me in the cab. Can we meet? I'll be in London until Thursday. Gerard.

Rebecca cupped the phone in her hands and ran her eyes over the message again and again.

Another ghost.

7

―――――

A FORTNIGHT after Joe's funeral, Rebecca stood above her suitcase, reviewing its contents. Uncertain how long she'd be gone, she had packed as she would for a weekend away. Just one small bag lay on the bed with her passport and telephone beside it. Her heart lifted when she snapped the bag closed. She'd surprised herself with her choice, but she had to act. She had to know why.

From her experience over the last fourteen days, Rebecca believed that she had developed an intimate knowledge of the five stages of grief. Concerned that Joe's comment about her inability to cope with grief was true, she'd spent hours sitting alone in the kitchen researching Elisabeth Kübler-Ross's model, struggling to identify where she was placed and how far there was to travel until the utopian realms of acceptance were reached – the journey over. But as she read case studies of the grief-stricken, she recognised the imprecision of the model. There was nothing exact about grief. The grey areas were vast and inconceivably murky. She had learnt as much after Luke's death seventeen years ago. It wasn't a tube ride from Bond Street to Bank, each stop signposted along the way.

Rebecca believed she'd accepted Joe's death weeks before he'd died in her arms, but perhaps she hadn't. Although mere snapshots, the visions of him were becoming more frequent, as was his voice in her head. Signs, surely, that there was still more to work through. Rutted in anger, Rebecca came to realise that acceptance wasn't her goal; Kübler-Ross had neglected to consider a sixth and most crucial stage – forgiveness.

Forgiveness seemed unreachable.

'Do you think this is wise?' Rebecca flinched then calmly closed her eyes, attempting to block out his voice. The visions were fleeting, the voice too if she was strong enough.

'I'm here. Turn around. Look at me.'

She did. Joe was standing in the doorway. He stepped forward to the foot of the bed.

Rebecca blinked hard and shook her head. She felt the hair prickle on the back of her neck. Then she rubbed her eyes, feeling slightly dizzy. It was midday; she was packing, about to go downstairs to wait for the cab. This couldn't be a dream. Apart from the appearance of Joe, everything in the room was perfectly normal, from the prints on the wall to the stale potpourri in the dish on the dresser. She pinched her upper arm. Awake.

'I've put your heart crossways, haven't I?' Joe laughed. It was an expression she had only heard Joe use.

'Talk to me.'

She shook her head as she desperately sought out one rational thought in her mind. A single word from her would acknowledge that Joe was in the room when he couldn't possibly be. She couldn't let him be. Rebecca closed her eyes again and pressed her fingers into her ears.

'Talk to me! Stop trying to shut me out,' he ordered.

Startled, she looked at him.

Joe gripped the railing at the foot of the bed. Rebecca stared at the fine black hair on his knuckles for a moment. She was neither scared nor comforted by his presence. Nevertheless, goosebumps rose like pins in a cushion along the length of her arms. As she examined his face and body, she attempted to date the manifestation standing only a few feet from her. It wasn't the Joe O'Neill who she had kissed goodbye, it was the Joe O' Neill of twenty years ago. His dark hair was only just greying at the temples and his green eyes were alert and mischievous. He wore faded jeans and a black Stranglers t-shirt that was emblazoned with a red raven. She had thrown that shirt in the bin a thousand years ago when it had become threadbare and frayed with age and overwear.

Joe was outraged when he had discovered her crime and had unsuccessfully searched the rubbish for it. Guilt quickly overwhelmed her and Rebecca had manically scoured Camden Market until she sourced a replacement. While the shirt she purchased wasn't identical to the one she had so callously discarded, Joe had been astonished by her gesture and embraced her more tightly than he ever had before. When they parted he had gazed at her sincerely. She had never felt so wanted. Then he kissed her – a fathomless kiss – and she'd struggled for breath.

Joe had wanted to lose himself in her that afternoon. They made love until the sun set. Three or four hours later they emerged and Joe made grilled cheese sandwiches for their supper. They ate them, legs intertwined, on the sofa as they watched television.

'Love is lovely, isn't it?' he'd said, in between bites of his sandwich.

Rebecca didn't need to ask him about why he was so grateful for a gift that cost less than ten pounds. His mother's suicide, his brother's internment, his difficult childhood in West Belfast ... There had been very little kindness or tenderness in Joe's life.

'What are you hoping to discover?' Ghost Joe asked her now.

Rebecca glared at him; her lips clenched tight.

'You're a stubborn one, *mo ghrá*. It's what I love about you the most.'

'Love!' she spat. 'Fucking bastard! How can you say you love me?'

'Do you doubt it?' Her eyes narrowed. 'Think carefully before you answer.'

That was the problem. She was certain Joe had loved her. There was nothing of which she was more confident. Love was the bedrock of their relationship. In the early years they had survived on nothing else.

'I don't doubt it,' her voice was even. She fiddled with the straps of her bag. She didn't want to love him, but she did.

'"*Don't*,"' he mimicked the clipped vowel sound. 'I remember when we met your accent was so relaxing it was a sedative. Your words rolled over me in gentle waves.'

'I've changed. Is that the point you're trying to make?'

'It's not. Just a mere observation.'

Then he was gone. A knock came at the door a second later while Rebecca was still staring into the space Joe had just occupied. She gathered her belongings and made her way out.

Rebecca sat opposite Angus in his Covent Garden office, waiting for him to speak. Redesigned and redecorated in various shades of toffee by Meredith, the room was sparse and minimal. As the elegant chair on which she sat hugged her back and bottom perfectly, Rebecca felt like an ill-placed, outdated curio.

She had found Angus attractive once, when he was her tutor. His dignified shyness and reserve was so enticing to a teenager from Gerringong. She had told Joe of her crush many years later, after they had shared two bottles of barolo at Il Portico. He'd laughed briefly, dismissing it as a cliché. Now she studied him as he absently tidied the papers, files and books on his desk, readying himself for what was to come. His tall, lean frame had broadened in the last twelve months, since he had turned fifty and begun to compete in triathlons and running events. Joe had quickly summed his friend's new pastime up as a mid-life crisis. Meredith, whose exercise regime consisted only of yoga and pilates, made no comment. However, Rebecca had been enthusiastic, perhaps too enthusiastic, she now realised. But she was glad her friend had discovered a passion in middle age.

She glanced at him. Despite the movement of his body, his mouth was a steel trap. Then he threw a book down onto the desk, pushed his fists firmly into his Gieves & Hawkes trousers and stalked to the window. Loosening his tie, he glanced warily at her overnight bag that stood by the entrance.

Rebecca rose and walked to him.

'Please, Angus. Talk to me about it. I can't go if I don't have your blessing.'

He looked at her gravely. Rebecca could see his resolve melting.

'Geneva? Really?' he finally said, wincing.

'I'm not after revenge. I just don't want to be angry forever. I still love him, you see.'

There was pain and confusion in Angus's eyes, as well as a little longing.

'How can I simply switch that emotion off, despite what he did? And I don't want to hate him. I could very easily hate him, but it doesn't make sense to. I don't want to be one of those bitter women who get drunk too quickly at dinner parties. I want to understand and I have to start somewhere. Geneva seems like the logical place,' Rebecca explained.

'Angus, I have to get away from London. Everything seems a little bit askew without Joe here.'

'Why don't you go home?'

'To Australia? Gerringong?' Rebecca laughed. 'I haven't been home since Luke died. I gave up my citizenship the moment I accepted the scholarship to City University.'

'I just thought the beach and the sun ... it was such a large part of your life once ... it might be ... regenerating or something,' Angus began.

'This isn't a book, Angus,' Rebecca said. 'I can't dive into the ocean and suddenly have the past and the pain –'

'Washed away,' Angus finished with a wry grin.

'Exactly.'

Angus poured a glass of water for them each from a large sterling silver pitcher. 'Modernist,' he remarked as Rebecca gazed at the condensation glistening its flanks. 'Meredith found it. Cost me a fortune.'

'The boy, his son, looked so much like him. That scowl and those eyes,' Rebecca sighed.

Angus nodded.

'He messaged me. He wanted to meet.'

'And did you?'

'It was tempting, so tempting. I stared at his text for

hours, thinking that he's half Joe. But I didn't ... I didn't even reply. Is that cowardly?'

'You did the right thing. You never know how mother bear might react.'

Rebecca nodded absently.

'I Googled her,' she said.

'Really?'

'She's not on Facebook. Well, not under her real name.'

'Sounds like you're stalking her.'

'Why did you tell me her full name if you didn't think I'd Google her? Surely you have as well.'

He glanced at her suitcase again. 'Perhaps.'

'She's an actuary analyst for a company called AKPH.'

'Yes, they're underwriters, I believe.'

'She's quite good at it, apparently. Recognised throughout the world as a "leader in the field". Written books on the subject.'

'They must be fascinating.'

Rebecca smiled at her loyal old friend.

'Why didn't you tell me the full story? You made her sound like a common old broker.'

Angus shook his head vaguely and sipped his water.

'Did you not want me to feel inadequate?'

He laughed quietly.

'You are far from inadequate.'

They sat without speaking for a long time. Rebecca gazed at the well-pressed middle-aged man opposite her and remembered her unkempt twentysomething tutor. Rebecca's crush had been immediate. When he recited *To Autumn* during their first tutorial her stomach had vaulted and swirled. His stammer, his halting, awkward speech, all his perceived inadequacies, had vanished under the spell of Keats's verse.

'*You're probably thinking I was trying to hide my inadequacies, hoping to convince you that, although Australian, I'm worthy of the scholarship,*' *Rebecca said when the other students had left the tutorial. She'd made a show of ordering her notes and books.* '*I'm not usually that vocal. Sorry.*'

'*Antipodeans,*' *Angus muttered with a crooked, bashful grin, flicking his eyes her way, easing her embarrassment.*

He pulled the chair out next to her.

'*You don't need to convince me of your right to be here. I read your story. It was enough to convince anyone. You're a very fine writer.*'

Rebecca felt the heat rise in her face.

'*And you're obviously quite familiar with the Romantics,*' *he said, in a lighter tone. Despite his scrappy appearance, he smelled recently laundered.*

'*I especially love Keats. A friend introduced me in high school.*'

Angus looked at her for a moment, nodding, acknowledging her response, as though he was about to speak. He was so close to speech; Rebecca could almost see the shapes of the words forming on his lips.

'*Well, keep up the good work,*' *he said stiffly, standing and collecting his satchel.*

As crushes do, hers had dissipated gradually as their friendship developed. Inseparable for a period until Joe, they had read each other's work, discussed books and films, and spent plutonic long weekends together in the Lakes District, attempting to conjure the magic of Wordsworth.

'A penny for your thoughts,' Angus said now, breaking their silence.

Rebecca shrugged and looked at her watch.

'I should probably get going.'

'Perhaps you should ... talk to somebody.'

'A therapist?'

He nodded.

Rebecca shook her head, cutting him off.

'I don't need a therapist ... well, I don't think I do,' she said, then paused.

'You know, it's as though the three of us were parasites, clinging to Joe, living off his dreams and success.'

Angus stared at her quizzically.

'When we met, you were a teacher, a part-time university tutor doing your doctorate and living in a share house in Brixton. You read poetry aloud for entertainment and wore jeans with holes in them. You shunned your background and spoke of "old money" with such disdain. You even smoked weed, if I recall.'

Angus chuckled, a little proudly.

'You built this company on your family's wealth and Joe's career, and that's fine, but at least you've built something.'

His eyes narrowed. 'You think I'm a sell out?'

'Of course not. You matured, that's all. You've built something to leave behind.'

Rebecca paused again before going on.

'Do you think Meredith would have ever gotten her romances published if not for Joe? She was in his circle and that gave her access to the entire industry. Joe made her work desirable, even though it was shit.'

Angus cleared his throat. 'Your books were very well-received by the critics.'

'But they didn't sell,' Rebecca fired back.

'Are you jealous of Meredith?' Angus asked.

'Of course I am!'

'But you're a far better writer.'

'It's not only about the writing.'

He nodded ruefully.

'It's just that now Joe's dead, you're both left with legacies. And Joe has left the most profound one. But I've been left with nothing. Do you see?'

'I see.'

'Looking back, I realise that I gave up so much of myself for Joe,' Rebecca continued, uncertain Angus really understood. 'I let him engulf me entirely but it was okay because I was happy and I thought we were building something together.' She swallowed. 'Turns out, we weren't. Now I need to let him go and create something of my own. Do you understand? The first step, I think, is knowing why he made certain choices.'

Rebecca needed Angus to understand. Before Joe, she had been consumed by Luke. She had left Australia to be something more than Luke Collins's twin. But she had allowed it to happen all over again. What did that say about her? she wondered. Was it even possible that she could be her own person?

'You gave up your dreams to further Joe's. You want to be a person other than Joe O'Neill's partner, assistant, editor, lover, dogsbody, sounding board, nurse ...'

'I have to be,' she stated.

'I understand perfectly,' Angus replied reassuringly.

The pair sighed then embraced; old friends contemplating past and future.

'I was talented, wasn't I? You were my tutor, my agent. Tell me.'

He nodded.

'You were my most gifted young writer. What's more, your books were published on their own merit. You had fresh ideas and passion and a way with language ... You wrote so beautifully because you loved it. Writing was as essential to you as ... as air ...' he trailed off.

'What's wrong?' she asked.

'What if ... hypothetically ... it had been me who had bought you that pint after Joe's lecture at the university and not Joe?'

She smiled and recalled the evening at The Well. Joe had delivered a lecture to her class. It was titled, 'Why People Need Poetry'. Joe was quite renowned by then, as much for his anti-establishment activities as for his writing.

Angus was thrilled when, after meeting Joe at a festival, he had secured a promise from the poet to lead Angus's creative writing tutorial the next time he was in London. As his black hair fell across his brow in thick locks, Joe had spoken fervently for almost two hours about technique, patterns and rhyme, and about caring for words and the resistance of words. Rebecca had found his tattooed fore-arms, muscled from working at the Belfast shipyards, as entrancing as his fire. He had recited poems by Housman, Dickinson, Keats and Stevens and had concluded that poetry helped people come to terms with their mortality. 'Poems take mankind beyond death', he had said. When the class had concluded, Rebecca's belly was filled with fire as well, a passion she had not experienced for a long time.

'By the time Joe had bought me that pint, Angus,' Rebecca remarked, 'I was already in love.'

8

———

'TELL ME ABOUT YOUR EDUCATION,' Eva said as she poured the coffee. 'What sort of student were you?'

Rebecca reached for the cup and sipped it slowly for a few seconds, drawing the blistering liquid through her lips to temper it. Eva's coffee made her sweat. Even with the air cooler turned to high, Rebecca perspired. Nevertheless, she never refused Eva's moka. She enjoyed the taste and it seemed to hone her thoughts. Everything in her mind – obscurities, faces and events that had faded over time like the ink on a letter – became clearer.

The doctor sat, put on her glasses and lifted her pen.

'I was an average student, a *very* average student. Just like most of the other kids in my hometown, except Heimo, of course. I was only interested in the beach, hanging out with Luke and my friends ...'

Eva stopped writing and removed her glasses momentarily in thought, put them on again then flicked back through her notes.

'But you have a Masters degree and a post doctorate.'

'My academic rise began when I broke my neck.'

'You *what*? How?' Eva threw her notepad on the steamer trunk then looked at her patient, removing her glasses once more. A degree of humoured frustration was evident in her hawk's gaze.

'In a surfing accident when I was fifteen,' Rebecca explained, shrugging. 'I was paralysed and spent a few days in the hospital.'

'Bruising?'

'And swelling. When I could move again, I was sent home, but I was housebound for six weeks and forbidden to surf for two months. During that time I discovered other interests. The schoolwork that my teachers sent home I completed, initially only out of boredom. But I found I was actually learning things and I liked it. There was nothing else to do, you see. So I spent time on assignments, considered the questions. I also began to read. Then I began to write. They were just ways of killing time, really, but I found I was quite good at them.'

'Do you remember the accident?'

'Yes, extremely clearly.' Rebecca said, staring hard at the doctor as she thought.

'It changed my life completely. If it wasn't for that single event, I'd probably be a hairdresser or a receptionist with three kids in a four-beddy in Gerringong.'

'I'LL PICK you up after work. I have to be back in Gerringong by five. I want you in the car park at four-thirty. I'm not going to scramble down to the beach looking for you.'

'Okay,' Rebecca said, offering her father a kiss. 'See ya then.'

'Bye,' Ray said. 'Be careful.' He kissed her forehead. 'Look after her, mate.'

Luke raised a hand and nodded.

The teenagers stood on the headland looking down at the beach. It was better than Christmas. The sun had barely risen and it glinted off the water like diamonds. Summer at The Farm tended to be flat, but in the winter, when the beach harnessed the southern swell, the surf was perfect – consistent and predictable. Exactly the conditions Rebecca loved.

A peppering of surfers bobbed among the seagulls waiting for a set. Rebecca and Luke didn't surf at The Farm often. Their mother or father needed to drive them and neither ever had the time. 'There are plenty of good surfing spots within walking distance,' they'd say. 'Why do you need to go all the way to The Farm?'

But Ray had a job in Shellharbour that day and he offered them a ride.

The pair smiled at each other and inhaled the crisp, briny air before making their way down the track. The last time they had scrambled down the dirt-and-sand hill, pushing through the scrub, Rebecca had been taller than her brother. That was last winter. In the summer between then and now, Luke had grown. His shoulders had broadened and his jaw had thickened. 'Fleshed out' was how their mum described it. Once school began in February, girls started showing up at the house, hanging around the front fence. Some even called out his name as if he was a rock star. Luke was oblivious to his newfound power and dismissed the girls. This made him even more magnetic. It made Rebecca happy when he opened the front door and told them to 'piss off'. She would outwardly mock his status as 'town spunk' while being silently gleeful at his indifference.

Their boards hit the water and they paddled out side by side beyond the break. They sat upright, surrendering to the swell of the ocean beneath them. Rebecca loved the anticipation, her long legs straddling the board, fading into the unseen depths. Her body was so alert it tingled. She looked to the horizon and contemplated what lay beyond ... but, she thought, nothing could be better than this, could it? The waiting was almost better than the ride.

She sensed the approach of a wave and glanced at Luke. He responded with an encouraging nod. He was the more adept surfer. Luke could always find the best take-off zone. There was no analysis involved, just intuition. Aware of the oncoming rush, she lay flat on her board and paddled wildly, her arms powered by expectancy. Then, gliding catlike to her feet, upright and unrestrained on the shoulder, Rebecca was electrified by the force of the water behind her, allowing her to move across, up and down the wave on her journey toward the beach. She was completely at the sea's mercy, at the very centre of nature, and it didn't frighten her in the least. She came off and was lost in the foam. When she surfaced, she spotted Luke riding in on a mushy. The wave petered out beneath him and he collapsed into the water. Then they paddled out together again.

They ate the lunch their mother had packed them – devon sandwiches, fruit and a can of Coke each. Luke burped, a loud, wet belch, and they laughed, then placed the remnants of their lunch in their backpacks and went out again.

The wind had picked up and the tide was low. All the other surfers had left. The twins had to walk out a long way before the water even reached their knees. When Rebecca finally sat upright and looked back she seemed miles away from the beach. A terrible knot gripped her stomach, as though she would never see home or Luke again.

After a few minutes, he called her name and she glanced behind her. The wave took her suddenly but she managed to rise to her feet. It was low and powerful and sent her hurtling towards the shore, and soon she could easily see the sandy bottom. Then, unexpectedly jacking up, the wave closed out over a section of sandbar and Rebecca was flipped off. Her head rammed into the ocean floor.

'HEIMO BECK'S HERE, LOVE,' *her mother said, walking into the sunroom.*

'I don't want to see him.'

'He's got flowers,' Joyce went on with a tolerant yet pointed smile. 'It's a nice gesture.' She pulled up the blinds and light flooded the room.

Rebecca groaned. 'Look at me!'

'You look fine. Come on in, Heimo.' Joyce walked to the television and turned it off.

'Can I get you two anything?'

Heimo looked at Rebecca. She wanted to run but she could barely walk so she just turned her head as far as the neck brace would allow.

'No thanks, Mrs Collins,' he answered.

The adolescent stood in the centre of the room dressed in his soccer kit, shifting his weight from foot to foot. He was tall, about the same height as Luke, and lean, but not skinny like some of the boys in their year. Rebecca liked his legs, the way his thigh muscles slightly bulged just above his knees.

His parents, who owned the only Italian restaurant in Gerringong, had immigrated from Germany in the 1960s. There was no taste for German cuisine in town in the '60s, so the Becks hired an Italian chef. Mr Beck, who was known by everyone as Hans, although his name was Tomas, had managed restaurants in Munich. They were the only Germans Rebecca knew. Joyce worked a few shifts a week for them at their restaurant, La Candela, waitressing, and Mrs Beck, who had been a music teacher in Germany, tutored in piano, violin and cello from home.

While Mrs Beck's knowledge and expertise paid no dividends with Rebecca, her own son played extremely well, although it wasn't a talent he ever boasted of. Each week he'd arrive at their house with an electric keyboard under one arm. Although they rarely talked at school, he and Luke would stay in the garage for hours. 'Jamming' Luke called it.

'How'd you go today?' Joyce asked.

Heimo ran his fingers through his thick brown hair.

'Alright. We drew two all.' He walked over to Rebecca who tried to turn her head even further.

'Mum wanted me to give you these.' He thrust a large bouquet at her.

'Oh, they're lovely. So colourful,' Joyce said, moving forward.

'Where are your manners, Rebecca?'

'Thanks.'

'I'll put them in water.' Joyce glared at her daughter, took the flowers and left the room.

Heimo sat next to her on the settee.

Irritated, Rebecca said, 'Luke's surfing.'

'I didn't come to see Luke,' he responded, pausing.

'Will you let me see your face?' His tone was kind, the phrasing of the question so sensitive that she turned towards him.

The Aussie kids, Luke's mates mainly, had christened Heimo 'Homo' in the fifth grade. The nickname had stuck, but Heimo never seemed to mind. A few of the girls had crushes on him. They said he was 'mysterious'. But he was just quiet. She liked his dark blue eyes. They saw beyond the obvious.

Heimo examined her injuries – the abrasions that littered her face and the two black eyes, silently documenting every graze and cut. The tenderness of his gaze was soothing.

'Luke won't talk about it. He shuts me down every time I mention you, but everyone's saying you broke your neck.'

'Fractured.' The term seemed less serious in Rebecca's mind.

She touched the swollen, purple flesh around her eyes. 'The doctor said the bruises might take weeks to fade.'

'They make your eyes seem even bluer.'

She smiled. He was the only person who hadn't exclaimed 'wow' or 'gross'. Even her father had taken to calling her 'racoon'.

'Do you remember it?'

'The last thing I remember was looking down and seeing the bottom of the ocean. The water was so clear it was like I could count every grain of sand if I wanted to. For a while I kept replaying it in my mind, even dreaming of it.'

Heimo nodded seriously, considering.

'But that's happening less and less now. Thank God.'

'That's your mind trying to classify the accident. Work out where the memory should slot into your brain.'

Rebecca looked at him.

'It was on a documentary.'

'Mum and Dad keep telling me that I could have died.'

Joyce tapped lightly on the doorframe. Heimo rose and smoothed his shorts. They were muddy. The flowers, now in a vase, were set on top of the television.

'Aren't they beautiful, Bec?' she said, beaming. 'I adore asters.'

'They're very beautiful.'

Joyce scooped the morning papers from the floor on her way out.

'When are you coming back to school?' Heimo asked.

'Six weeks, the doctor said. But he reckons the neck brace can come off in a fortnight. I'm bored already.'

'Would you mind if I came and visited again? Just to keep you company, I mean?'

'That'd be nice.'

R*EBECCA LAY in bed and listened to the sounds of the household. Heels on the wooden floor, a toilet flush, plates being stacked in the sink, goodbyes then the screen door slamming, one, two, three times. The brace had come off and the severity of her injuries had diminished. The bruising on her face had faded to a bilious yellowy green, but her mum insisted that she stay home for another month and no surfing until the school holidays - doctor's orders. When she finally got up, she roamed the house with her cereal bowl, wondering how she'd fill another day.*

Homework and assignments were usually her first job. She'd stretch out the tasks for as long as possible, adding detail and concocting intricate, colourful borders appropriate to the subject area. But her day really began at eleven, when General Hospital started. It was followed by Days of Our Lives then The Young and the Restless. By the time her parents came home she was immersed in the quiz shows. She barely saw Luke. He ran in from school, threw her schoolwork at her, dumped his things and went surfing until dinner. It was as though she repelled him.

She missed him, and was angry; after all, she was the one who had broken her neck.

'He's taken it very hard,' Joyce said, keeping the peace. 'He'll come around. Give him time.'

Believing their bond was deeper than the ocean, Rebecca was hurt and confused at his behaviour.

She attempted to put herself in her brother's shoes. She felt him then, his fear and the anger seeped through from her, leaving her deflated.

She eased herself onto the settee and placed the bowl on the floor. The sun through the glass walls burned her legs and reminded her that it was the first day of spring. Her eyes scanned the room and a petal from Heimo's flowers fell to the floor. The once pert buds drooped forlornly. He said he would call in this afternoon. *A weird quiver filled her belly and she closed her eyes, enjoying the sensation.*

When she opened them, her attention fell on the bookcase. The four pine shelves stood against the brick wall of the original house. Her father had built the sunroom himself when she and Luke were in kindergarten. The bookcase now struck her as odd, out of place, even though it had stood in the same position since she was six. She couldn't remember her parents ever reading books. Ray read the newspaper and Joyce read magazines. She and Luke read the surf report in the afternoon paper.

Rebecca rose, drawn in that direction. She ran her fingers along the rows – biographies of sportsmen, a joke book, cookbooks, a few Reader's Digest *anthologies and a book called* Raising Twins *by Dr Jonathon Nowicki. The image of identical twin girls wearing matching pink dresses and sitting at a children's table was displayed on the spine. Kneeling on the tiles, she examined the lower shelves where a series of hardcovers rested –* The Complete Agatha Christie *– chronologically ordered from one to fifteen. They bore the* Time Life *logo. When had her mother sent away for those? she wondered, as she drew one from its position. The image on the glossy dust jacket featured an old-fashioned telephone left off the hook. There were drops of blood around the receiver and the author's name was written in a bold Art Deco font. She crossed her legs and opened the cover. It complained with a creak, stretching its spine for the first time.*

Rebecca began to read.

9

———

'WHAT WAS *wrong with you out there today?'* Luke said as they walked home.

She shrugged. 'It's been two months. I'm rusty.'

'You dropped in on Nev.'

Disappointment was written all over his face, paralysing her all over again. Although they hadn't spoken about it, she knew he'd been living for this day since the accident. For him, things could finally go back to normal. No neck brace, no bruising. Full movement. It would be as though Rebecca had never broken her neck.

'It wasn't intentional,' she lied. 'Like I said, I'm rusty.'

'They'll give you the benefit of the doubt once, but ...'

'Why do you take it all so seriously? I'm sorry, okay!' Luke stopped, open-mouthed, as Rebecca stormed through the back gate and threw her board on the grass. She ran into the house and into her bedroom, slamming the door behind her.

She peeled off her wetsuit and jumped into bed in her swimmers, pulling the doona over her head. Ashamed of herself and angry with Luke for making her get in the water again, she began to cry. Soon she heard the hose. Luke washing off the boards. The sound prompted her to sob even harder. There was a tap at the door.

'Love. Are you alright? You didn't hurt yourself out there, did you?' Her mother entered slowly. Rebecca felt her hand on her back through the covers.

'What's wrong? You two have a fight?' Her mother eased her from her cocoon.

'I hate this room!' she screamed. 'I'm too old for pink.'

'Okay ... We can change the colour and I suppose you're a little beyond Barbie,' her mother said, glancing at her doona cover. 'But I don't think that's what you're upset about.'

Her mother drew Rebecca into her arms.

'I just don't like it as much.'

'Surfing?'

Rebecca nodded.

'If you're frightened, that's natural.'

'A little, I s'pose.' She wiped her teary face with the corner of her sheet. 'But it's more that ... there's just more to life, you know? There has to be. But Luke's obsessed.'

Her mother glanced at the books on her bedside table and bit her lip.

'You have to tell him then, Love. Just be honest. It's probably just a case of you maturing faster than your brother. Just because you're twins doesn't mean ...' She studied her daughter's distress.

'Girls mature earlier, you know. They develop faster than boys.'

Rebecca sank into her mattress. Heimo was going to Germany in December for the Christmas holidays. He and his parents did so every year. This year he was going alone. Heimo was given space to grow and mature, to develop into his own person. Since the accident, Rebecca had begun to fear she would always be half of a whole.

'It's true there's a big wide world out there ...' Joyce rose and *placed her hand on the pile of books. 'It's great that you're reading. Your dad and I think it's fantastic, but what's in these is make-believe. Don't forget about what's real, what's right here.' She stroked her daughter's tangled hair.*

'Luke's never liked change, you know that. Talk to him.'

Rebecca nodded and smiled half-heartedly. She glanced through the window. Luke stood on the lawn between the boards, looking towards the ocean. Tears began to surface again.

'Tea's nearly ready,' Joyce said, leaving the room.

She knew his every thought. Watching him out there, she knew exactly what he was feeling. Mostly it was an overwhelming love that was all at once consoling and terrifying. But there was also anger and an acute pain that came with the realisation that nothing could remain the same forever, no matter how much you fought against it or denied it.

Luke didn't come in for the evening meal. Rebecca found him after dinner sitting on the grassy verge of the beach. The sun had all but set. Luke was illuminated by a street light, his long hair streaming around his head in the wind. Rebecca stood behind him for a time, considering what to say, where to begin. Her stomach eddied.

Luke stubbed his cigarette into the ground.

'You did it on purpose, didn't you? You surfed like a quimby out there today on purpose.'

Rebecca approached and sat by his side. Be honest, her mother had advised.

'Yeah.' Rebecca tugged at a blade of grass and then another. 'It just doesn't mean as much to me any more. I wanted today to be perfect for you, but I hated that I was doing it for you and not myself. I felt like you forced me to go out there again.'

'You were scared?'

'No, not really. I just can't handle ... I shouldn't have to be the one to make you happy.'

Luke stared at her for a moment.

'It's all those books you've been reading, isn't it?' he said. 'And the writing. I've seen you writing in that notebook. You hide it in your top drawer.'

Being absent from school and lacking activity for so long meant Rebecca hadn't been tired at night. As the household slept she had taken to turning on her lamp and writing, scribbling in her notebook until she had stripped herself of every word, exhausted. It was like she was shedding her skin and becoming someone different. When she was writing, anything was possible. Her world became bigger. In the quiet of the house, her senses were alert. She would write about things, small things, she had observed during the day – a blow fly trapped, darting frantically around the window pane, or her father nodding off on the lounge, beer can in hand, after he'd finished work for the day. Or Luke standing on the beach, assessing the conditions, reading the swell.

'I don't hide it. You can read it if you like.'

He turned away without responding.

'Perhaps you already have.'

He shot her a look.

'Why would I want to read about you getting wet for Heimo Beck?'

'You're gross, Luke!' Rebecca leapt to her feet and marched towards the water. The onshore breeze was cold, but she didn't feel it.

Within seconds he was by her side, his arm around her shoulders.

'Fuck off,' she said, pulling away.

'Listen,' he shouted into the wind, gripping her arms, keeping hold. 'You and surfing are all that make sense to me sometimes. If I haven't got you ...'

'You're hurting me.'

He dropped his hands.

Rebecca stared at him, struggling to figure him out. She brushed his hair from his face and he looked at her hopefully. The tears resting in his pale blue eyes made her ache.

'When you came off your board and you didn't stand up,' he said, 'it was like I was trying to swim through cement. If it hadn't been for that old guy walking his dog ...'

Luke wiped his eyes with the heels of his hands. Rebecca's throat thickened and she rested her head against his chest. His arms closed around her body and they relaxed into each other, taking comfort from the intimacy. She felt Luke's lips against her hair. For a moment, Rebecca felt safe again.

'I thought we were immortal, you and me, that we'd be surfing The Farm forever.'

'But we're not immortal,' Rebecca replied, breaking away. 'I think it's alright if we try some different things. Doesn't mean you're not my best friend any more.'

'Am I?'

'Always.'

'You too,' he said then paused. 'It's really hard though, Becca. After what happened, I just want to keep you even closer.'

'But we can't get any closer, Luke. We're twins. And you can't keep me safe all the time.'

He nodded. Rebecca hoped he understood.

'I won't be surfing as much,' she went on gently. 'I've found something else. I don't know if I'm any good at it and it's harder than I thought, but I love it. It makes me feel special ... Anyway, when it comes to surfing I'm a rank amateur compared to you. You could be the next Tom Carroll.'

Luke sighed and placed his hands on his narrow hips, transfixed by the movement of the water.

'I'm sorry for what I said about Heimo. I like him. He's a good guy.'

'He's just a friend and I don't write about him.'

'What then?'

'They're mostly descriptions of things that strike me as beautiful – the waves, a bird or a flower, Mum's fingers when she's icing a cake.' Rebecca paused then. She felt at one with him again.

'Or when you're out there and you pull into a barrel and it closes over you. You're lost to me for a second and I'm scared, really scared, but you always come out the other end, grinning like an idiot. It's the most beautiful thing I've ever seen.'

'AND THAT WAS THE TRUTH,' Rebecca said to Eva. 'Luke on a board was the most beautiful, the purest thing to watch.'

Eva pushed a tissue box closer to her patient. Rebecca plucked one out and blew her nose.

'Take a few deep breaths,' the doctor advised.

She did so and soon became calm.

'After Luke died the words became more difficult. They no longer poured out of me like water. I'd fuss with a single page, sometimes a single sentence for days. It was torture. In the end, I gave up. Whatever transitory gift I'd been touched by was absent without Luke.'

10

Eva led Rebecca down the narrow hallway to her office. The doctor was slightly hunched and she shuffled in her flat slippers, sandpaper on the tiled floor.

Copies of each of Rebecca's three books were stacked on the steamer trunk. 'You're an extremely talented writer,' Eva said.

'You read them?' Rebecca wondered where Eva had found them. They'd been out of print for years.

Eva nodded and reached for one of the novels, *Breathless*, Rebecca's first. Yellow sticky notes loomed above some pages. She flicked through the book for a moment then read aloud.

Deb stared at the canvas. It had become dark in the hours she'd been standing in the corner of her room fixed to the floor, unmoving; so dark all she could see were shadows. Her bladder was bursting. Suddenly she gripped the work and hurried it to the backyard, her shins knocking painfully against the frame. Hurling it into the incinerator bin, she was certain it was the right decision. Worthy of burning. A sacrifice to Minerva. Flames lit her face and danced in her eyes. Taking the smoke into her lungs, she fought against the urge to cough or retch, hoping to absorb each blackened particle.

Rebecca hated hearing her work read aloud. Shying away from public readings when her books were released, it always seemed that her words were never meant to be voiced. Although she remembered the scene Eva quoted, she couldn't remember writing it. Where had she been? In the bedroom at Camden? In the London Library while she waited for Joe to finish a lecture or research?

'Deb, the main character in this book, is an artist. She wants to escape. She wants something bigger than her small town can give her. Deb "sacrifices" what she considers to be her best, her truest work – a portrait of her teacher, her guru.'

Rebecca looked out the open window. The sky was cloud-covered but the temperature had already risen into the thirties. The ancient cooler sat silent in the corner.

'She's at once ... expelling him while drawing him in.'

'I suppose you could interpret it in that way,' Rebecca replied.

'Is there another way?'

'Deb wants out of Hawks Bluff. She hopes to start over somewhere else, make her own mark. But she's struggling to let go, to move away from her teacher's influence. The painting symbolises her past; she has to burn it before she can move on.'

'I see.' Eva closed the novel and placed it on the steamer trunk then looked back at her notes.

'*Shelter* was published in 2000, the year Luke died. It was your last novel, yes?'

Rebecca checked her watch, impatient. It was almost eleven.

'We talked about this on Tuesday. Luke was my muse, you said.'

Eva thumbed through her note pad.

'I don't believe I did say that. You inferred it.' Eva lifted her head and removed her glasses, scratching her temple with an arm.

'But muses are myths. Water nymphs, they say.' She frowned. 'Even so, it seems odd to me that you wrote and published three books in eight years then nothing.'

Rebecca unbuttoned the cuffs of her shirt and rolled up the sleeves.

'To be honest, even though my books received good reviews, they never sold well. By the late 90s Joe's career had taken off and was consuming most of our time. There were too many distractions. Maybe I used Luke's death as an excuse not to write.'

'Doesn't the best art challenge death?'

'Is that "Death" with a capital "D"?'

Eva laughed.

'Perhaps.'

'So, is art really just a way of giving Death the bird?'

'Yes, I suppose it is. Isn't that what Joe believed? Art, poetry were a means of defying Death?'

'He did. But I don't.'

Eva seemed to ignore her patient's comment, continuing to unravel a thread.

'I know other writers. The way they describe the process, it seems quite addictive, all-consuming. I have written a book myself and I experienced a little of that. It was cathartic, I suppose. Others liken the process to the gestation of a child.'

'Yes. The birth is seeing your book, your baby, in a shop for the first time. It's indescribable.'

'The joy?'

'It was an odd experience for me,' Rebecca said.

REBECCA HURRIED *along Charing Cross Road through the peak-hour foot traffic. She should leave her visit until late, Angus had advised. Bookstores never unpack the stock the moment it arrives. He'd wanted to join her, be by her side when she saw it on the shelves, but she'd declined his offer. She wasn't certain how she'd react when she saw her novel on a shelf in a shop.*

'It's best to be alone the first time, mo ghrá,' Joe had said, 'to take in the breadth of your achievement. I faced all kinds of demons when I saw my first collection in Hatchards. It was as though heaven and hell collided on Piccadilly.'

He wouldn't explain any further.

Rebecca hadn't known what Joe had meant but now, halting a few shops from Foyles, she was beginning to understand. As she moved closer to the store, the excitement she had felt leaving the flat gave way to a strange sense of dread. Rebecca had never felt so vulnerable, as though she were shedding her clothes one piece at a time. Everyone she passed glanced her way in shock, she imagined. But there was no turning back. The words were out there.

Momentum pushed her on, through the door towards a sign that read 'New Releases'. The store was busy. Over-coated customers, killing time while waiting for friends or on their way home, milled around. They picked up a book, read the blurb then replaced it before wandering to another shelf or out the door and onto the street.

Two towers (one five books higher than the other) of her novel stood on a display in the centre of the shop. The books were perfectly aligned, the title and her name evident in gold lettering on the spine. Upright copies like crenellations rested atop each stack, displaying the cover.

Contrary to Angus's counsel, Rebecca had chosen a small, boutique publisher, Rough Cup Press. During her meeting with them they had boasted of authenticity and personal attention to the author and their work. Rebecca was sold on them immediately. Her work seemed too delicate to leave in the calloused hands of a big publishing house.

It was the first time Rebecca had seen her book en masse. Single proof copies and mock-ups of the cover had been sent to her, but she had never examined a version of her book that was completely complete, pristine and polished. There'd been a delay with the printer and the review copies had been late ... Now, confronted by them all, she felt sick.

The dust jacket was a wash of blue, scored with a brush stroke of imperial yellow vaguely in the shape of a human body, blurred but recognisable. Effervescent bubbles whooshed from the form disappearing behind the letters of the title, Breathless. Tears began to form behind Rebecca's eyes. She picked up the book, pressing it against her brow.

'If you smell it, you have to buy it,' a shop assistant said as she approached.

Rebecca looked at her, took in her narrow face and friendly smile for a moment, said 'I'm sorry,' then hastily replaced the book on the pile.

'I'm just joking,' the girl went on, picking up a copy.

'It's a fantastic cover, isn't it? Just came in today. The manager plans to move it into the window tomorrow. It's just so eye-catching. The reviews are very positive as well.'

'Really?'

The girl nodded, examining Rebecca more closely.

'Are you okay?'

Rebecca nodded.

'Let me know if you need any help. The publisher has promised to send us some copies signed by the author, if you're interested. They should be here in two or three days. Just let me know and I'll put one aside.' The girl moved to the opposite side of the display and began neatening piles.

'Thanks,' Rebecca said offhandedly, remembering Joe's words.

Heaven and hell.

In the space of three minutes a lifetime had been dredged up from the depths and laid naked in front of the world.

EVA SCRATCHED HER HEAD, thinking for a moment.

'Because the subject matter was so personal?'

'Perhaps,' Rebecca replied, hoping to move on.

But Eva wasn't ready to move on. She waited. Rebecca's eyes scanned the room, skirting the picture rails and the pretty, decorative cornices that were in need of dusting and paint.

'I guess once you get to the point of seeing your book in a shop, once the process ends, I mean, it's the culmination of so many different emotions ...' Rebecca paused. 'A bit like crossing the finish line of a marathon. The runners always break down. They're usually a mess. But I went back with Joe and Angus, a few days later. By then they'd put my book in the window. To see it behind glass, displayed ... I was over the moon. Completely euphoric.'

'It can't have been easy to stop writing.'

Rebecca looked away. 'In the big scheme of things ... in the context of my life at the time, it just didn't seem important.'

Eva pushed on. 'When I finally completed my book after many years, I experienced a great sense of joy. I was riding a strange, self-satisfied high for many days afterwards.'

'It's a wonderful sensation,' Rebecca agreed. 'As though you've reached the summit of Everest.'

'Exactly.'

'It's addictive.'

'And you went cold turkey.'

'I suppose I did.' Rebecca looked at her hands clenched in her lap. Eva was searching for a more precise reason. How did her failure to write link to Luke's death? But she couldn't go any further. A door closed and she couldn't find the key.

Eva studied Rebecca's face for a few seconds then turned her notepad to a clean page.

'Let's talk about Heimo.'

Rebecca cleared her throat and her shoulders relaxed.

'Childhood sweethearts, yes?'

'No, not really. We grew up together but lost touch when we went to university. I moved to London and Heimo studied in Sydney.'

'Then you met again recently, in Geneva?'

'That's right. He recommended seeing you.'

'How did you feel when you saw him again after how many ...' she flicked back through pages, *fft, fft, fft*, 'after twenty-seven years?'

'Good,' Rebecca answered. 'Wonderful, in fact.'

11

A CLERK NAMED PAUL, a greying, impeccably presented man in a slim-fitting, pale charcoal suit, checked her passport and scanned her credit card. Apart from the tap of Paul's keyboard, the lobby was silent. Rebecca examined her surroundings. The space was clean, smooth and slate-coloured – industrial.

'Have you any idea when you might like to check out?' he asked, raising his eyes from the computer monitor, his fingers hovering above the keys like birds' feet.

'No. My trip is open-ended ... so far.'

He pressed the return key with a glint of satisfaction.

'Are you familiar with Geneva?' he asked gravely, as he waited for the printer to whir into action.

'No. I've never visited before,' she answered. 'But I'm looking forward to getting to know the city.'

Rebecca tapped her fingers on the counter. 'Is Rue de Berne very far, do you know?'

He shook his head casually. 'It's in the financial district, about a fifteen-minute drive away. There is a bus stop ten metres from the hotel or, if you require it, the concierge can arrange for a taxi or a car for you.'

'Thank you, I'll let you know …'

'Also, the number fifty-six bus runs frequently – it will get you there,' Paul added. 'Or, of course, you can choose to walk. It is not more than thirty minutes by foot along the lakefront then through the city. It is very pleasant at this time of year.'

Rebecca nodded appreciatively, enjoying Paul's willingness to be of assistance and his assured directness. While she loved living in London, she would never describe Londoners as helpful or direct. As an Australian born and raised in a small seaside town, it had taken many years to grow accustomed to Londoners' preference to grunt rather than say 'excuse me,' and their near pathological fear of eye contact.

Paul snatched a document from below the counter, perused it quickly, then pushed the paper across the sleek marble surface with straightened fingers. He handed her a pen then slid a large bronze bowl displaying pomegranates, shining crimson, a couple of centimetres to the right.

'Check the details, please,' he instructed. 'Then sign your name here.'

He pointed to a line at the bottom of the form. He closed her passport and placed her credit card on it. Out of habit, Rebecca went to push her hair behind her ears before reading the page. Smiling to herself, she signed her name. Paul took the form with his left hand and slid her passport and credit card across the counter with his right. Rebecca smiled again. She knew it was a stereotype, but the efficiency of Paul's movement was as precise as a Swiss watch. Londoners weren't famous for their accuracy either.

'Guten tag, Herr Beck,' Paul said, looking over Rebecca's shoulder.

When she heard the name, Rebecca turned instinctively and looked at the man standing behind her. He acknowledged Paul with a nod, without taking his eyes from his phone. Heimo Beck. She turned back to the clerk quickly, her heart racing, although she wasn't sure why. Joyce had sent her a photograph of Heimo and his kids a few years ago, thinking Rebecca might be interested in seeing her 'old friend'. Rebecca had stared at the photograph for an age. Heimo was lying on the grass on his side, in a park with his kids. They were all wearing shorts. The boy and girl were all limbs and goofy grins as they wrestled with their father. His daughter's arm obscured his face and Rebecca was disappointed, left wondering who the boy she'd loved had become and why her mother had sent her such an unsatisfactory image of him. Were her mother and Mrs Beck engaging in a passive-aggressive game of one-upmanship? Mrs Beck had grandchildren; Joyce did not. The photograph had felt like a message: breed, or else. Rebecca had hid the photograph in a volume of Keats's poetry.

Now, from the brief glimpse of Heimo she'd just stolen in the lobby, she could see he had matured into a very handsome man. His close-cropped hair and jaw-hugging beard suited him. She caught herself growing warm.

He was a doctor, she knew. 'A Macquarie Street specialist,' her mother had boasted over the telephone from Gerringong some years ago, as though she somehow had a hand in his success. But Rebecca had never sought him out online. It struck her as disloyal.

She didn't think he had recognised her. Even if he was expecting to see her, with her short hair he might not ...

'You have been placed in the front cottage because you requested a view of the lake.' Paul went on to Rebecca. She wondered if she should speak to Heimo. A lump rose in her throat. 'The cottage is part of the original hotel, although none of the original fittings remain. Julie will show you the way.'

'Thank you,' Rebecca replied quietly as a pretty young woman appeared by her side. She was dressed in an identical suit to Paul's. Julie interlaced her fingers in front of her body as she waited for Rebecca to place her belongings in her handbag. She should say something. But what if he didn't remember her or worse, didn't want to remember her? Their last meeting had ended so strangely. Then she noticed her hands shaking and took a moment to steady herself before she turned.

'This way, please, Ms Collins,' Julie said, leading the way.

Rebecca didn't look Heimo's way as she passed, keeping her gaze on Julie's straight back and sleek blonde ponytail. But she felt his eyes on her.

***

WHEN THEY ENTERED THE ROOM, Julie paced its length and pulled back the heavy curtains.

'Oh, it's beautiful,' Rebecca remarked as light flooded the space. Lake Geneva, cheerfully animated by the sun glinting on the surface, was only metres away through the expansive windows. Rebecca moved closer to the life played out in front of her – ferries, yachts and the occasional eager windsurfer, struggling to remain upright on the windless day. She wanted to be out there, in it immediately; craved to be wet and cool and at the mercy of unseen forces. She hadn't seen water so blue, so crisp, since Gerringong. Even on a cloudless summer's day, the Thames was repellent. She stared at the lake and imagined herself diving into its crystalline depths.

'Such a dramatic backdrop with the mountains and sky and –' Rebecca began.

'The Jura Mountains, yes.' Julie responded crisply in a French accent, cutting short Rebecca's rhapsodic praise.

Julie smiled fleetingly, took a few steps to her left and slid open a screen door made up of louvered opaque shutters. 'This is the bedroom ...' Julie stepped lightly around the enormous bed and parted the curtains. The same view of Lake Geneva lay behind them. Rebecca immediately began looking forward to waking up.

The room was entirely decorated in shades of latte. It was a colour Rebecca had heard Meredith speak of endlessly when she was having her bathrooms renovated. The curtains, carpet, walls, sofa and billowing duvet that seemed to hover just above the mattress were all varying shades of light brown. Joe had never paid any attention to where they stayed when travelling. Whether he was camping in a soggy field in Whitstable or residing in five-star accommodation Paris, it had made no difference. But Rebecca enjoyed the comforts of a posh hotel room.

'It's all beautiful, thank you,' Rebecca said.

'You are a writer, I believe, Ms Collins,' Julie said.

Rebecca had read about this trend in *The Times* – hoteliers and restaurant staff Googling their guests to form a connection.

'Sort of, I suppose.'

'We have a library in the salon,' Julie announced.

'Thank you. I'll head down there soon.'

'The bar opens at five o'clock,' she added. 'Is there anything else I can help you with?'

Rebecca was tempted to ask about Heimo.

'No, thank you. You've been extremely helpful.'

'HERR BECK. CAN I HELP YOU?' Paul repeated.

Heimo glanced at the clerk then back to Rebecca who was walking towards the elevator. He stood speechless for a second.

'Was that Rebecca Collins?' he asked, stepping up to the reception counter. He was certain it was. He had seen her face only briefly, but he was certain it was her. 'She's an old friend.'

Staring at her back as she walked towards the elevators, he recognised her broad shoulders and shapely legs. Apart from the short hair there was no mistaking her, but Heimo was a scientist. It was routine for him to check then double check the evidence.

'Yes, it was.' Paul said, nodding.

Heimo turned back and watched as the elevator doors closed on her.

'Is there anything else I can help you with?' the clerk asked.

Unable to recall his original query or request, he shook his head.

'No, that was all.'

He wandered to the couches in the lobby and sat, running his fingers through his hair. It wasn't until then that he noticed the furious rhythm of his heart.

---

*H*EIMO CUSTOMARILY ATE *his lunch at school with the handful of outsiders in his year — the few Ginos, Slopes and Pakis who had found each other adrift in a sea of white during the early weeks of Year 7. None of them were good friends, really, they were just boys to eat lunch with, to sit with so their exclusion wasn't so obvious. Heimo's name excluded him. It labelled him 'wog'.*

There were benefits to this arrangement. The boys could swap notes if they were absent and offer one another help with homework. They discussed soccer and made jokes about their parents' preference for SBS World News over Neighbours, and the salami sandwiches, noodles and samosas their mothers packed in their lunch boxes.

When Heimo saw Luke Collins approaching the group one lunchtime, he steeled himself. Typically, Luke left them alone. It was Luke's friends who enjoyed teasing them, demanding money, threatening to flush them or bash them. Luke was never a part of it, but he was always in the background. An observer.

But people change.

Physical harm was not Heimo's concern. Luke was small for his age and skinny. His legs reminded Heimo of a joint of lamb once all the meat had been eaten. Heimo was solid and stood at least a foot taller. What troubled Heimo were words. Luke was smart. He used words sparingly and to great effect. Heimo had witnessed him cut kids and teachers down with a single phrase — tone honed, each word razor-edged — then leave them for dead. Every remark was so apt, so accurate, so perfectly timed that often, like a doting groupie, Heimo found himself concealing a grin, stifling his laughter and silently applauding Luke for his perception and wit.

Luke sat down next to him on the cold metal seat. The other boys stopped eating, stealthily sliding their lunches back into their bags.

'My sister says you play the piano.'

Heimo nodded.

'She reckons you're pretty good.'

Hoping to conceal his elation that Rebecca thought his playing 'pretty good', Heimo shrugged, expressionless. Speech would lure Luke in. He wanted to remain remote, distant. Then he'd be protected from what was coming.

'Do you want to jam this arvo?'

'Jam?' Heimo looked him in the eye, hoping to detect a grain of humour, an ounce of mockery. Then he could tell Luke Collins to 'Piss off.' But all he observed was warmth, kindness.

'Yeah, play music. I play guitar. I want to get better, start a band.'

Start a band ... Surely, Luke was setting him up, waiting for Heimo to take the bait and show some enthusiasm for the scheme. The others thought so too. Heimo could tell by their body language, the slow edging away, the concern etching deep ditches in their brows. Drawing in breath, Heimo prepared himself for the punchline.

'Do you have a keyboard? We've got one, but it's old. Not even sure if it would work any more,' Luke went on, ploughing through Heimo's skepticism.

Was it possible Luke Collins was being genuine? Heimo wondered. Perhaps he was looking for something different, hoping to break away from the brain-dead morons he called 'mates'. To make a friend of Luke Collins would really be something, he thought. To stand in his glow would be something.

'Yeah. I can bring it.'

'Cool. I'll see you at four. That alright?'

Heimo nodded again, the tension gradually draining from his body. 'See you then.'

The other boys advised Heimo to not show up. Was he completely stupid? Did he have a death wish? they asked. It was a trap, they said. Jamie Rooney, Nev and Stevo would be waiting when he got there, waiting to laugh at him or worse, egg him. He'd never live it down, they warned.

Heimo ignored them. His desire to be Luke Collins's friend far outweighed any fear he had.

Only Luke was at home when he knocked on the door at precisely 4 pm. Luke had cleared a space among the surfboards, skateboards and boxes in the garage. They 'jammed' for more than two hours. It was the beginning of a weekly ritual.

Why was he remembering that now? Heimo wondered as the elevator doors opened. He pressed the button. As they slid shut he realised it was because of Rebecca.

Luke hadn't worn his hair short very often. But when it grew into a matted, tangled and unruly mess, his vexed mother would shave his head in the kitchen. Luke hated it but he bore it. At the instant Rebecca turned from the reception counter and he saw her profile, Heimo thought it had been Luke.

WHEN HEIMO RETURNED to his room, he opened his laptop with the intention of editing a journal article a colleague had emailed him. After reading the abstract at least four times, he gave up and closed the computer. He needed a drink but the bar didn't open until five.

Blast from the past. That was the expression. Such a cliché, but so accurate, he thought. Heimo's breathing was still rapid and his hands were trembling slightly. He'd been jolted out of his typical composure by the glimpse of a girl, a woman, he hadn't seen in a quarter of a century. His mind skipped from memory to memory. Doors unlocked and opened. Rebecca emerged. There was a time when she occupied space in every thought that came into his mind.

The heartbreak of so long ago had dissolved but there were still traces of her pulsing through his bloodstream, triggering his senses. He could still feel it when he gave his heart its legs.

He sighed deeply then rested back on the sofa. Struggling to think of his children or work or anything that might soothe him, he eventually gave his mind free rein to explore. He did this occasionally, usually when he was stressed. Nurturing the mind, he often thought, was like nurturing a child. Sometimes it needed free play.

An image of a girl emerged. Monica. When he was sixteen his parents sent him to Munich to visit his grandparents over the Christmas holidays. At the urging of his cousin, who was astounded Heimo was still a virgin, he had sex with a girl he met at a concert.

He squeezed his eyes tight, attempting to recall the name of the band. He could picture them easily – grim and pale in black denim ... *Todesengel.*

'In English, it's 'Angel of Death',' Monica shouted above the hammering music.

Monica was also grim and pale in black denim. She was slightly older than Heimo and spoke English perfectly. Monica snuck him into her bedroom in her parents' home and once they were finished, she promptly let him out the front door, directing him to the nearest underground station in precise, clear utterances. On the train ride home, with his cheek pressed against the frosted window he thought of Rebecca and his disloyalty overwhelmed any sense of masculine accomplishment he might have felt when he had rolled off Monica thirty minutes earlier.

Although he and Rebecca weren't dating and had no claims on the other, he hated himself for his weakness, for giving in to his cousin's goading. In his imaginings, his first time would be with her. But there was nothing he could do to reverse the situation. He would never be a virgin again.

There was a low rumble of thunder in the distance and Heimo opened his eyes, finding a darkened room. He checked his phone. It was almost five. He sighed again.

He always came back to Rebecca.

12

———

As she showered in the hotel bathroom, Rebecca thought of Heimo Beck. Seeing him after so many years in the lobby had sent a familiar surge through her body, a thrilling rush of longing. Wrapping herself in a lavender-scented bathrobe, she lay down on the bed. Ancient history, she thought, closing her eyes, attempting to dismiss her feelings.

———

'History?' he asked.

Rebecca started when he sat down beside her.

She looked up from her book and into Heimo's face, nodding.

'Last exam.'

'I've got physics.'

'I know.'

They heard the librarian, Mrs Hardy, behind them replacing books on the shelf. They sat silent, heads down, until she moved away.

'Has Luke studied?'

'No.'

'Why did he take physics in the first place?'

'His idea of a joke.'

Heimo made that peculiar noise he often did when a situation completely baffled him, a deep click of discontent that emanated from the back of his throat.

There was no one else in the library so early, except Mrs Hardy. Rebecca enjoyed being there for the quiet, the order and for the grassy, tangy scent of books.

Apart from English, she and Heimo hadn't chosen any of the same subjects for their senior years, but they had taken to studying together every morning before the day's exams. Heimo was determined to study medicine, but Rebecca wasn't certain in what direction to head. Her mother wanted her to do teaching at Wollongong. It was an easy commute and Dad said he'd buy her a cheap car.

Heimo's hair was neatly combed and his shirt still tucked. When his foot rubbed against hers under the table, she felt a strange flutter in the bottom of her belly. Not unpleasant, just unusual.

After her accident two years before, they had become friends. They'd often hang out together at the beach or the milk bar, sometimes with Luke, but mostly on their own. This year, though, something had changed. They both felt it. But they hadn't kissed. Kathy Leary liked to point out that Heimo and Bec 'weren't official'.

Sometimes when they were together Heimo's hand would brush her arm, hair or thigh. Rebecca suspected, hoped, that those brief touches, those short-lived moments of what might be, were intentional. Looking at him now, she was certain. There was a sparkle in his eyes, playful and sensual, as though he was wise to a secret, as if he knew something about her that even she didn't.

'I got you this.'

He produced a small wrapped parcel from his bag. It was book-sized.

'It's a present for being my study buddy.'

She laughed. He had never used the term before and it seemed so ridiculous spilling from his lips. Rebecca carefully unwrapped the gift from the floral-print paper.

The Complete Poems of John Keats. A picture of the poet, a pensive young man resting his chin in his palm, featured on the cover.

'I know you enjoyed Coleridge when we did him. Keats is even better. He's my favourite.'

'You have a favourite poet?' Rebecca asked, flicking through the pages. 'You're a romantic.'

Heimo shrugged bashfully. Rebecca wondered if she was the only person who knew that about him.

'Thanks. It's lovely. Thoughtful.'

Aware her words didn't come close to describing how she felt, she kissed him softly on the cheek. Then she felt his hand on her thigh through the pleats of her skirt.

'Do you want to come over tonight, you know, as a sort of celebration for getting through the trials?' He looked at her squarely. 'I've got soccer training but if you come over about seven-thirty we could watch TV or listen to some records ...'

Heimo paused before adding. 'Mum and Dad'll be at the restaurant 'til late.'

Rebecca nodded, anxious and excited by the possibility.

SHE'D BEEN into the store on Fern Street – Top Drawer – only once before, when her mother had wanted a good pair of panty-hose to wear to her cousin's wedding. They cost a fortune, she had commented when her husband spotted her stockinged legs as she slid into the car. He had wolf-whistled appreciatively. Rebecca knew the owner of Top Drawer, Suzie Bramble; she was Luke's friend Nev's mother. Mrs Bramble's hair was always styled in a neat bob. Rebecca had never seen her without high heels and a thin strand of pearls cascading into her cleavage.

For as long as Rebecca could remember, Top Drawer held a place on Fern Street between the takeaway and Barb's Cuts, but she had only been in there that once. The store was a mystery to her, an ever-present mystery. It wasn't an everyday shop. Top Drawer was where the women of Gerringong shopped when they wanted something special to wear under their ordinary slacks, skirts and dresses. She'd never seen the place busy and her parents mused occasionally how it was that Suzie Bramble kept the business afloat. Family money was the conclusion they reached. Now Rebecca wanted something special herself, so she went in. It was a coming-of-age after all. Was she ready? she asked herself. She wasn't sure. Rose scent, pungent and savage, clawed its way along her nostrils and nestled into the back of her throat, fuelling her doubts.

Bras, underpants, nighties and pyjamas hung on racks. One of each size to try. Most of the stock lay in glossy white drawers that lined the walls, although the bronze handles were a little tarnished. Rebecca took a pink lacy bra off the rail and looked at the size as Mrs Bramble moved out from behind the counter.

'What are you looking for, Love?'

'I'm not sure.' She hung the bra back on the rack and shrugged. 'I don't even know what size I am.'

'Well, that's not uncommon. More's the shame. Here, let me measure you.' Mrs Bramble slipped the tape measure from around her neck as she approached. Rebecca heard it slither against her skin.

'Raise your arms.'

Rebecca did as instructed and was quickly measured.

'Right. I'd say you were a 10, possibly a 12B.' Mrs Bramble removed the pink bra that had caught Rebecca's eye from the rack. 'Do you fancy this one? It's lovely, a silk-cotton blend. Berlei. And I have a pair of matching panties.'

Rebecca hated the word 'panty'. She thought it was a word only perverts should use.

Stepping back, Mrs Bramble took in Rebecca's form. 'You're very slim hipped. I'm sure a 10 will do in the panties.' She handed Rebecca the appropriately sized bras and the panties from the rack. 'Dressing room is behind you.'

Mrs Bramble followed and pulled the curtain closed. 'Call me when you have them on.'

Clutching the hangers, staring at her reflection as she stood against a backdrop of pink velvet, Rebecca wondered why she was even there. Never desiring pretty trimmings, she now found herself willing the underwear to fit, nervous at the prospect of how she would look once it was on. If anything happened with Heimo, if tonight got to that point, she wanted it to be just as she had imagined it. She wanted whatever happened to be special. And she'd imagined herself in pretty, matching underwear. Rebecca toed off her school shoes and began peeling the tights from her legs.

'Okay, Mrs Bramble. I'm ready.'

The curtain swept back. Mrs Bramble tugged mercilessly at the bra straps with her index fingers and cupped Rebecca's breasts from behind as though weighing their heft or assessing the firmness of two peaches. She examined Rebecca in the mirror.

'How does it feel?'

'Good. Comfortable,' Rebecca answered as indifferently as possible. In truth, she didn't care how they felt, Rebecca was amazed at her transformation. The pink fabric glowed against the shadow of her tan and her breasts seemed fuller, rounder. Apparent was a waist and a cleavage and, while in need of shaving, her legs appeared thinner and longer, more befitting a comic-book super heroine than a schoolgirl from Gerringong who was possibly, conceivably, about to embark on her first sexual encounter.

'You look gorgeous. The panties fit nicely too. Are they for anyone special?'

Rebecca glanced in the mirror at Mrs Bramble's wide, curious eyes. It was an odd question to be asking her son's seventeen-year-old classmate, she thought. Was she hoping the answer would be Nev or did she simply have a nose for gossip?

'No.' She hoped to shrug the question off. 'Just getting sick of the stuff Mum buys me from Kmart. It never fits properly.'

'Well, women have to be measured. A badly fitted bra can cause all sorts of problems. But this one ...', she said, gazing at Rebecca's body admiringly, 'fits you perfectly.'

THE FINAL TRACK ENDED. 'All My Life'. Heimo rose from the sofa to change albums.

'What next?' he asked, removing Echo & the Bunnymen from the turntable. 'U2 or REM?'

'U2,' she answered from the floor as she studied his collection, pulling the sleeves from the shelf to examine the covers and the track listings.

'You've got everything – all the new releases. Are you a secret millionaire or something?'

'My grandparents send them to me from Munich. Everything is cheaper there.'

'Where the Streets Have No Name' began and, satisfied with the volume, Heimo sat down behind her on the patterned carpet of the lounge room floor. He was so close she could sense his *warmth but she wasn't certain what she should do. Then she felt his fingers in her hair.*

'I've always loved your hair. Even when we were in kindergarten and I sat behind you, I remember being mesmerised by it. It was so much more interesting than Mrs Finlay.'

She nodded, barely able to breathe.

'It's so dark at the top and then the curls get lighter and lighter as they travel down your back. The tips are as white as milk teeth.'

As white as milk teeth. He was quoting someone, she was sure. Although she didn't recall the origins of the simile, Rebecca was pleased by Heimo's efforts to romance her.

Rebecca could feel herself shaking but Heimo didn't seem nervous at all. His voice was assured and his hand steady.

'I think I've had a crush on you since then ... since kindy.'

Her heart was pounding loud and fast, in sync with the beat set by Larry Mullen Jr. Rebecca wanted to voice her feelings – that she had always felt the same – but her mouth was dry and her tongue like sandpaper.

'Will you let me read your writing some time?' he went on. 'That story, the one Mrs Brennan read out last week, was ... it was brilliant.'

'If you want. Some of it's pretty ordinary, though.'

'I've watched you when you write. You light up.' He pushed back her hair and kissed her neck. Floating, Rebecca closed her eyes and let her head fall forward. 'It makes me want to know you better ...'

The song ended and Larry Mullen Jr's drumbeat filled the lounge room once again, this time more intensely. 'I Still Haven't Found What I'm Looking For'.

'I love this song,' Rebecca said. 'Kathy Leary reckons you look like Bono.'

'I'm not interested in Kathy Leary.'

Heimo wrapped his arms around her body, his hands resting on her thighs.

'I think you're beautiful and smart,' he said then, turning her to face him. 'But we don't have to do anything if you're not ready.'

She still had her jumper on and she was beginning to perspire.

'I am ready ... it feels like the right thing to do. Not the right thing, but ... the natural thing. You know?'

'I know.'

'And I trust you.'

Heimo took her hands and lifted her to her feet, then led her down the hallway towards the bedrooms, with the gospel-sounds of Bono's voice fading behind them. When they got to his bedroom, Heimo entered first and turned on a lamp. His room was tidy, monastic. The bed was made and his clothes put away. Rebecca looked around her for a moment at the books stacked neatly on his desk, at the brown-and-white striped curtains and his simple blue doona cover. No posters or pennants, toys or games; no leftovers from childhood. Three soccer trophies standing in a line on a chest of drawers were the only sign of Heimo once being a kid. This was a grown-up's room.

She smiled at him, a half-smile which she hoped displayed assurance. Heimo stared at her; the intensity of his eyes was unnerving. She pulled her jumper over her head and threw it on the bed. Then she took off her t-shirt. His eyes flashed wide for an instant. She had surprised him. A small kernel of confidence took root in her chest.

'Your turn,' she said.

Heimo pulled off his t-shirt and let it fall to the ground. His chest was hairless and slightly muscled. Rebecca traced its valleys and hills with her eyes. Tiny goosebumps rose like prickles all over his torso.

She unbuttoned her jeans and eased them over her hips. As she kicked them off her feet, she heard Heimo gasp.

'What?'

'You're so beautiful,' he said, moving closer. 'Can I touch you?'

She licked her lips and swallowed, nodding. He walked to her and placed his hand on her breast, cupping it gently. His breathing was still steady but deeper now and an expression of great concern washed over his face. He unhooked her new bra and drew the straps down her arms.

Taking a step back, he took her in for a moment. Then she moved to him, lifted his hand and placed it on her breast again. As he caressed it softly, a sense of longing gripped her, as though everything inside her was reaching for him. If she didn't feel him too she would die. He was still wearing the shorts he'd worn at training. Rebecca slipped her hands inside the waistband and drew them to the floor. Their hips met and she could feel his erection. But they didn't kiss. An unspoken agreement had been reached. A kiss would be the trigger, a starter gun spurring them towards a finish line.

From then events occurred in slow motion or fast-forward, she wasn't certain. When Rebecca recalled the night later — the next day, the next year — she saw only flashes of colour and noise, a stuttering home movie reel, dulled by emotion and distance. Yet at the time, in the moment, each sensation had been hot iron and every sound rang crystal clear. Every heartbeat pealed and Heimo's fingers were charged, snapping and hissing as they traced the curve of her breasts and hips, firing her towards one inevitability. They were soon lying face to face on his bed, naked.

'Your eyes are as blue and deep as the ocean,' she whispered into the warmth of his breath.

Their bodies came together.

A booming knock at the front door made them pull back. Rebecca wasn't even sure the sound was real. Startled out of the moment, awoken from a dream, they were both panting hard and it took a few seconds for either to speak.

'Your parents?' Heimo asked as he pulled on his t-shirt and reached for his shorts.

'I don't think so ...' Rebecca said, confused. Suddenly aware and embarrassed by her nudity, she grabbed her clothes and began to dress.

As Heimo made his way towards to front door there was another round of banging. He opened the door casually, not wanting to look like he had anything to hide.

Luke stood there alone and barefoot. His t-shirt was ripped at the neck and his skateboard rested under one foot.

'The Joshua Tree. Good album. Fancy some company?' Luke held a six-pack of beer in front of him.

Rebecca joined Heimo at the door.

'Not particularly,' she said, her face emotionless. 'Go home.'

Luke looked at her, then slowly back to Heimo.

'Thanks, mate, but we're good. I'll walk Rebecca home a bit later,' Heimo said.

Luke swayed slightly on his feet.

'What have you been up to?'

'Just listening to records,' Heimo answered. 'We had pizza.'

Luke's eyes closed for a second and he stumbled towards them, dropping the beer. The smash resounded in the empty street and a light came on across the road. Heimo caught him.

'Sorry, mate,' Luke said.

'Be careful of the glass,' Rebecca said. 'Neither of you have shoes on.'

Heimo guided him to the swing seat on the balcony. 'I should get him home.'

Rebecca sighed and hastily sized up the reality of the situation.

'I'll take him.'

She glared at Luke on the swing. She turned back to Heimo. She was barely able to meet his eyes.

'You should stay and clean up before your mum and dad get back. This'll be hard to explain.'

'Will you be alright?'

She shrugged.

'I'm sorry, Heimo.'

'That's okay. I'm sorry, too.'

HEIMO WALKED BACK *to his room, reeking of beer and lost opportunity. Rebecca's jumper, bra and underpants were on the floor where she had dropped them, where he had dropped them. Picking up the underwear, he placed them on his bed, carefully approximating the position of her chest and hips. Laying down beside them, he felt the fabric between his fingers. They were new – even of colour and apple-crisp, sour-sweet. He placed his nose against the bra and breathed in her unclouded scent, resonant of coconut and chocolate.*

'Fuck you, Luke,' he said out loud as he clutched his aching balls.

13

THE SIBLINGS WALKED *in silence most of the way home.*

'Nev told me you went into his mum's shop today. You and Heimo seem to be moving pretty fast all of a sudden. I just didn't want you doing anything stupid.'

Rebecca stopped.

'Stupid? You mean stupid like fucking every girl I see? Stupid like flunking out at school, or stupid like getting stoned every chance I get?'

'Just stay out of it.'

After she led Luke to bed, Rebecca filled a schooner glass with water in the kitchen. Only minutes had passed before she returned to the bedroom. Luke was asleep. She placed the glass on the floor beside his bed and stood over him, looking at his still face.

Rebecca knew she should want to punch him, shake him awake and tell him how much he had disappointed her, scream until he realised how much she had begun to hate being his twin. Yet, she loved him more than anyone. More than Heimo, more than her parents. But she hated him, too. So much. She hated him for interrupting them, for trying to protect her.

And she hated him for loving her.

Rebecca sat down on the bed, trying to figure him out. She examined the cut on her brother's lip, tracing the curve of his mouth, her mouth, with a finger. Who had he fought? Nev? Had Nev said something about her? Luke would defend her honour no matter what, she knew.

Perhaps Luke was right. Perhaps she and Heimo were moving too fast. Certainly too fast for Luke to handle. It occurred to her then that they weren't pulling apart from one another; she was speeding away from him. Luke remained fixed. He was rock; a proud, jutting sea stack slowly being eroded by the inevitable movement and change around him. Luke was incapable of adapting. That's just how he was made.

But she wasn't.

———

FOLLOWING A RESTLESS SLEEP, Rebecca was woken by the doorbell just after ten. Within seconds, her mum poked her head through the door.

'It's Heimo, Love. He wants to talk to you.'

Rebecca groaned.

'What happened last night? Luke's out the front with him now.'

'Nothing.'

'Luke's got a fat lip. Did he get in a fight?'

'Ask him,' Rebecca snapped. Her mother left the room, grimacing concern and suspicion.

As Rebecca made her way down the hall, she heard their voices.

'Sorry, mate. I was pissed. Sorry I wrecked your night.'

She couldn't hear Heimo's response, but when she reached the door she saw them shaking hands. Then Luke shuffled across the veranda and indoors. He was still wearing the same clothes, a cut lip and a black eye. He looked at his sister as he passed her in the hall. Rebecca ignored him.

Heimo was sitting on the front step and Rebecca lowered herself by his side.

'I've got your stuff here,' Heimo handed her a plastic shopping bag. 'Your jumper and ...'

Rebecca took the bag and rummaged inside. He had folded her bra and pants in her jumper. 'Thanks.'

Mr Kramer backed his van out from his driveway next door. He raised his hand at the teenagers. They waved back then were quiet until the noise of his engine had disappeared.

'There's a play I'd like to see in Wollongong. The Crucible. Will you come with me? We could go next week?' Heimo said.

'I don't know ...'

'We can take it more slowly.'

'It's not that.'

Heimo was an only child. It was impossible for her to explain the peculiar dynamics of her relationship with her twin, how Luke's sadness became her own and how she wasn't capable of living with that darkness inside her. She was moving too fast but Heimo had nothing to do with it.

He waited for her to go on. 'What is it then?'

'Maybe we should just wait until the HSC is over. Wait until we have more time.'

Heimo made the strange clicking noise in his throat again.

She didn't dare look at him. She could smell his disappointment and confusion.

'Right. Okay.'

'I'm sorry.'

'You sure?'

'Yeah. I think it's for the best,' she said, rising. 'To ease up until we don't have any other distractions.'

When her hand touched the doorknob, she stopped, hastily

weighing up her decision, measuring the severity of the seed of
regret that was fast taking root in her heart. She didn't fully
understand why she had to choose between Heimo and Luke, but
she knew that she had to, at least for now.

HEIMO LOOKED AT HIS WATCH: five minutes to five. Thunder murmured in the distance. He walked to the bathroom and brushed his teeth, attempting to shake off the memory of that morning when Rebecca had left him on the veranda. He remembered walking home and going straight into his bedroom, swearing to himself to steer clear of the brother and sister. His heart had ached, literally ached, and there was no scientific reason why. There was something about Luke and Rebecca, their bond, that made him furious.

Now, closing his eyes, he took slow deep breaths.

He had loved them both. That was the problem.

14

———————

REBECCA FINALLY ROSE and dressed then sat on the bed in her room, waiting until a little after five before she appeared in the salon. She turned to the window. Flashes of lightning illuminated a darkened sky. Nickel-coloured clouds had moved in over the mountains while she'd been in the bathroom and she heard a faint growl of thunder.

She rolled back on the bed, turned on the lamp and opened the drawers of the table. A bible and an assortment of power adaptors. They were so neatly arranged that she wished she had use for them. She closed the drawer and checked her phone. There was a new message from Gerard.

I am home. Can I call you?

Rebecca sighed, rubbed her forehead then scrolled up to reread the stream.

Can we meet? Please.

I want to know all of my father.

Do you have time to talk?

I want to know more about my father. Please can we meet?

Joe's son was persistent, dogged. An inherited characteristic.

Then a new message.

No one needs to know.

'Why don't you just delete them?' She heard Joe comment, and she closed her eyes. It was a question she had asked herself many times. Why hadn't she messaged Gerard instructing him to stop? Or threatened to tell his mother?

'It's the connection, I suppose,' she heard herself responding. 'Despite how angry I am, I still love you and Gerard is a part of you. He is the last O'Neill.'

Silence. It was a few minutes before Rebecca opened her eyes. Feeling slightly silly at discussing the matter with a 'ghost', she rose cautiously and sat up straight. Joe was perched by her feet at the foot of her bed, looking at her. So close, so real. The piece of hair he was always pushing off his forehead, the stubble on his cheeks and chin and the pinhead mole to the right of his nose – all so real. How thoroughly she must have scrutinised him in life to reimagine him in this way, in such unfailing detail. Was that normal? she wondered. Then he raised an eyebrow and gave her that look, that mischievous, teasing expression, the prologue to a quip or a barb.

'I saw you sizing up Heimo Beck, *mo ghrá*,' Joe said now. 'Why did you never tell me about him?'

Rebecca's heart raced and her blood surged, her cheeks suddenly alight. Embarrassed and ashamed, she felt like a schoolgirl again. She leapt from the bed, grabbed her swipe card and ran from the room.

When she reached the salon she was breathless. Stopping outside for a few minutes to recover herself, she wondered what Joe's appearance meant. Because if it didn't mean something then she was surely going mad. Rebecca closed her eyes for a moment to dam the tears she felt rising and took a deep breath.

There was no such thing as ghosts, she told herself, opening her eyes. Sorrow and shock were responsible for her mental state, her hallucinations. Her grief had concocted this figment of imagination from her over-wrought mind. Time was all she needed. Time healed all wounds, didn't it? She took a few more deep breaths until her light-headedness passed, then entered the salon.

There were several people already occupying tables and stools, mostly couples and groups. Rain pounded the floor-to-ceiling windows and each crack of thunder prompted an awed gasp from a few of the female clientele. Candles had been lit on the tables, a countermeasure against the unseasonal darkness brought about by the storm.

Rebecca went straight to the bar and ordered a glass of wine. Unable to call to mind any of the varieties she liked, or focus on the wine list, she let the barman choose. He presented her with a glass of local Gamay, produced in the vineyard behind the hotel. Rebecca drank it so quickly she was unable to recognise any of the flavours. While she feigned interest as the barman went on to describe the characteristics of the grape – the sweet cherry undertones – she concentrated closely on the journey of the liquid from her throat to her stomach. Then she waited until its vital force seeped into every part of her body, compelling her shoulders and breath to relax. By the time she had finished the glass, the wine's job was complete.

With her thoughts reassuringly blurred and her stomach warm, Rebecca glanced around the room. Heimo was seated alone at a small table in the corner looking at his phone, his thumb scrolling down the screen. A glass of beer rested within reach. She turned back hastily and ordered another glass of wine.

When the barman placed her second glass on the bar,

she took a long sip immediately. Why was she so nervous? she wondered. They had been kids. It was almost thirty years ago. They shared a friendship, nothing more. But, if she was honest with herself, it had been more. Until two weeks ago, Heimo had been her only heartbreak. And somehow, in that microcosmic, insular world they had shared as teenagers, Heimo's betrayal seemed worse that Joe's.

They had been kids, she reminded herself, making a decision. Gripping the stem of her wine glass, she approached Heimo's table.

'Heimo Beck, I presume.'

He looked up from his phone and the intensity of his dark blue gaze (eyes as blue and as deep as the ocean) startled her for an instant.

'I thought it was you. I mean, I knew it was you,' he said, standing. 'But you've changed.' He offered her a seat.

'Older, you mean.'

'No.' They sat. 'Your hair.'

She rubbed a hand over her head.

He smiled.

Heimo's appearance had changed very little, she thought. He was simply an older version of the young man she'd yearned after. A few wrinkles, the beard, the odd fleck of grey in his hair ... Images rearranged and updated themselves in her mind.

They sighed in unison then glanced at each other sheepishly, searching for the teenagers they remembered in each other, scouring the past for a memory to anchor them to. Rebecca raised her glass to her lips then set her glass down.

'I was thinking about your record collection the other day,' Rebecca said. 'You had everything. I was so jealous. Do you still have it?'

'They're boxed up in my garage,' he answered, picking up his phone. 'All that music is on here now.'

'More portable, but you can't look at the covers.'

They were quiet for a moment. Rebecca stared into her wine but she sensed Heimo's eyes on her.

'I was sorry to read about Joe,' he said. 'How are you?'

'Up and down. Mostly somewhere in the middle.' She picked up her glass and brought it to her lips again, hoping the wine would offer her inspiration. 'What brings you to Geneva? Work?' she asked, desperate to change the subject.

His phone vibrated on the table and his eyes shot to the screen.

'Excuse me. I have to take this.' He scooped up the device, pressing it to his ear, then rushed out of the salon.

Odd, she thought, but he was a doctor, a 'Macquarie Street specialist'. Rebecca waited almost fifteen minutes for his return. When he didn't, ruffled and wounded, she moved across the room to the safety of the hotel's well-stocked bookshelf.

Scanning the alphabetically arranged collection, she came across an English version of *The Tempest*, a play she had studied in high school. She removed the slim volume from the shelf. The image on the cover, a tornado's funnel stretching down to the ocean, was depicted in varying degrees of charcoal and grey. 'William Shakespeare', the title and the other text on the cover, were printed in azure. Rebecca looked to the window. Heavy rain peppered the glass, although the thunder had retreated, now a mere moan far away.

As she sat transfixed by the patterns made by the raindrops edging down the window, she recalled the chorus of moans and grumbles that had issued from her classmates when their English teacher Mr McDermott had handed out the texts. Bruce McDermott, a large man with a full beard who lived with his wife in a modest weatherboard just two doors down from the 1920s bungalow where Rebecca lived, was a man with a great love of literature but with little knowledge of how to teach it. The class struggled with Shakespeare's language and the Italian names; only the best readers were allowed parts. After a week, Mr McDermott, resigned to his fate as an English teacher at a middling south coast high school where the students viewed education as little more than an interruption to surfing, showed the class a BBC production of the play on video. They raucously mocked Prospero's wig and the fake sets. Rebecca was disappointed with her teacher's efforts and the brief, simplistic analysis of the play he offered. She liked the idea that books were the source of Prospero's power.

Flicking through the pages of the play, Rebecca came across Ariel's song.

Full fathom five thy father lies;
Of his bones are coral made;
Those are pearls that were his eyes;
Nothing of him that doth fade,
But doth suffer a sea-change
Into something rich and strange.
Sea-nymphs hourly ring his knell:
Ding-dong.
Hark! now I hear them — Ding-dong, bell.

The lines brought Luke to her mind, although they never had before. The wine had made her gloomy. She sat down and began to read, in no hurry to return to her room tonight.

BY THE TIME the salon closed at midnight, Rebecca had finished the play and had reread her favourite scenes. She walked to the hotel's entrance, hugging the book to her chest.

The lake that had so warmly greeted her on arrival at the hotel now appeared unfriendly in the dark, pitted by the stinging rain. The doorman scurried to her side and opened the door. She hadn't wanted to exit, but now she felt obliged to and stepped out onto the footpath, shielded from the weather by the hotel's large red awning. The air possessed a vicious bite. She'd forgotten to grab a jacket when she fled her room. 'Fled' wasn't a word used in normal conversation. Had she ever *fled* before? Had speaking to visions of her recently deceased partner been a dream? she now wondered. The hours between then and now and the wine had cushioned the memory.

Her stomach grumbled. She'd not eaten since the plane.

'Are any restaurants still open?' she asked the doorman.

'No, Ms Collins, but the hotel has twenty-four-hour room service.'

'Thank you,' she responded, stepping inside. 'I'll look at the menu when I get back to my room.'

REBECCA STOOD outside her door for some time before drawing her room card from the pocket of her jeans. The fine hairs on the back of her neck rose like quills. She inserted the card into the lock slowly. The light failed to turn green. She inserted and removed it again, this time quickly. The light turned green but her hand refused to turn the door handle. Joe isn't alive and he isn't a ghost, she told herself as she mustered her courage and inserted the card a third time.

Entering, Rebecca glanced into the bedroom, craning her neck to see the entirety of the space. Then she walked cautiously into the bathroom. All clear. She relaxed. On her way back into the sitting room, she slipped off her shoes and slid the room service menu off the bedside table, scanning the first page briefly. When she looked up, Joe was seated on the sofa with his legs crossed and his right arm strewn across the back, forcing the wings of the raven on his t-shirt to spread across his chest at a peculiar angle.

Rebecca's throat tightened and she looked away. When she looked back a moment later, he was still there.

'What unnerves you so, *mo ghrá*?' he asked. 'Is it my presence or what my presence means?'

There was no shutting him out. There never was. He was, quite literally, larger than life. But this wasn't Joe. She knew it was a manifestation of her anger, grief and confusion – emotions that are difficult to suppress. Perhaps she should see a therapist, as Angus had suggested.

'Is there a difference?' she responded.

'There's always a difference,' he replied.

'What are you?' she went on, unable and unwilling to interpret his answer. 'A phantom of my overwrought psyche?'

'I suppose,' he said. 'It might help to talk to me.'

'I don't want to talk. I want to understand.'

'Understand what?' he asked. 'My death?'

She laughed. 'Christ no! You smoked two packets of cigarettes a day from the age of twelve. You got throat cancer. You died a horrible death. That I understand.'

Joe laughed.

She lowered her gaze to her hands.

'What I can't understand is Karina Bonnay and the children.'

'They had nothing to do with you,' he said.

'Karina Bonnay has everything to do with me!' she seethed. 'Was it the children you wanted?'

He eyed her warily as she halted and calmed herself. Rebecca never expected one day she'd be sitting in a hotel room shouting at a ghost. What was happening to her? Sitting beside Joe, she closed her eyes and cradled her head in her hands. Pressing firmly against her temples, she hoped to drive him out, like St Patrick had banished the snakes.

'Do you recall us babysitting Hugh?' Joe asked. Rebecca nodded. 'We were always so desperate to cuddle him, read him books, sing him lullabies ... Simultaneously, we were terrified we'd drop him or lose him or forget him in the bath.

'We'd have made grand parents, *mo ghrá*. It just wasn't to be.'

'I sat next to a woman and a young baby on the plane today,' Rebecca began quietly, raising her head. 'When we were taking off, the mother put the little boy to her breast, you know, so his ears could equalise ...'

Joe nodded.

'I stared at the scene for a long time, amazed at how the roundness of his tiny head mirrored so perfectly the roundness of his mother's breast. They seemed so seamlessly fused. Mother and child will always be bonded, united, in a such a primal way ... Am I making sense?'

Tears began to pool in her eyes.

'Yes, perfect sense,' Joe murmured.

'Then once they parted, when the plane had levelled out, I was suddenly overcome with hatred for the mother. It was the fiercest resentment I've ever felt.' Rebecca began to feel again the tight-fisted anger in her chest, burning for release.

She was crying now, the tears running unheeded down her cheeks.

'What have I turned into?' she asked.

He gazed at her levelly. She wanted to fall into his arms at that moment, but she was frightened of how deep she might plummet.

'Why couldn't that have been me?' she whimpered through the sobs, but the questions kept coming, leaving no time for answers. 'Why did you choose her over me? Were you punishing me?'

Rebecca stared at her husband, pleading.

Joe looked at her lovingly and shook his head.

'Oh, no. Never,' he said softly.

'After Luke, after everything ...' he said, trying to explain. 'It was like something in you switched off. The light that had always shone switched off, just like that.' He clicked his fingers. 'I could see you trying, but way down deep there was nothing. Just blank space. I knew I'd lost you and I was grieving. Karina was a way, I suppose, of working through that grief.

'It's not your fault. It's not mine, either.' He frowned, thinking. 'We should have been braver, gotten our hands dirty. We should have talked about what was raw and sharp. But we blunted our feelings with silence.'

REBECCA WOKE in the early hours of the morning. That night she'd gone to bed restless and distressed, Joe's words and their implications tumbling around her mind like balls in a bingo wheel.

She sat up and scanned the room. Joe was gone. He had been there when she fell asleep, sitting under the light of a reading lamp. A guardian angel.

Wide awake, she checked her phone and read Gerard's messages again.

No one needs to know

To meet the boy seemed wrong, clandestine, immoral.

She typed quickly.

I'm in Geneva. When and where?

Then she pressed the blue arrow.

Within seconds her screen lit up.

Starbucks in the old town? Place de Longemalle 4 pm

Rebecca bit her lip, contemplating the wisdom of her decision. She typed a final message.

Thanks

Then she switched off her phone.

15

———

REBECCA OPENED the door at eight. Heimo was standing on the other side holding two takeaway coffee cups. The aroma triggered her stomach, which growled with neglect. She had forgotten to eat last night.

'Did I wake you?' he asked. She was still wearing her pyjamas.

She shook her head then ran her hands over her hair to flatten it. A habit. Joe often joked that her bed head was terminal.

He smiled, briefly yet warmly.

'I'm sorry about last night. Can I come in?'

Heimo sat on the sofa and Rebecca accepted one of the cups. He wore shorts and Rebecca glanced at the legs she was once so fond of.

'I feel like we need to clear the air but I'm not certain of what,' Rebecca said.

'I know what you mean.'

They sat and Heimo leant forward with his elbows on his knees, rubbing his palms together.

'I wanted to be at Luke's funeral ... I was so upset, no

distressed is a better word, when Mum told me he died,' Heimo said. 'I wanted to be there. I was in Munich, working.'

'That's okay. Mum and Dad got your card. It was thoughtful.'

'I couldn't express what I'd hoped to. I can't even imagine how his death affected you. I wanted to talk to you about it ...'

Rebecca's chest tightened. It was impossible to put into words the sensation of being entirely unstitched and robbed of her stuffing – the matter that made her matter. She didn't even want to try. After Luke, for a time, she was a rag doll.

She shook her head, absolving him.

'It's okay. These things are so difficult to talk about, especially long distance. I know how you felt about Luke and he did too. In a way, it would have made it harder. No one knew Luke like we did. It helped me remain detached. If we'd spoken ...' Rebecca's eyes began to moisten and she brought the cup to her lips. 'I still reckon you two should have started a band.'

Heimo wiped a tear from his cheek.

'We made some pretty beautiful music together in your parents' garage.' He winked.

It was easy to talk about Luke with Heimo and it lifted her mood. Nobody in London had met her twin, had shared him or been touched by his humour, sensitivity and tolerance. They had never seen his brilliance on a board or the dexterity of his fingers across six strings. Although flawed beneath the surface, Luke had been a work of art. Rebecca and Heimo saw his imperfections, the cracks and chips in his veneer, and they both loved and hated him for them. Even her parents had never fully and openly acknowledged him as he was.

'It wasn't a surfing accident, Heimo,' Rebecca said. 'It was suicide.'

She had never shared this with anyone.

Heimo tilted his head and leaned in closer.

'But Mum said the death was an accident ... she showed me the newspapers. How do you know it wasn't?'

'I just know.' There was no mistaking her tone.

'Remember Matt Shephard?'

Heimo nodded.

'He was editor of the *Illawarra Mercury* at the time. He was Luke's mate and he wanted to protect Luke's reputation, I suppose. An accident is more acceptable than suicide. Mum and Dad went along with it. They didn't want to face it, even though Luke's state of mind at the time didn't suggest anything else.'

Heimo made a noise, a low, intrigued *humpf.*

'Had you seen him recently?'

Their eyes met. It was as though Heimo saw more than other people, as though he could see right through her. It was always like that.

'I spoke to him on the phone a couple of months before it happened. He was a mess, falling apart. Then I couldn't reach him. His phone was disconnected or he moved out of the house he was renting. I was never sure where he was. When I asked Mum, she said he was staying with a mate. She told me he was alright but didn't want to speak to me.'

Heimo took her hand, squeezed gently and stroked her knuckles with his thumb. They sat without speaking. Somehow, he knew what she was reliving. There were no words he could offer to assuage her feelings.

'Since Joe died, I'm thinking of Luke more often. It's weird.'

'Not really.'

'I suppose Joe's death has triggered something in my mind ...'

'Opened something,' he corrected.

'Opened?'

He nodded.

She thought for a moment. 'That makes sense.'

Rebecca remembered Heimo at fifteen, sitting in the sunroom explaining to her why she was reliving her accident. He always seemed to know what was going on in her head.

'Why did you run off last night?' she asked, hoping to discover what was going on in his.

Heimo sighed but didn't release her hand, instead gripping it tighter. Although having to twist his body uncomfortably, his other hand moved unconsciously to the pocket of his shorts where his phone lay between the layers of fabric.

'I recently divorced. After twenty years of marriage my wife left me for a colleague a year and a half ago. She said I worked too much. She lives with him and my children in the house I bought and renovated in Melbourne. Now I seem to spend my life waiting for my kids to call. I miss them. Last night in the salon, my son rang. Then I was embarrassed, I suppose. I didn't know how to explain it without seeming like a fool.'

'Do your children blame you for the break up?' Rebecca queried, moving closer to him along the sofa so their thighs touched. She stroked his fingers. His skin had hardened over time.

'No, not at all. But they're teenagers and, despite spending hours on Instagram, TikTok and Snapchat, they never have time to ring their father,' he grinned.

It seemed strange to her that Heimo identified as a

father. There was an entire portion of his life that she'd missed, where he had transformed into someone new. It was odd how that happened when a person had children, she thought. Her mum hadn't been known as 'Joyce'; she was 'the twins' mum'. But Rebecca would never be defined as a parent. That would never be her identity.

When Luke was living she always viewed herself as a sister first. Never a daughter or a student or a lover, not even a writer. At the very centre of her, at the point in her soul from which everything else about her sprang, at her nucleus, she was Luke's sister. That knowledge coloured and inspired her. Although she fought against it, Luke had been her lifespring and she had been his. What was she now? she wondered. What lay at her source?

'Would you like to see some photos?'

Rebecca nodded, yawned and rubbed her face. He scrolled through what seemed like hundreds of images, attempting to find a suitable picture. The photographs that were stored in her phone were mostly of Joe or Hugh (another couple's child), striking landscapes, memorable meals or performers on stage – common images captured by the childless.

Heimo handed her the phone and Rebecca studied the girl and boy on the screen. They were striking, with dark hair and their father's cobalt eyes. The girl wore heavy charcoal eyeliner, a lip ring and a scowl.

'Your daughter ...' Rebecca began.

'Anna,' Heimo said.

'Anna looks ...' Rebecca searched for a suitable description. Alternative, angry, scary ... 'artistic,' she finally decided upon.

Heimo nodded. 'She's in a band. She plays guitar.'

Rebecca noticed an almost imperceptible flurry of satisfaction sweep over his face.

'Do you still play piano?' she asked. 'You were so good, you and Luke both.'

Heimo laughed.

'We were so serious. So dedicated to creating a new sound when all we were doing was imitating old ones. I still play sometimes, at Christmas parties, that sort of thing.'

'And why are you here in Geneva, alone?' she asked, handing back the phone.

'My friends suggested that when the divorce papers were signed I should do something for myself for closure. A full stop, if you like, on that chapter of my life.'

'Was that a good suggestion?'

Heimo shrugged. 'Yes and no.'

He took her hand again. Intimacies had been shared. His touch warmed her from the inside out.

'I've always wanted to come to Geneva. The university has been asking me for years ...' he said, then stopped.

'I've Googled you,' he said. 'Kept track of your life.'

'Oh,' Rebecca, her face warming again, didn't know how to respond.

'I read your books, too. They were very good. I gave them to Anna to read, so she could understand how I grew up. You captured it all so perfectly. I recognised Gerringong.'

He looked her directly in the face, searching for something.

'I recognised Luke as well.'

16

Although it made her journey longer, Rebecca had made a habit of walking along the beach to her appointments. Sand under her feet was an evocative preparation for her sessions. The sun bit her shoulders and back, prompting her to stop and look at the waves, imagining their sting were she to run into the surf. Two boys, young men, kneeled on the beach waxing their boards, smooth, amber backs hunched as they worked. The urgent scratch of the block against the board and the scent of coconut were so familiar. She breathed in deeply then took in their hurriedness, their constant glimpses at the waves, as though they might be too late, as though the waves might run out. Drinking in the scene a final time, she turned and continued towards Campbell Parade.

A spicy, pungent odour wafted to her nose from under the door.

'Luke, open up.' Rebecca heard a click and the door opened a crack.

Luke resumed his seat on the floor, cross-legged, shirtless.

Several books lay open around him. A bong rested between his thighs.

'How long have you been doing that stuff?' she asked, gesturing disapprovingly towards the bong.

'Reading?' He grinned through heavy lids. His bedroom was stuffy and rank with an earthy stench that hung in the smoke-filled air. U2 spun on the turntable, the volume turned low.

'Drugs.'

'A while.'

Rebecca hadn't seen him much that summer. She hadn't been surfing with him as frequently, preferring to read or write. If she went to the beach, it was to sit alongside Heimo on the sand, plunging into the waves when they grew hot, then resuming their positions on their respective beach towels again.

She realised that Luke was struggling to reconcile himself to the change in their relationship. They both knew it was strained and the stress was compounding. A tug-of-war of wills.

She circled the festering room, stepping over the dirty clothes, cups, plates and ashtrays that littered the floor then cleared a space for herself on the bed behind him.

'And what about this?' Rebecca poked his shoulder blade.

'It's Pisces.'

'I know it's Pisces.'

'Do you know what it means?'

She nodded and caught his eyes in the mirrored wardrobe staring at her, startling in their stubbornness. The tattoo was a challenge.

Her mother said Luke's 'shiftlessness' was just a phase. After the holidays, when he was back at school, everything would sort itself out. School was 'the best place for him', but they'd given him an ulti-matum – school or a job. But he didn't want to go back to school and he didn't want a job, so Rebecca's parents thought they had won.

'Nev said he saw you and Heimo at the café, having milkshakes.'

'Is he spying on me?'

'Nuh. Have you fucked him yet?'

'You're disgusting!' Rebecca kicked him hard in his thigh. 'None of your business.'

He laughed then, quietly, with eyes half closed.

'You're so responsible. Little Miss Responsible.'

Rebecca wasn't certain if Luke's observation was meant as an insult or a compliment.

'We're friends, that's all,' she said after a moment. 'You'd better air this place out before Dad gets here. He's home early today to take me to the dentist. I'm getting my braces off.'

He took no notice and placed his mouth in the chamber of the bong. Holding a lighter to the weed, he inhaled deeply. Rebecca turned her head. It sickened her. She opened a window then glanced at the books on the floor. Children standing in hospital gowns or lying naked on operating tables stared back at her. Then there were the images of corpses and autopsies, also children.

It took her a moment to realise they were all twins.

Rebecca's stomach heaved. As she looked away, she caught a glimpse of herself and Luke in the wardrobe doors. Even at sixteen, their faces were so similar. He gazed back at her. His eyes were no longer sleepy; there was something in them she didn't recognise. What she saw was as disturbing to her as the books.

'What have you got these for?' she asked.

He took another drag, blowing the smoke out slowly.

'In Auschwitz, Mengele used to do medical experiments on twins. He'd inject them with diseases, try to change their eye colour, remove their organs and limbs, then swap them around and wait to see if the kids survived. They all died.'

'It's gross, Luke. Depressing.'

'We've always been a mystery.'

'You're stoned.'

'Yeah.'

Rebecca rose and felt dizzy. She went to the window.

'If twins had kids,' Luke said. 'What do you think they'd look like? Genetic freaks or perfect clones?'

Rebecca's heart beat faster. He was stoned, that's all. He won't even remember this conversation tomorrow, she thought.

'I miss you, Becca.' Luke reached for her. 'I don't know how to love you …'

'What do you mean?'

He shook his head. 'I just miss you.'

His tone pierced her heart and she turned. She stared at his hand floating in air. It was larger than hers, but they shared the same slender fingers and square nails.

'I miss you, too.' She went to him and he drew her down into his lap.

Bound together, they rested like that for a moment until they heard their father's car in the driveway.

EVA ROSE FROM HER DESK. She walked to the printer that lived behind the door that led into the kitchen. She drew a piece of paper from the tray. As Eva walked through to the living room, she read the words aloud, enunciating each word, each syllable.

Two from one you came.

Wailing leviathans from primeval mire

Returned, defeated by God.

Apocalypse.

TWO FROM ONE.

You came. Whole.
Who remembers you?
The living lost, yet paths reflected in slender ribs,
Intersecting in the other.

BITTER WOUNDS WEEPING *petals on sand,*
   Crushed, dried shells like bones or fossils.

CLEAVED, *forever cleaved ...*
   Trails of blood streaming time
   And distance
   Bearing the stigmata and the passion.

Eva finished the final stanza more loudly, as though a glorious light would shine on the poem's meaning. *Galatia*, written by Joe O'Neill in 2002. She had found it online, a random site. The poem had never been published in a formal collection.

She interpreted it as Joe's portrayal of Rebecca and Luke's relationship. Why, she pondered, had Joe written it with such weight, in biblical terms? References to blood and the stigmata, suggestions of resurrection and sacrifice ... What had Joe seen that the psychiatrist couldn't see now? Removing her glasses, Eva rubbed the bridge of her nose then threw the paper onto her desk.

Rebecca was due for her appointment in fifteen minutes. Eva wandered to the window and raised the blind. She picked up the binoculars she kept on the windowsill and held them against her eyes, waiting to spot her patient crossing Campbell Parade. Rebecca was always early. It was amazing what people revealed when they thought they weren't being watched. Eva didn't make a habit of spying on her patients; she used the binoculars to gain a different perspective when she was nutting things out. Gazing out of her window toward the horizon occasionally offered her startling clarity on otherwise murky ideas. Today, the trashy little object she'd picked up in a Two Dollar store allowed her to gain a different perspective on Rebecca.

At five minutes to ten Eva saw her patient walk up the beach with thongs in hand. Rebecca dropped them when she reached the footpath and slipped her feet into them while she waited for the walk sign. She was wearing a light green, plaid sundress tied at the waist. Long-limbed and straight-backed, Rebecca was a remarkably attractive woman, Eva thought as she watched her patient walk calmly across the road. Rebecca stopped at the traffic island and checked her watch, then turned, looking back at the beach. Despite the number of tourists congregated there on the hot day taking photographs, Rebecca seemed oblivious to them all as she gazed unmoving into the horizon. Unable to see her expression, Eva wondered what she was contemplating.

When the lights changed, Rebecca and a few pedestrians stepped onto the road. A Vespa sped by, ignoring the signal, missing Rebecca and a few tourists by millimetres. The pedestrians shouted abuse after the wayward rider, who tooted his horn in retaliation. But Rebecca didn't miss a beat. She walked on, unfazed.

'What's going on in there, Rebecca Collins?' the doctor said to herself, lowering the binoculars. 'What won't you tell me?'

Within seconds, Eva heard the buzz of her intercom.

17

———

'I watched you just now, walking up the beach and crossing the road,' Eva said. 'You seemed lost in thought. So lost that you were nearly hit by a scooter.'

Rebecca shrugged, hoping to throw off the question.

'Really?'

'Yes. What were you thinking about?'

'I can't remember to be honest. Emails I have to get back to, friends I said I'd catch up with ... you know.'

She crossed her legs and smoothed the fabric of her skirt over her knees.

'That's a very pretty dress.'

'Joe bought it for me years ago, on a whim. He thought it would suit me. I haven't worn it in ages. I don't even know why I packed it.'

Perspiring from her walk to the doctor's office, she ran her hand across her top lip.

Eva put her glasses on then picked up her notepad and pen. Rebecca knew this indicated the beginning of the session.

'Let's talk about Joe today. Tell me about your relationship.'

Eva's questions were so broad, so open-ended. Rebecca never knew where to begin or where to end. She sighed, readying herself for the plunge. Turning towards the window as she considered what to say, the heat rippled in waves off the tin roof below. She stared into the brightness. She wondered how she could encapsulate her and Joe in the space of an hour.

'Joe was very funny, absurd at times, but there was a darkness in him as well. His life had been so lacking in beauty. It was marred by so much ugliness – the death of his brother and mother. The IRA attempted to recruit him when he was thirteen. Even at that age he was self-willed, dogged in his belief that violence was not the way forward. His brother Brendan kept him safe. No one dared touch him.

'A primal sense of vengeance was rooted in the community, as well as a skewed sense of honour. Joe didn't have that but as a child, he watched as it was played out. It coloured his entire outlook, I think, his entire world view. When we first met, he spoke a great deal about death and our legacies as human beings. Perhaps that's what attracted me – I made him happy. And I did. I know I did. I think I inspired him too. Artistically, I mean. That sounds very arrogant, but I'm sure that was part of it. I know he loved me. I'm certain of it.'

'You made him happy, provided some light in his life.'

'Yes.'

'What did Joe do for you? How did Joe make *you* feel?'

Rebecca felt her chest tighten. She looked away.

'He made me feel ...' she said, pausing before looking back to Eva.

'He made me feel special.'

Eva nodded.

'He made me feel real.'

She nodded again. Eva poured her patient a glass of iced water from an old wine bottle. She wanted Rebecca to have a moment before they took the next step.

'I believe there's a darkness in you, too, Rebecca,' she began. 'Your books are evidence of that.'

Rebecca sipped her water and considered Eva's observation.

'I wrote from my experience, I suppose.'

'Tell me.'

Rebecca sipped at the water. When she finished, she wiped her hand of condensation on her thigh.

'Writing helped me make sense of growing up in a small town, growing up as a twin ... as Luke's twin. But later, when I moved to England, I became scared of sadness. It's a natural emotion, right? It's normal to be sad, occasionally.'

She took another sip of water.

'Yet, at the first sign of a bad mood or a gloomy thought, I'd panic and put on a happy face. I felt like it was my responsibility to maintain the light ... Joe screamed at me once when he was ill. "It's okay to be sad, I am fuckin' dying," he said.

'I buried my sorrow for a very long time. I stubbornly refused to give it its head. I was afraid if I let it out, it would consume me, like it had Luke ... I was terrified that his kind of sorrow might be in me as well, and that I wouldn't be able to contain it.'

'But sorrow must have surfaced sometimes,' Eva mused. 'It's extremely difficult to sustain that sort of front.'

'I agree.'

Rebecca's chest began to tighten again.

'Was there a time when ...?'

'When Luke died.'

Eva waited for her patient to elaborate.

'There were simply no words to describe to Joe how it affected me. I couldn't voice it. I still can't.' She paused. 'He told me in Geneva that after Luke died, there was "just blank space" left where I had been.'

'What do you think he meant?'

Rebecca rose and walked to the portable cooler in the corner of the room. She stood with her back to it, the cold air billowing her skirt and drying her back and thighs of perspiration. *Just blank space* ... Trying to understand those three words had occupied most of her time in the last few months. She had come to no solid conclusions.

'There was a hole left, I guess, after Luke died. It couldn't be filled. Not by Joe, not by anyone. No matter how hard I tried to conceal it, Joe felt it as strongly as I did and it pushed him away. I pushed him away.'

She turned to the window and gazed out, wanting to escape. But there was no view. Eva's office was at the back of the apartment building, overlooking roofs and a narrow laneway just wide enough for a garbage truck.

'When you picture Joe, what do you see?' Eva asked, after a moment.

Rebecca closed her eyes and took in the image that appeared.

'Joe in his forties, seated at his desk in our Islington flat. A lamp illuminates his face, which is resting in a hand. In that hand sits a slow-burning cigarette. He is writing with the other hand, his left. It's curled around the pencil like a claw. His hair is messy and he has dark rings under his eyes, but his expression is entirely serene.' She paused. 'He's at home.'

Opening her eyes, she moved back to the sofa and took a seat.

'He was talented and passionate, outspoken and funny. He made me laugh every day and he challenged me every day. He still does, even in his current incorporeal state.'

Eva smiled. 'Go on.'

'I think Joe placed himself above usual convention. He refused to adhere to any norms.'

'Do you consider him amoral?'

'No, not at all. But he was instinctual. It probably began during childhood. Death was ever-present and he often had to live by his wits. His writing was a kind of therapy, I suppose. He'd place words on a page – free associate, I guess – then shift them around until they made his world make sense.'

It was a strange but satisfying experience to be analysing Joe in this way, like a character in a book, once the book is finished.

'He could be bad-tempered and moody as though the world had failed him, as though he was disappointed with everyone in it. But he was also gentle and kind and forgiving. Naïve, too. He believed that words could change the world.'

'You don't agree?'

Rebecca shrugged.

'I used to think they could change me.' She frowned and closed her eyes, searching for the most accurate words. 'Purge me.'

'Of what?'

'I'm not sure.' Rebecca looked at the doctor squarely. 'Then Luke's death changed everything.'

Eva nodded as she scrawled Rebecca's thoughts onto the page. Then, lifting her pen and closing her eyes, she thought for a moment before writing *Two from one you came.*

'There were no half measures for Joe,' Rebecca went on. 'He swore like a trooper, drank like a fish and smoked like a chimney. He'd hate me describing him like this, in clichés. He hated clichés. But that's what he was like. Joe was a stereotype, a trope, yet completely authentic at the same time.'

Reading back over her notes, Eva laughed. Rebecca looked at her, curious.

Eva explained. 'Joe may have been putting up a front, too, do you think? Perhaps he adopted a persona. Perhaps you were more alike than you realised, Rebecca. You lessen your tragedy because, in your eyes, Joe's tragedy was on a much grander scale, an international scale. But yours is no less.'

Rebecca sighed and steepled her fingers in front of her face.

'So that drew us together?'

'And also pushed you apart.'

The patient nodded gravely. 'We were doomed from the beginning?'

'Not at all. You were together for almost thirty years. I'd say for the most part your stars were aligned.'

Eva paused for a moment. She removed her glasses before asking her next question.

'Why did you never marry or have children?'

Rebecca shifted. She never enjoyed answering this question because she wasn't certain of the answer.

'We discussed it occasionally, but we always decided against it. We were happy as we were, I suppose. Now, in hindsight ...' Rebecca held open her hands and feigned bemusement.

'Karina.'

'Yes. Karina.'

'How did you feel when you met her in Geneva?'

'I had hoped to hate her,' Rebecca said. 'I hoped to push her to the ground and tear out her hair, claw at her cheeks until she bled, until she cried for mercy and apologised.'

Eva chuckled.

Rebecca straightened her hem over her knees and rubbed the course fabric – Madras cotton – between her fingertips.

'I wanted so much to hate her. There is part of me that did. And, I guess, still does.'

18

REBECCA WAITED outside Karina Bonnay's office on the Rue de Berne. It was lodged at the back of the Allianz Building. She hadn't made an appointment. Once courage arrived, she didn't dare hesitate.

As she waited, her eyes wandered around the office, at the prints on the wall – all modern, tasteful; rented from a gallery, she imagined. The clock on the wall ticked on and the initial surge of courage that had propelled her into this office began to peter out.

Meeting Gerard had been a mistake.

They had sat in Starbucks for two hours drinking coffee, talking about Joe. Gerard's resemblance to his father was remarkable and Rebecca's thoughts immediately drifted to her own imagined children, the children she might have given birth to and raised into thoughtful and eloquent teenagers. Gerard might have been her son. With a different accent and her own high cheekbones, he might have been her son.

'How would your mother react if she knew you were with me?' she had asked.

He shrugged. 'I'm not sure. She is being very protective right now.'

'Why did you want to talk to me so badly?'

'I was curious about you and about Dad.'

Hearing him call Joe 'Dad' startled her. She had excused herself and went to the bathroom then sat in the cubicle with her head in her hands, feeling desolate and lonely. She didn't leave the toilet until she heard the knock of another customer.

When she and Gerard parted, they had embraced and he kissed her on each cheek. He was warm and his face was soft and velvety. He and Joe were the same height and they shared the same stocky build. She found it disconcerting.

'By the way,' she said as they had begun to go their separate ways. 'How did you get my number?'

'Dad gave it to me. In case of an emergency. He told me about you the last time I saw him.'

Joe must have been worried he'd die in Geneva, Rebecca thought. It intrigued her that he had conspired with his son.

'I should go,' Gerard said. 'Mum will get worried. Can we meet again?'

'Of course,' Rebecca replied in the moment, instantly basking in the conspiracy and the pain she might be inflicting on Karina.

Now she was regretting her response. It had been casual and cowardly.

'Karina shouldn't be too much longer,' the assistant interrupted.

Rebecca's eyes shot to the young woman behind the desk and her chest tightened between her breasts. Her breathing became shallow. Then the nausea came.

What was she doing here? she asked herself, seeking out the exit.

Slow, deep breaths, Angus had advised.

'Are you feeling okay?' Karina's assistant said, offering Rebecca a concerned glance.

'I'm fine,' Rebecca answered, struggling to draw oxygen into her lungs; it felt like sucking porridge through a straw.

'Karina is just finishing up some work. She knows you're here. Can I get you anything?'

Rebecca shook her head. Slowly, with each laboured breath, her chest began to loosen and her airways widened. By the time Karina Bonnay's office door opened five minutes later, the nausea had subsided. But when she rose, her head reeled. Focusing on Karina's elegant heart-shaped face and shimmering hair, she sucked in a final deep breath, refusing to faint in front of her.

Karina held out her hand and ran her eyes quickly over Rebecca's head, noting the alteration since the funeral.

'Please, come in, Rebecca.' Her face was expressionless. 'Sophie, will you get us some coffee?' The assistant rose.

After she closed the office door, Karina gestured to a sofa by the window. Rebecca sat, uncertain who should be the first to speak. It was Rebecca's quest, but it was Karina Bonnay's office.

'I'm so glad you came, Rebecca,' Karina began, perching herself onto the edge of the sofa. Pleasantries didn't come easily for her, Rebecca could tell.

'Thank you for seeing me.'

Sophie entered bearing a tray laden with a coffee pot, cups and a selection of mini pastries arranged in rounds on a plate. She placed it on the coffee table in front of the sofa and Karina poured the coffee.

Silence followed, neither woman knowing how to proceed. They glanced at one another warily. As Rebecca searched for an opening to their dialogue, she remembered that just as her heart ached for the loss of Joe, so did Karina's. Rebecca recalled her bedraggled form a few weeks before at the funeral, the injured bird. Honesty paved the way forward. Or as much honesty as Rebecca was willing to allow.

Rebecca smiled with a forced warmth she hoped was inconspicuous and placed her cup in its saucer.

'I loved Joe and so did you. I saw that at his funeral. I have no ill feelings towards you or ... your children, but it would be stupid, don't you think, to ignore each other? To be honest, I wish I could, but I can't. I feel stuck, as though I can't move on without knowing more about you.'

Karina sipped her coffee thoughtfully for a moment.

'What do you mean by stuck?'

'I'm stuck, I suppose, in the rubble,' Rebecca explained.

'An unusual metaphor,' Karina replied. She was strangely unemotional, so altered from the woman who Rebecca had met on the steps of St Paul's. She supposed that grief had strange effects on people.

'That's just how I see it,' Rebecca went on. 'Joe and I had such a strong relationship, or so I always thought. When I saw Gerard in the cab ...

'You know his name?'

'Angus Redmeyer filled me in on the details.' When had she become so adept a liar? she wondered. The fiction steadied her.

'When I saw him in the cab,' she continued, 'the foundations of my relationship with Joe crumbled around me. I was suddenly embarrassed and humiliated and extremely lost.'

'What do you want?' Karina asked, her wide curious eyes eager for Rebecca's response. It was the first animation Rebecca had seen.

'I'm not going to contest Joe's will or cause any difficulties of that kind. But I need to understand what went wrong with Joe and me.'

'What if nothing went wrong?' Karina queried.

Rebecca bit her lip. She'd planned to be civilised, the bigger person, because she wasn't certain whether, under normal circumstances, Karina might be a woman she might like and admire. But her coolness, her level tone was too much for Rebecca to bear.

'What does that say about Joe, then?' Rebecca asked. 'That he was a natural born cheat? That lying and hurting people was sport?'

Karina looked at her. Her eyes were as sharp as lights on still water.

'I just mean that perhaps there was nothing obvious. Or perhaps there were signs you –'

'When Joe was alive,' Rebecca put in quickly, 'did you know about me?'

She nodded. 'Joe was honest with me from the very beginning.'

Rebecca winced. Did she deserve that?

'But the children didn't. I didn't tell them anything until he died. The news reports ... It was better coming from me.'

Gerard did know about me, Rebecca wanted to shout. Instead she shifted her gaze to the floor, struggling to tamp down her spite.

'If you knew about me, how could you be with him?' Rebecca's voice rose.

'Because I know he loved me. And I saw it in the way he looked at Gerard when he was born, and then Marie. Sometimes relationships are unorthodox. It wasn't an ideal situation for any of us, but I was willing to compromise to be with him.'

Insurers rarely compromised, thought Rebecca. The children, she guessed, were Karina's insurance.

Karina slid her cup onto its saucer then put it back on the tray very deliberately.

'I'm having lunch with my children today. Would you like to join us?'

Rebecca eyed her doubtfully, confused. She had already decided she didn't like Karina. But she longed to witness an aspect of her character that might be the one that had appealed to Joe. Rebecca needed to know what had attracted him to this woman.

'I think it would be beneficial for the children. They're already asking questions, especially Gerard. They're curious.'

'Yes, I would. Thank you.'

Karina wrote her address on a notepad that lay on the coffee table. She tore off the page deftly and handed it to Rebecca. 'Twelve o'clock.'

KARINA'S APARTMENT was situated high in a modern block in the residential suburb of Sécheron. The doors to the apartment's balcony were open when Rebecca arrived and, stepping outside, she took in the view over the rooftops of the city, attempting to pinpoint her hotel in the distance. Gazing down at the road, she watched the cars moving slowly up the street, their drivers searching for a free space. It struck Rebecca as odd that despite the action below, there was no sound. If this were London, she thought, the sounds of horns and angry voices would be rebounding between the buildings like gunfire. But the Genevese were polite and restrained, always, as they drove around the city in their energy-efficient cars.

By the time Karina returned with a glass of wine, Rebecca's stomach had twisted itself into tight knots at the thought of seeing Gerard again. The children were yet to arrive from school.

'It's quite an elegant ballet going on down there.'

'Car spaces are highly prized in Geneva,' Karina explained. 'Parking is unrestricted for the two hours over lunchtime. If you then set your disc for a following hour you can achieve the unimaginable – three hours free of the tyranny of the parking police!'

'How long have you lived in this apartment?' Rebecca asked.

'Nearly sixteen years,' she replied, sweeping some leaves with her foot into a corner. She had removed her heels and now wore red clog-like shoes. 'I moved in just before Gerard was born ...'

There was silence.

'This is all still very fresh for the children,' Karina confessed seriously, after a moment. 'Please, remember they have only recently lost their father.'

'Of course,' she replied, flatly, her jaw tensing.

The women heard the front door slam.

'Ah, here they are,' Karina said, her face brightening. She stepped inside and for Rebecca the air became thin.

Rebecca followed her into the sunny living room. The boy and girl removed their backpacks and hung them on hooks near the door. When they turned they noticed their mother standing with Rebecca.

The girl smiled timidly. Gerard frowned, intrigued. Rebecca looked at him, hoping to explain without words, enjoying the subterfuge.

'Gerard. Marie,' Karina began. 'This is Rebecca Collins, your father's partner.'

Rebecca had never heard such an odd introduction and she hesitated.

'It's lovely to meet you both.' She approached them with an outstretched arm. Gerard took her hand first, then was followed by his sister.

Marie resembled Joe too, with her distinct green eyes and her heart-shaped mouth but, seeing Gerard now in the stark light of the apartment, Rebecca was shocked at his uncanny likeness to his father. Besides the physical, there was a presence, an aura of self-confidence that was so like Joe's. His rooted stance and the obstinate tilt of his chin were painfully familiar.

She took a deep breath and smiled.

'You're probably both wondering why I'm here. The answer is quite simply that I'd like to get to know you both, a little, if you'll let me. I loved your father very much and, seeing you two standing there, I'm happy, in a weird way, that you were born.'

They laughed shyly.

'It seems that Joe, in his life, created something much more enduring than words on a page, something much more valuable.'

'Where are you from?' Marie then asked, interested, approaching Rebecca.

'Australia.'

'Did Dad ever live there?' Gerard queried.

Rebecca shook her head, her tension easing. Gerard seemed comfortable with the deception.

'Joe only visited Australia once. He concluded that humans weren't meant to fly that far.'

They laughed, recognising Joe in the joke.

'What's it like there, in Australia?' Gerard said, his brow creased with interest.

'Very beautiful,' she replied slowly, studying his intense emerald eyes in the daylight. 'Very different from Europe. I grew up by the ocean –'

'Can you windsurf? Sail?' Gerard cut in.

'Gerard windsurfs and sails on the lake in summer,' his mother explained. 'It's his passion.'

Rebecca shook her head.

'I surf. Well, I did, once. I'm not sure I could even stand up on a board now.'

Karina gradually eased away from the group into the kitchen.

'So ... who's the reader?' Rebecca asked, indicating the long white shelves that lined two walls of the room. They were bursting with books stacked in trendy higgledy-piggledy disorder. Mostly fiction. A few economic texts she assumed to be Karina's.

'That's Marie,' Gerard answered. 'She writes, too.'

It had been Gerard who she thought would have been the writer.

'Do you write, too?' Rebecca asked, looking at Gerard.

'No,' Marie replied. 'He's only interested in sports.'

Rebecca smiled as she glanced around the room for signs of Joe. Apart from the heaving bookshelves, there were none.

'You should pick her brain,' Gerard said to his sister, the colloquialism flat-footed on his tongue. 'She's a writer too,' he added in a low voice, so his mother didn't hear from the kitchen.

Rebecca shot him a quick glance. What had Joe told him about her? she wondered.

'What do you write?' the girl asked.

'Fiction. I'm more of an editor and proofreader now, but once upon a time I wrote fiction.'

'When did you start? Were you as young as me?' Marie was eager.

'No, a little older. It wasn't until I was fifteen,' Rebecca explained, frowning. 'You see, I had an accident and I was home from school for a long time. I got bored, so I started to read. Then I thought I'd try writing. That's how it began for me.'

Marie nodded, thinking.

'Do you have children?' the girl asked as they took their seats at the table. 'I mean, do we have any brothers or sisters?'

'No. Joe and I never had children,' Rebecca answered quickly.

'Oh,' the girl responded, perplexed by the idea. 'Why?'

'It was never the right time.'

Marie frowned, not quite understanding.

To Rebecca's relief, Karina emerged from the kitchen. The subject was forgotten when she placed a large bowl of pasta in the centre of the table. The pasta was coated in a rich tomato sauce, laced with onions and sausage. Alongside the pasta, Karina placed an equally robust salad of green leaves, potato, corn, egg and some sort of grain – quinoa, Rebecca guessed.

Before Karina sat, she placed an affectionate hand on the shoulders of her children and drew them both closer for a moment. Rebecca saw that it was a pointed gesture, aimed to unsettle her.

She experienced a deep and acute stab of jealousy that forced her to quickly avert her eyes from the scene.

OVER LUNCH the children quizzed Rebecca incessantly about Joe and, surprisingly, her own childhood in Australia.

'... and the scorching heat in summer is like nothing you've ever experienced,' she said, eager more than ever to capture the exoticism of her birthplace. 'Some days, it feels as if your skin is cooking and the only relief is to run into the ocean and stay there until the sun sets.'

Gerard nodded seriously, considering her descriptions.

'Australia, life near the ocean, the struggles teenagers face growing up in small seaside communities ... it's what I used to write about,' she finished.

The three sets of eyes taking her in made her mortifyingly aware of her own foreignness.

'Karina,' Rebecca began, shifting the conversation away from herself. 'Tell me about your work.'

'I don't think you'll be very interested.'

'I'll be the judge of that,' Rebecca said. 'The world of insurance is completely new to me.'

'Well, in layman's terms, at the most basic level, I use data and statistics to measure risk for the company. Once I have the figures, I turn them into colourful charts and graphs for the various teams in AKPH to utilise when developing new products, projecting future results or repricing existing products.'

Aware she was being patronised, Rebecca persisted. 'And at its most complex level?'

'I create the modelling software that other insurance companies use to measure risk.'

Rebecca couldn't imagine Joe being with a woman who was so boring, so composed, so completely flush. Passionless. What's more, she made a career in an industry that Joe despised. Rebecca had hoped that over lunch she might witness another facet to Karina, a pinch of spirit to round her out, but there was nothing. She attempted to play out a dialogue between Karina and Joe in her mind. It was stilted, awkward and destined for conflict. How did he ever fall in love with her? Rebecca wondered.

'Where did you and Joe meet?' Rebecca asked, determined to find answers.

The eyes of Gerard and Marie darted from their food to their mother. The group had been in constant discussion for almost an hour but this strand in the conversation had been avoided by everyone.

'Vienna. In an airport lounge in 2000,' she explained with a rare smile. 'Both our flights were delayed. Joe had just presented at a seminar for conflict resolution at the Hofburg. I had been visiting my sister.'

Rebecca cast her mind back. She had helped Joe with that presentation. It was detailed and moving, as were all of Joe's speeches. But she hadn't travelled to Vienna with him as planned. She had been packed and ready to go but then her mother rang to inform her that Luke was missing, presumed dead. She and Joe had gone to Heathrow together the following morning in a cab. When they reached the terminal, they had hugged tightly.

'Are you sure you don't want me to come?' he asked at the gate, placing his bag on the floor. 'I really think I should come with you. You're more important than conflict resolution.'

'Everything will be okay,' she answered, forcing a reassuring smile. 'Besides, it's too late now. You're committed to Vienna. I'm certain the entire seminar rests on your presentation. I'll be fine, I promise. But I'll miss you.'

He kissed her. It was a kiss so filled with love and compassion that she began to sob.

'You're a brave one, mo ghrá, to go back alone,' he said. 'It's exactly what I love about you the most.'

A certain misgiving coloured his tone. Rebecca felt a block of ice begin to form in her belly.

Then they parted and went their separate ways.

'WHAT DID YOU SEE IN HER?' Rebecca asked. She was seated on a bench opposite the Jet d'Eau, tracking the column of water with her eyes.

'It was Karina's levelness that attracted me.' Joe replied.

'Was I too emotional? Unstable?'

Joe shook his head.

'It wasn't a competition.' He shifted on the seat and faced her. 'Karina possessed a quality I needed at that time.'

Rebecca inhaled deeply. 'I just can't get my head around ...'

'The attraction.'

'Yeah.'

'Who would have ever put us together, *mo ghrá*,' Joe responded. 'Our ages, backgrounds, experiences ... they were worlds apart. Literally. Yet, that night at The Well I couldn't keep my eyes off you. I couldn't stop listening to you speak. I was completely spellbound. If someone had tried to take me away from you that night, I would have ripped their head off. I was drawn to you like the moon draws the sea.'

'Poetic.'

Joe sighed. 'All I'm saying is that attraction ...'

'Love.'

'... isn't logical.'

A small group of people – sightseers – stopped alongside Rebecca's bench to admire the fountain. They spoke French as they photographed the Geneva icon. She realised what

Joe was explaining was feasible, reasonable even, but she didn't want to forgive him.

'Is that how it was with Karina? Were you spellbound?'

'Not at all. It was different. Karina isn't you.'

The sightseers glanced at her then moved on.

'So Joe met Karina in 2000 but they didn't become "attached", according to Karina, until a year or so after that when they ran into each other in Paris. But to think that if I had just let him come with me to Australia ...'

Eva took off her glasses and closed her eyes for a moment.

'It sounds like an extremely uncomfortable lunch.' She opened her eyes, stared hard at Rebecca.

'When you left, how did you feel?'

'For want of a more powerful adjective, *awful*. Exhausted, angry, sad ... at a complete loss. I went there looking for an answer and I walked out even more devastated and confused than I was before. I realised it was a mistake; it was a stupid thing to do.'

'But very courageous,' Eva remarked.

Rebecca looked at her, surprised.

'To confront her as you did, to go looking for those answers,' Eva clarified.

'Thanks, but it just felt stupid to me.'

Eva smiled.

'Have you always been like this, Rebecca? Would you define yourself as a courageous person?'

'I LOVE THIS SONG,' Katie Bates said, squeezing Rebecca's arm.

Luke was playing guitar and singing 'Fifty Years', his plangent keening stirring a few girls to tears. The shadows cast by the flames danced on his face, making him more of a mystery than he was already. Sharon Mason swayed by his side, eyes closed. Drunk. A 'sure thing' was how Luke described her when Rebecca had questioned his choice of date for the party.

'Yeah, it's great.' Rebecca pulled her jumper over her head. 'I'm going for a walk.'

Katie nodded.

'Wanna come?'

'Nah, I'll keep your beer warm,' the girl giggled.

Rebecca left the bonfire and her friends who sat around it, glad of the privacy. Would she miss them when she was gone? she wondered, looking back at the pure lapping heat of the flames.

Staring at the darkening horizon, Rebecca didn't feel the water wash over her feet. She closed her eyes, hoping to capture the sound of the surf – the distant rumble, the thunderclap when the waves broke then the rush against the sand. Capture it, and somehow bank it for when she was no longer there.

'He's so talented. Mum reckons he could be a professional.'

Rebecca opened her eyes slowly. It was Heimo. She hadn't heard his approach over the sand. Her heart beat faster.

She nodded. 'Luke's got many talents.'

'What do you think he'll do?'

Rebecca shrugged.

'He just wants to surf. Dad's trying to get him an apprenticeship. What about you?' She studied his profile as he answered.

'*I'll see what my results look like.*'

'*Same.*' *She swallowed. Heimo made a noise, part sigh, part hum – a low deep-throated humph – and Rebecca glanced at him.*

'*I was just wondering if you were going out with anyone,*' *he said.*

Rebecca shook her head. He knew she wasn't. While all thoughts of romance had been postponed since the night that Luke, drunk, had come to Heimo's door, she and Heimo still seemed to wind up occupying the same space at school or at the beach. They were drawn to each other. There was a luscious sense of anticipation and intimacy each time they were together. They wanted one another. Although unspoken, that was no secret. Nevertheless, it was just like Heimo to ask.

She was leaving next year. She'd made the decision and signed the letter of acceptance to London's City University. Then the letter was posted, placed in a tub behind the counter.

'*It'll get there in a flash,*' *Keith the postmaster had said.* '*Something important?*'

'*No. Just a letter to a penfriend,*' *Rebecca had replied before leaving. She almost turned back to retrieve the envelope. But, really, there was no choice. She had to leave. She had to make a break, even if that meant leaving Heimo, too.*

'*Well, I was thinking about the formal ...*' *Heimo began, bringing her back to the moment.*

'*Homo!*' *a voice called from behind them. It was an ugly, aggressive, beer-fuelled voice.*

Heimo didn't flinch but Rebecca turned. It was Jamie Rooney.

'*Hey, Homo, who invited you?*'

'*Everyone from our year was invited, you moron,*' *Rebecca called.*

Heimo touched her arm. '*I don't think logic is going to work. Let it go.*'

There were others gathering by Jamie's side now – Johnno

Campbell, Stevo Harrison and Phil McKenzie – the 'bottom feeders', her dad called them. Even though they had left school, they had been invited – they'd been part of their original year.

'What kind of pussy are you, letting a girl fight your battles for you? You must be a homo.' Jamie laughed; his mates joined in.

'I should go,' Heimo said to Rebecca.

He began to walk back up the beach towards the bonfire, but his path was blocked by Jamie. Heimo stood at least a foot taller than him, but Jamie was stocky and broad, a house brick standing on end. Rebecca moved closer, as did Jamie's mates.

'Where do you think you're goin'?' Jamie asked.

'Home.'

Rebecca was amazed at Heimo's level tone. She was breathing hard and her insides began to seethe. Jamie wasn't going to move aside, back down. He wanted a fight.

He pushed Heimo's shoulders with both hands but Heimo didn't stumble. His feet were firmly rooted in the soft sand. Johnno, Stevo and Phil took a few steps closer, grinning like lunatics.

'Luke!' Rebecca cried out until her voice broke.

The music stopped. Jamie and his friends were startled by Rebecca's scream. Heimo took his chance and bolted down to the surf, to the hard sand and along the beach, his arms pumping wildly and his feet kicking up the water. The bottom feeders took off behind him and Rebecca saw Heimo stumble in the dark. The pack was on him in a second.

'Luke!' she cried again then ran towards the brawl.

When she reached them, Heimo lay on the shoreline, his body balled up. Jamie and his mates were kicking him in a frenzy, venting a lifetime of small-town frustration. She heard Heimo moan each time a foot connected solidly with his body.

'Lay off, inbreds!' Rebecca yelled when she reached them, grabbing Stevo by the collar and pulling him back. He rounded *and struck her in the face. The impact of the blow sent her flying onto her back, clutching her cheek.*

'Becca!' Luke sprinted towards her. She was crying, trying to stand. He pulled her away from the scene then shouted. Luke never shouted. Rebecca couldn't even remember him raising his voice.

'You fuckin' hurt her and I'll kill you, I swear,' Luke yelled, approaching Stevo, fists balled.

Backing away, Stevo raised both hands. Luke ran at him, punching him hard in the side of the head. Stevo crumpled onto the sand.

'Now, piss off, fags. You're not welcome,' he shouted.

Jamie and the others halted. They glared at Luke. He was their mate, their leader. Rebecca read the confusion in their eyes.

Luke ran at Jamie then and struck him in the chin. Jamie hadn't expected it, hadn't seen it coming. Rebecca heard a crunch. Jamie's nose? His jaw? Jamie tried to stand but he couldn't find his balance as the waves battered his legs.

'Four on one ... bloody cowards,' Luke continued, standing over Jamie.

Others from the party had followed Luke to the scene. The bottom feeders backed off. Johnno helped Jamie to his feet. He was clutching his jaw.

'You okay?' Katie whispered when she reached Rebecca. She lifted Rebecca's hand from her cheek and examined the injury.

'You'll have a shiner tomorrow.'

Heimo cautiously unwound his body. Rebecca scrambled to her feet and tried to see how much they'd hurt him. There was no blood that she could see. But it was dark, the moon a thin sickle in the sky. Rebecca gingerly checked her own teeth with her tongue.

'Piss off,' Luke said with finality.

Rebecca saw her brother's shoulders relax as they walked away.

'Okay, show's over,' he said to everyone else.

LUKE AND REBECCA walked Heimo home. He was shaking at first, then he gradually calmed, but he moved carefully and slowly, wincing now and again. His hair, shorts and t-shirt were wet and caked in sand. No one spoke.

When they reached his house, Heimo opened the gate. The windows were black. Heimo rested one hand on the fence and clutched the other across his abdomen.

'Thanks,' he said to them both, head lowered. He sighed.

Luke shrugged and removed a packet of Drum tobacco from his pocket then crouched on the footpath.

Rebecca and Heimo watched Luke and his nimble fingers as he rolled a cigarette, turning the cylinder until it was just right. Once it was lit, Luke rose and sauntered a few houses along Boona Avenue.

'I'm sorry that happened,' Rebecca said after a minute. They were Luke's friends. She felt responsible. Guilt by association.

'They're idiots. They always have been. They've been wanting to do that since kindergarten.'

'I s'pose.'

'What are you going to tell your mum about your face?' He touched her cheekbone softly. His fingers were icy.

'I'll say I did it surfing. What about you?'

The front lights went on in Heimo's house. Rebecca started. They were running out of time.

'I don't know.' He paused. 'Maybe the truth,' he added.

Rebecca exhaled, gripping the picket fence in her hands.

'Well, I suppose I should go.'

Heimo nodded. He breathed in and flinched. His hand moved to his ribs.

'*Do you think they'll forgive you? Jamie and the others, I mean. They looked pretty shocked that you sided with Heimo.*'

'*Don't care. I don't need them.*'

Rebecca placed her arms around his neck and hugged him tight.

'*It took a lot of guts. Thanks.*'

'*I felt you tonight, Becca.*'

She broke away.

'*You were shit-scared for Heimo, weren't you?*'

She nodded.

'*But you kept running. Shit-scared yet fuckin' fearless.*'

'Are you okay?' she asked.

Heimo nodded, teeth clenched.

'Thanks, again,' he finally said, defeated.

'Sure. See ya.'

Rebecca walked away towards Luke. She heard the do
close.

'Did he ask you?' Luke said. Rebecca shot him a look. 'To t
formal?'

She shook her head. They ambled slowly to the end of t
street and looked towards the beach and the glow of the bonfire.

'Do you want to go back to the party?' Rebecca asked. 'Shar
will be waiting for you.'

'Nah.' They rounded the corner.

'He told me he was going to ask you. It was like he was aski
my permission or something.'

Rebecca pressed her hands into the pockets of her shorts.

'What do you two talk about?' she asked.

'Stuff.'

'It's just that I can't ...'

'Music, sport. Shit like that.' Luke paused, stamped out h
cigarette on the ground. 'Heimo's interesting.'

Rebecca looked at him strangely. 'Yeah, he is.'

'You really like him, don't you?' Luke asked.

'Yeah.'

'He'll ask you.'

'We'll see.'

They continued in silence until they reached their hous
Mum had left the front light on for them. They stopped at th
gate. Rebecca leaned over and unlatched it.

'When did you learn to fight?' she asked. Luke's ferocity at th
beach had stunned her, impressed her even. She wanted to kno
from where it had come.

'It was just instinct.'

20

___

WHEN REBECCA ENTERED the hotel after lunch at Karina's, the concierge waved to her from behind his desk.

'Ms Collins,' he said, rising. 'There's a gentleman, an English gentleman, in the salon waiting for you. He arrived thirty minutes ago.'

Rebecca was not surprised when she saw Angus standing in front of the bookshelf, hands in pockets, perusing the collection. He was wearing pressed chinos and loafers – his travelling attire. Rebecca's heart swelled at the sight of him. She couldn't face going back to an empty room, or worse, a room with Joe in it.

When she entered the salon further, Heimo was there as well, standing at the bar in running shorts and trainers. Flushed and perspiring, he brought a bottle of water to his lips as he nodded at her. His eyes lingered on her face for a moment, concerned. Uncertain who to acknowledge first, Rebecca stepped into the centre of the space.

'Look what the cat dragged in,' Rebecca said.

Angus turned and approached. She pecked him on the cheek quickly. He removed his hands from his pockets and, as he was about to embrace her, she said, 'I'd like you to meet an old friend. We went to school together.' Rebecca led Angus towards the bar.

'Angus Redmeyer, this is Heimo Beck.'

The men shook hands. Rebecca stood by and listened as the pair exchanged small talk about the etymology of their names, Angus's flight and running (a mutual interest). Rebecca's eyes moved back and forth as they spoke. Joining in the conversation seemed too hard. Before long, Heimo excused himself extremely politely. Rebecca caught him glance back at the salon as he waited for the elevator.

'What are you doing here?' she asked Angus.

'I hadn't heard anything from you ...'

'It's only been a week. A simple telephone call would have saved you a trip.'

'I suppose ... I missed you.' He pushed his hands into his pockets. 'Is there some place we could go to talk?'

———

'You seem slightly glassy,' Angus said in Rebecca's room. 'Is everything alright?'

'Not really.' She opened a bottle of water and swigged it greedily. She ran her hand across her mouth. 'Will you stay a while?'

'I'm going to order us something to drink.'

'That's a good idea.'

———

They sat together on the sofa watching the sun become a fierce orange glow over the lake. The window shimmered against its intensity. Then she looked at him, turning his way.

'What happened today?' he asked

'Nothing.' Rebecca hated lying to Angus, but she wasn't ready to discuss her lunch with Karina. She didn't want to face her own shortfalls. Angus had warned her off and he had been right.

When the wine arrived, they finished the bottle. Rebecca was silent as Angus spoke about Hugh and work, the current manuscripts he was reading and a book launch he had attended the night before. He'd caught up with so-and-so there. So-and-so was quite a talent back in the day. Do you remember? His first book ... what was it called? Rebecca shrugged. Haven't seen him in years. Left his wife a year ago ... do you remember her? Pretty girl, but a great deal younger. Doomed to fail, when you think about it. Rebecca had nodded, agreed and uh-huhed without really listening.

Then Rebecca wanted to sleep, so without preamble she walked into the bedroom, lay down on the bed and closed her eyes. When she woke a few hours later, Angus was beside her, perfectly still, his arms crossed over his heart like a marble knight on his tomb.

His eyes shot open as he sensed her presence.

'I didn't mean to wake you,' Rebecca said.

'I wasn't asleep. What's wrong?'

'Nothing.'

After the diagnosis, she and Joe had made love only once. Doctors move fast. Within days of learning he had throat cancer, Joe was in surgery, connected to machines and drips. Then, distracted by his ongoing illness or exhausted and nauseous from his treatment, Joe had asked Rebecca to sleep in the spare room. She had reluctantly agreed. Despite his increasing frailty and sickness, Rebecca had never stopped pining for the touch of his skin against hers.

Now she rolled against Angus and nestled into his side.

They sighed in unison then lay in silence, each in contemplation. Angus fingered her cropped curls absently as her mind skipped briskly from Karina to Heimo to Angus and finally to Joe.

'Do you remember when Joe ...' Angus trailed off. 'I'm sorry.'

'Don't be. You can talk about him. You're grieving too,' Rebecca said.

'I was just thinking about that night when he accepted the T. S. Eliot Prize,' Angus said. A smile broke out on her face. Rebecca remembered the evening vividly. 'By the time he stood up on stage to make his speech he was well and truly pissed ...'

Rebecca cut in. 'And he said, "Now that Thatcher has been deposed and peace has been restored in Northern Ireland, my brand of dissent and style of poetry is suddenly trendy..."'

'"And I would just like to say to you all,"' Angus continued, '"Go fuck yourselves!"'

Angus did a decent Irish accent and Rebecca laughed. Angus joined in and they hugged tighter, wrapped in the comfort of a shared memory.

'The funniest thing was,' Angus continued, 'the bastard got a standing ovation!'

<hr>

REBECCA'S MOUTH curled into a smile in her dreamy half-slumber. Being held, the physical contact – Rebecca hadn't realised she was so in need. Basic thermodynamics, she guessed. Angus rolled towards her and they hugged again.

'Thank you for staying ... for being here,' she whispered.

That was all they said for a while, but Rebecca couldn't return to sleep. With the setting sun, she had grown cold. The embers of their warmth had died and reality shone crisp and clean in the darkness. She focused on the outline of it, turning it over in her mind.

'Are you and Meredith happy?'

Angus shifted slightly. 'To be honest, we're more like friends, I suppose, than husband and wife. It doesn't make for an entirely satisfactory relationship.'

'Why don't you separate?' she asked.

'Plenty of reasons – complacency, convenience ...'

It didn't seem like an adequate response.

'I'm sorry.'

'What for?'

'For your unsatisfactory marriage.'

He laughed.

'Do you think there are any couples left in the world who are happy? I mean truly happy?' she went on. 'Who have given themselves to each other completely?'

'What's happened?' he asked, propping himself up on an elbow and looking at her. 'Is it something to do with that fellow in the bar?'

'Heimo?'

Angus nodded.

'No. We ran into each other here. A complete coincidence. I told you.'

'Have you seen Karina Bonnay yet?'

'I'm beginning to think that's a mistake as well,' she said, evading the question.

'I'm worried about you, Rebecca. Will you come home with me?'

'To London?' she asked.

He nodded.

'London's not home.'

'Do you want me to stay?' Angus asked.

'No. You should go soon. I'll keep in better contact. I promise.'

IT WAS NOT YET four-thirty in the morning when Angus woke her as he rose from the bed and walked into the bathroom, his hands locked above his head as he stretched his long arms towards the ceiling. She heard the faint crack of a joint. In the dim light from the living room, she watched him ready himself with the satisfaction that is gained from watching another person do an unpleasant task when you don't have to. She didn't alert him to the fact she was awake, enjoying her study of his unconscious movements. When he leant over the bed to kiss her goodbye, she feigned sleep.

He kissed her forehead, picked up his bag then left the room quietly.

She opened her eyes when she heard the door click shut.

'He loves you. He always has.'

'I know.' Rebecca turned. Joe was propped against the bedhead, his legs crossed at the ankles.

'Do you ever ask yourself "what if"?'

'About Angus?'

Joe nodded.

'Sometimes. He would never had done what you did.'

'But he just did! I thought it was an extremely surprising twist.'

'Nothing happened.'

'You don't have to have sex to be unfaithful.'

'Still waters, I suppose.'

'What's going on in the depths of your mind?'

Rebecca drew the duvet over her shoulders.

'We shared twenty-seven birthdays together,' he said. 'Fifty-four celebrations. Yours were always sad, despite how hard I worked to make them special, happy. Balloons and flowers, restaurants, trips away ...'

'They were just birthdays.'

'I knew you were thinking of Luke. You never voiced it, but on your birthday you felt his absence ever so strongly, didn't you? I was aware. I should have tried a different tack.'

Joe sighed. 'So many scars. I saw them ... I saw them all. I should have done more.'

'You did enough.'

'Were you not happy with your life, *mo ghrá*?'

'Very happy, but now ... it doesn't look the same as it once did.'

21

———

Eva searched her desk for a pen that worked, scribbling curls on scraps of paper until she found one. She sat again and brought her glasses down onto her nose.

'Go on,' she said. 'I'm sorry. I need to throw all the old ones out.'

'I met Brian in Montmartre, in a café called Le Chat Noir. I met him when Joe took me to Paris after Luke died. Joe was involved in a writers' residency at the Irish embassy. I think it was December. December 2000. It was my birthday while we were there. Thirtieth. We were there for a month. Joe was busy every day – he was gaining fame by then. Left to my own devices, I'd wander around the city, stopping in cafés. Hours would go by and I wouldn't even notice, oblivious. Nothing could make me feel. I was breathing, but barely functioning.

'During the second week, I began visiting Sacré-Cœur. It was the apse. The mosaic of Christ in the apse looked like Luke. It was uncanny. His cat-like eyes and high cheekbones were just like my brother's. I was addicted to the image. I'd dream of it during the night, then return each morning, hoping it might change me, repair me. But after hours of sitting in the church, I'd leave broken and return to the embassy. It was a long walk – about forty minutes. I'd take the same route every day. Le Chat Noir was on the way, not far from Sacré-Cœur.'

Rebecca paused and looked towards the open windows. Eva's portable air conditioner was away being repaired. The scratch of Eva's pen stopped.

'Did you pray?'

'Never.'

Rebecca wiped her top lip and continued.

'There must have been hundreds of cafés on the hill down to Le Chat Noir, but they were all so touristy. You know, the kinds where the waiters wear berets. This one was rough around the edges. There were tattered promotional posters of 80s bands on the walls. They were all by the same artist, painted in the same caricatural style. Even before I walked through the door, my nose would be filled with that wonderful combination of cigarette smoke and coffee. I remember the toilet cubicle was so small I had to sit on the toilet sideways. The place was a warren of rooms and bars, but only the front bar was open during the day.'

Eva nodded. 'And Brian?'

'Brian was always there at the same time as me. He sat at the same table in his suit, a briefcase next to his feet. He was always on his BlackBerry. I'd never seen one before.'

'You were attracted to him?'

'Attracted? I was definitely attracted to him. Brian was handsome – dark, well-built, neat; clean and tidy in the All-American style.'

'During my fourth visit to Le Chat Noir, I tripped on a step on my way to the bathroom. Old wooden steps shaped like pieces of driftwood joined the rooms. I guess they were relics from the original building. It was lunchtime and the café was full. On my hands and knees, I sensed my face reddening, then I felt hands on my arms. They were so firm. Brian helped me to my feet. He smiled. His teeth were straight and white. My heart fluttered. I know that's a silly, romantic description, but I felt my heart flutter.

'"Are you alright?" he asked, guiding me to a seat. His voice was deep and resonant.

'He brought me another *café au lait* and a baguette with ham and cheese. "You never eat," he said. "You should eat." That baguette was the best thing I'd ever eaten. We sat together and he told me about his job (a realtor) and his reason for being in Paris (a conference). He was thirty-one, a successful team manager. He aimed to be the MD of his own brokerage by thirty-five. Brian told me all this while I ate my baguette.'

'When I was leaving, I approached the counter to pay. Brian clutched my hand as I was searching for my wallet in my handbag. "It's on me," he said.'

'"*Merci. Je vais bien. Je te verrai demain,*" I replied, proud to have pronounced each word flawlessly.'

Eva smiled.

'"Tomorrow?" he said. "Why should we wait?"'

'He was flirting and, normally, I wouldn't be attracted to such an obvious come on, but I felt something. It felt good to feel something after not feeling anything for so long. I didn't want to refuse him. It was selfish and stupid, I know.'

'Did you think that at the time?' Eva asked.

Rebecca shook her head.

'We caught a taxi to his hotel. The Four Seasons, I think. Then we made love and everything in me came alive. I hummed for hours afterwards. How was that possible? How could sex with a stranger make that happen?'

Eva considered the question for a moment, then focused on her notes.

'Go on.'

Rebecca nodded.

'This was our pattern for the next fortnight until I left Paris. We'd meet at the cafe, catch a taxi to The Four Seasons and make love. I'd look forward to the next day the moment I kissed him goodbye on the street outside the hotel.

'The bed was always made with hospital corners with crisp, white sheets. I loved lying down in his cold, clean bed. Everything was spotless. When I went to the toilet, the bowl sparkled and the taps on the sink gleamed.'

Eva stopped writing and looked at her patient squarely above her glasses.

'I don't consider myself promiscuous. There's been less than a handful of men. Tame by most comparisons, I'd imagine. You see, it's not the physical act of intercourse that was important,' Rebecca leant forward to ensure Eva understood. 'It was the connection. The spark or force, the feeling that you're at the centre of something you can't control. To be lost in it, unaware of everything else. Surfing was like that, as was writing ...

'The sex was always different and we often made love more than once in an afternoon. Afterwards we'd lie in bed just talking. To be honest, Brian would do most of the talking. He had such big dreams and a way of speaking that made me believe he'd achieve them all.'

'Brian was full of hope, had prospects for the future,' Eva said, pausing to think. 'He was the antithesis of Luke,' she pointed out.

Rebecca frowned. 'I suppose he was.'

'Joe, too, yes?' Eva went on.

'Yes.' Rebecca shook her head slowly. 'How did I not see that?'

The doctor shrugged.

'You would only recognise it if you were searching for connections, like we are now.' Her gaze returned to her notes. 'Go on.'

'Whenever I got back to the embassy after being with Brian, I'd hop straight in the shower and reluctantly wash him away. Joe asked me why I was washing my hair every day. I told him that Paris was a very dirty city. It was the only time I was unfaithful.'

Eva glanced at her for a moment.

'Describe to me the way Brian made you feel,' she asked.

Rebecca closed her eyes and tried to conjure the memories of those afternoons. The stuffiness of Eva's office made it difficult to remember Brian and his hotel room where everything had smelt white.

'Try to condense your feelings into a single word,' Eva prompted.

'Free,' she replied immediately.

'So when you weren't with Brian you felt trapped?'

'I could scarcely move.'

'Trapped by what?'

'Sadness.'

'Why couldn't Joe free you?'

Rebecca leaned forward and poured herself a glass of water.

'When he was working, when Joe was in the midst of a piece of writing, he had the ability to block everything else out. He was lost in it. Nothing else was important.'

'Did that make you angry, especially considering the circumstances?'

She thought for a time on the question before nodding.

'Furious. I didn't want to talk about Luke, I couldn't, but I wanted Joe to hold me, feel me and somehow know what was going on inside my head. It was as though the act of an embrace, a real, genuine embrace might have dissolved a little of my pain. But work was a barrier between us. His focus was elsewhere and he ... Joe was rarely present. Looking back, I think I must have done it out of spite, out of anger ... although I don't think I realised that, then. At the time, I just wanted to feel. I never told Brian about Luke or Joe, or what I was going through. But he somehow understood what I needed.'

'Did you ever see Brian again?'

'No, I never did. But I have thought of him a lot in the last couple of years, since Joe got sick. I was so angry when Joe was diagnosed.'

'At Joe?'

'Partly. I'd tried to get him to stop smoking hundreds of times and he refused. But really, I was angry at the world. I guess I saw myself as "fortune's fool".'

'*Romeo and Juliet?*'

Rebecca nodded.

Eva opened her notebook to a fresh page.

'Did you say goodbye to Brian?'

Rebecca shook her head.

'Goodbyes are important. Brian lives in your memory untarnished, blameless –'

'But sometimes goodbyes can sully a relationship,' Rebecca interrupted. 'You can say things you don't mean, or you don't say things that are important.'

'Did you say goodbye to Joe?' Eva asked.

Rebecca crossed her legs. She scratched her scalp rapidly, itchy in the heat.

'Not in so many words,' she replied. 'I couldn't say the

actual word. "Goodbye" didn't seem to do the circumstance justice. How can you say goodbye forever after twenty-eight years? The word wasn't big enough, grand enough.' Rebecca rubbed her temples, as if to ease the immensity of the experience.

'But I was with him. I was with him to the end. I read to him and talked to him. Then I kissed him. I suppose that's the same.'

'And Luke?' Eva asked, scrutinising her patient over her spectacles.

Rebecca shook her head. 'He committed suicide. I couldn't.'

'Before that, I mean, when you left Australia. I imagine it must have been hard to say goodbye to your twin and move to the opposite side of the world?'

Rebecca's eyes instantly pooled. She blinked purposefully two or three times.

'It was incredibly difficult.'

'I'M GOING NOW. Dad's taking me to the train. Half time.'

Luke threw the comic he was reading to the floor – it landed among clothes, dirty plates and ashtrays – then picked up the guitar from beside his bed, his smooth tanned chest defiant in the face of July's cool nip. Brushing his matted hair from his eyes, he began playing Bon Jovi's latest, 'Living in Sin'.

'So, this is it,' he said.

They hadn't spent any time together since the summer. They hadn't talked. But Rebecca had to say goodbye.

Rebecca stared at him for a moment, her insides hollowing out, uttering words she should not.

'Why don't you come with me?'

'To the station?' he asked.

'To London.'

'Nah. I've got everything I need right here.'

'There are girls and beer in London, too.' Rebecca smiled.

'No beaches, but,' he shot back, staring at his fingers as they caught the strings.

Rebecca sat on the bed and placed her hand over his to silence the music. She wanted him to realise this was serious. They might not see each other for years. Despite everything that had happened, they were still connected. He looked at her, finally. His blue eyes were her own.

'Don't worry about me, Bec. You always wanted to escape. Not me, but.'

Her throat tightened. She hadn't always. He felt as miserable as she did – she knew it.

Rebecca rose. 'I better go. Dad wants to get back for the second half.'

Her fingertips hovered above the door handle.

'Hey,' he called. She turned hopefully. He cleared his throat, his eyes still focused on the strings. 'Will you come back? I mean, if I ever need you?'

Wiping her cheek with the sleeve of her jumper, she nodded.

'See ya.'

'See ya.' Rebecca departed, agonisingly aware of the deficit in her words.

'I love you, Becca,' Luke said so softly, Rebecca wasn't certain if she was intended to hear. 'I always will.'

'Me too. I love you, too.'

As she walked down the hall to the front door, the doleful chords from his guitar followed her, spiking her heart with each faltering step.

22

———

Heimo was naturally inquisitive. He always had been. He found discovering more about a topic, an issue or a person stimulating. It made him feel as though a further significant brushstroke had been added to his portrait or another major movement added to the symphony of his life. He believed that humans are a sum of their experiences and their knowledge. No occurrence was wasted. This belief had helped him reconcile the breakdown of his marriage.

So when Heimo left the hotel that morning for his 5am run and saw Rebecca's friend leaving as well, clearly on his way to the airport, he began to wonder about their relationship. Of course, it could have been entirely innocent, he surmised. Rebecca had explained that she and Redmeyer were friends. He might have slept on the sofa or on the floor of her room, thought Heimo.

But he found himself tallying the time since Joe O'Neill's death. Rebecca had nursed Joe for almost two years, the newspapers claimed, through a violent, crippling illness. It must have been lonely and difficult. He measured the role that grief plays on the human mind; it may have made

Rebecca need physical consolation. But Rebecca cared for people, especially those she loved. Empathy is what made her such a good writer. It was difficult for Heimo to contemplate Rebecca having an affair during the period of Joe's illness, or sleeping with another man so soon after Joe's death, old friend or not.

Yesterday, before Rebecca had arrived, Heimo had watched Redmeyer in the salon. The fierce way he pushed his hands into his trouser pockets and his distracted perusal of the bookshelves reminded Heimo of a schoolboy waiting outside the headmaster's office.

He remembered the expression on her face when she entered the salon and saw Redmeyer. It wasn't love or even tenderness. It was more a fine blend of relief and gratitude. An eyebrow had raised and she closed her eyes briefly. It was the look you gave someone when they hand you a cold drink on a hot day. It was that *I really need this* kind of look. Rebecca wasn't in love with her friend, Heimo was sure. But he suspected that Redmeyer was in love with her.

Heimo closed his laptop, unable to concentrate. The more important question he should be asking, he realised, was: why was he so curious? A mild pang of jealousy had tweaked his chest when he saw Redmeyer leaving. The feeling must have been born from that fleeting moment they had together when they were teenagers. Yet he had no claim on Rebecca. While he wanted to know more about her, he didn't feel he had the right to.

'WHY HAVE YOU BEEN AVOIDING ME?' Rebecca asked as he answered the door the next morning.

Heimo stepped back. She brushed past him as she

entered. She smelled fresh, soapy, like she had just showered.

'Angus.' Heimo cleared his throat. 'I saw him leaving the hotel when I was coming down for my run yesterday. I assumed ...'

Rebecca sighed, knowingly.

'He's a friend, my best friend. My first London friend. That's all. There was a time when we shared almost everything.'

Heimo frowned and sat down, offering her a seat. He looked at her, wanting more.

'Angus is ... was ... Joe's agent.' Rebecca placed her head in her hands for a moment.

'He was my tutor at university. Angus was the first person to read my manuscripts.'

He was silent, wishing it had been him who had read her manuscripts first, angry at himself for wanting it so.

'That's significant, you know,' she continued. 'To be *that* person. To trust someone *that* much.'

Heimo leaned forward. 'I know. I believe you.'

'I'm not sure why, but it's important that you believe me.' She straightened and looked at him directly.

'To find you here, in Geneva of all places. How weird is that? I have to believe it's fate or destiny ... I know you don't believe in that stuff but how else can you explain it? The two people I cared about most, loved most, are now gone. Then you turn up.'

Heimo let her speak and find her thoughts, enjoying being led down the different pathways of her mind.

'It must *mean* something to have you back in my life. I want to be friends with you, build or rebuild a relationship. I don't mean like when were kids, but we had a connection then, right? An intellectual connection. We enjoyed being around each other.'

Agreement came in the form of a solemn nod.

'I can see you searching for the girl you used to know, the girl you wanted to know better years ago. I like that. It's like a gap has been closed. No Joe, no Angus. There's just you and me on the beach. I like that you still see me in that way, because I'm not that person any more and I wish I was. But nothing is ever simple. It wasn't then and it's not now.' Heimo considered her words for a moment. She was right. He was seeking out the memory of a girl he once knew – it was all he had.

She took in a deep breath.

'So much has happened since Joe died and I'm struggling, Heimo. I'm gasping for air.'

Looking at her now, seeing her as an adult, as a woman, he knew that he still wanted to know her better.

'Tell me,' he said.

Rebecca began to speak, slowly, unemotionally at first. He could see her ordering the events in her mind – Joe's cancer, his death, the funeral, Karina and the children – and she soon began to speak more easily. Eventually, the words poured out in a liberating torrent. This was completely normal, he thought – the deluge that follows admission. He had witnessed it hundreds of times before. When it was out, she began to cry softly.

'Is this catharsis?' she asked with a feeble smile. 'Remember in English when Mr McDermott explained catharsis?'

Heimo moved closer and took her hands. 'He wrote the word on the board and the boys in the back row sniggered.'

'*Cats arses.*' Rebecca's whimpers quickly became fierce, uncontrolled sobbing.

He placed his arm around her shoulder.

'I hope this is it,' she said. 'I hope this is the end.'

Rebecca inhaled a reviving breath as Heimo held her. He sat silently, waiting for her to go on.

'When I left Karina's apartment, I started wondering about accountability. Was it all Joe's choice? Or had there been things I'd done to bring that relationship about, make him look for someone else? Was she a better person than me? More accomplished, more qualified, more beautiful? Was it the children?'

Heimo looked at her, watching as confusion flickered across her face. Her last question triggered a memory in him.

'But you and Joe ...?'

Rebecca eased away. Shaking her head, she wiped her nose. Composed, she allowed herself to speak.

'It was never the right time for us.'

He wanted to ask her more, but he didn't press for exactitude. That would come in time.

'WHAT DO YOU SPECIALISE IN?' Rebecca asked as they waited for their coffee. The café Heimo had led her to sat on a hill in the old town, next to a church.

'I'm a neuroscientist,' Heimo answered as though it was the most common profession in the world.

Rebecca thought she'd misheard him. The café was noisy, every oak table filled with chattering couples and groups.

'Pardon?'

'Neuroscience is my specialty.'

The waitress, a serious girl with a pretty, shy face, placed the coffee on the table then took their orders for breakfast.

After the girl retreated, Rebecca said, 'Mum made it sound like you were an ENT.'

Heimo shook his head and stirred his coffee. 'My parents still don't understand what I do.'

He went on to explain his study of medicine, then later neurology, all over the world – New York, Munich and Tel Aviv.

'But,' he concluded, 'I found myself interested in the chemicals at play in the brain and how they could be altered to treat not only diseases and mental illness, but conditions such as PTSD.'

'What are you working on now?'

'The connection between memory and emotion.'

'Tell me about it,' Rebecca said and leant back in her chair. The sun spilled through the glass and across the table then fell noiselessly to the floor. She liked to listen to him. His voice had matured and deepened over time and his accent had been polished, the rough edges buffed away, slicing through the low harmony of background conversation.

He took a sip of his coffee and licked his spoon.

'Okay. Let's say a young woman is brutally assaulted: robbed, bashed, left for dead. For the rest of her life when she remembers the attack, the exact fear that she experienced at the time resurfaces also. It's paralysing, so she attempts to repress the memory, which leads to further emotional complications.'

Rebecca nodded in understanding.

'Our memories work a little bit like a Wikipedia page,' he continued. 'We can go in and alter a memory and so can other people. While the brain will readily adopt a false memory merely by the power of suggestion, there is no way to remove a memory, despite what Hollywood tells us.

'It's impossible to pluck out a single memory without destroying others. But I believe there is a way to erase the emotion associated with the memory by using medication. Consequently, the young woman could then relive the moment or discuss it with family, with the police or with a jury, without reliving the terror connected to it. Removing that emotional connection to the memory gives her the chance to go on and live a "normal" life.'

'Wow,' Rebecca said. 'Grief, regret, anger, blame ... all the bad emotions could be wiped out ... theoretically. And, I suppose, theoretically, it could work on positive emotions, too?'

Heimo, curious, raised his eyebrows. 'Go on.'

She was pleased to impress him, prove her intellect hadn't dulled over the years.

'For instance, drug addicts. If they're unable to recall the feelings associated with a high – bliss, euphoria, et cetera – addicts might, much more easily, get clean.'

'Exactly,' Heimo said, smiling. 'But while we've had success with rats in the lab, we're a long way from running human trials.'

She frowned. 'What about depression?'

'Depression is more complicated because there's not always just one incident that causes the disorder.'

Rebecca nodded. 'In some cases though, there can be a trigger, right? A trauma that sparks the sadness?'

'Yes, but depression is a combination of biological, emotional and environmental factors. In many cases, it occurs for no apparent reason. Yes, sometimes one event *can* spark major depression in a person that's had no symptoms in the past ...A major physical trauma or the loss of employment, for instance.'

Heimo frowned at her. 'What are you thinking about?'

Rebecca scanned her memories quickly, rewinding at high speed, searching for the moment it all began. 'It was when I broke my neck,' she uttered without meaning to.

Heimo glanced at her, surprised. 'What?'

'He blamed himself.'

Heimo reached for her hand across the table.

'Luke was diagnosed with psychotic depression.' Rebecca remembered that Luke had been so ashamed when the psychiatrist had told him. The word 'psychotic' was loaded. Rebecca had been by his side when the doctor had delivered the diagnosis.

'I know,' Heimo said gently. Rebecca looked at him, confused. 'He told me. I went home in at the beginning of 2000. He told me then.'

———

THE SAME WAITRESS wordlessly placed their breakfasts in front of them – scrambled eggs for Rebecca and a fruit plate with yoghurt for Heimo.

'Do you know what got me interested in neuroscience in the first place?' he asked, picking up a slice of watermelon.

Rebecca shook her head.

'The letter you wrote me from London.'

She swallowed then placed her knife and fork on the table. 'You got that.'

'I still have it.'

'But you never replied.'

'It disturbed me. I was rattled for days. I must have read it a hundred times. The way you described your connection with Luke was unnerving, but it made sense of a lot of things and I understood why you had to leave. There was no point to replying. But I began to wonder about the connection. I didn't believe it was psychic. I thought it had to be chemical.'

Rebecca had always considered the bond with her twin as spiritual or extrasensory. She had never thought of it from a scientific point of view. But Heimo – rational, cool Heimo – had. She wanted to kiss him, but they were too old to kiss in public.

'You must help a lot of people.'

Heimo shrugged. 'I'd like to think so.'

'Writing is so internal, so solitary. Writers are so obsessed with what's going on inside their own heads, they're not worried about anybody else's.'

'Joe wasn't. He wanted to make a difference to the world, didn't he?'

She nodded. 'Joe was special.'

'Is that why you stopped writing?' Heimo asked. 'You didn't feel as though you were helping anybody?'

'I stopped because my well ran dry.'

As Heimo paid the bill, Rebecca checked her phone. Her screen was gridlocked by a loud and insistent queue of messages demanding her attention.

Will you meet me for lunch on Saturday at the yacht club?

The first. Sent over two hours ago, just as she was leaving the hotel.

There is something I need to show you. Please

The second. Sent one hour and twenty minutes ago.

I also need to discuss something. G

The third. More desperate.

Please. My lunch break is at 1.

The fourth. Emphatic.

I have something of dad's that I want you to see.

The fifth. Enticing.

I'm lost. Will you help me?

The sixth. The baited hook.

Rebecca glanced at Heimo, waiting in a line of customers, her fingers levitating just above her phone. She heard Heimo's voice thank the staff.

Then she typed.

I can make it. 1pm Saturday. Message me the address. Rebecca.

Gerard sent the destination within seconds.

23

WHEN REBECCA ARRIVED for her next appointment, Eva had rearranged the furniture in her office. The desk was no longer under the window and the sofa was facing the wall on which the bold geometric painting hung. Eva sat under the print. And the steamer trunk was gone. Where was the steamer trunk? It had been replaced by a staid glass coffee table. Rebecca scanned the room. She found it behind the door.

Rebecca sat. She felt exposed without the steamer trunk.

'I found this at the library.' Eva held up a copy of Joe's second collection of poems, *Peace Lines*. Rebecca remembered the edition. The cover art featured a series of interlocking walls that formed a maze.

'One poem I thought was particularly interesting.' She opened the small volume to a page bookmarked with a shopping receipt.

'*Mo chailín rua fiáin*. Did I say that correctly?'

'Very good.'

'*My Wild-Haired Girl*.'

Rebecca nodded, astounded at Eva's depth of research.

Joe had hundreds of poems published, some in English, others in Irish. Had she read and translated each one, searching out a clue?

'It was written in 1991, so you had been with Joe for ...'

'About two years,' Rebecca put in.

'"Misguided love" ... "Demons leavening" ... "Vital sustenance."' Eva read random words and lines from the page then the final line. '"A banshee's scream of silent fury, released."'

Eva removed her glasses and looked at Rebecca squarely, demanding a response with her hawk's eyes.

'He was trying to understand me. Writing was the way Joe found truth in the things he didn't understand.'

'And Joe had found the truth in you.'

'Partly.'

'Is this poem why you cut your hair?'

Rebecca nodded.

Eva smiled, pleased with her discovery.

THEIR MEETING HAD BEEN STILTED and awkward, strangers pretending to be siblings. Luke studied her from the opposite side of the dining table. She could feel his eyes on her. He wasn't eating the turkey and pork that his mother had piled onto his plate. He brought the beer to his lips. While her parents and grandparents quizzed her about London – 'Did it rain all the time?', 'Is the beer really warm?',' Have you met the Queen?' – Luke stayed quiet. Neil Diamond singing 'I'll Be Home for Christmas' played on the stereo too loudly and Rebecca found herself straining, leaning across the table to hear their questions.

'Listen to her posh accent,' her father repeated when Rebecca

said words such as 'answer' and 'France'. She wasn't sure whether he was impressed or ashamed.

She glanced at Luke instinctively for help. He didn't react.

As Joyce cleared the plates from the table, Luke pushed out his chair and retrieved another beer from the fridge, then went out the back door. Rebecca felt guilty discussing her new life and she tried to make it seem dull, as though nothing was working out for her. Luke, unemployed, was sharing a house in Bomaderry with a 'bunch of losers' her father had told her when she arrived home the day before.

Dreading this moment and her brother's seething attention, on the flight to Sydney she had drunk four vodka tonics then taken the sleeping pill Joe had given her at Heathrow as he saw her off. She woke with a hangover as the plane was landing and made her way to the bus feeling nauseous and dazed.

'We'll have a break before the plum pudding,' Joyce said, as Rebecca entered the kitchen with the leftover roast potatoes. The tuberous mountain seemed untouched. She must have cooked a hundred, Rebecca thought.

'Go out and talk to Luke. I'm so worried about him, Love. He's so troubled. Your dad's gotten him jobs — nothing flash, just labouring — but Luke never shows up. He's happy to be on the dole, smoking pot and surfing. He never talks to me any more.'

'He never did.' Joyce shot her a look. 'What do you mean by troubled?'

'Bec, he's different, changed a lot since you left. Troubled.' Her mother's face was flushed and moisture gathered on her top lip. She'd been cooking since sunrise.

Rebecca frowned and grabbed the paper crown from her head, rolling it into a tight ball in her fist. Mum handed her the cling film and she slid it into its home in the drawer next to the stove.

'He's missed you. He doesn't say so, but he has. It might help if you talk to him. I'm so glad you're home. I'm at my wits' end.'

Her daughter nodded then turned on the taps, waving her hand under the water until it was hot.

'I'll help you wash up, first.'

'Do it now.'

Rebecca looked out the window. The spray of the surf was visible over the back fence. Luke lay flat on the lawn beneath the spinning clothes line with his hands beneath his head, the beer bottle beside him. Mum nudged her towards the door.

Rebecca approached across the grass. Overcast and humid, the atmosphere intimated a storm. When they were kids, they would have gone for a surf now, in the break between lunch and pudding as the adults dozed and sweated in the lounge room.

'You're skinnier,' Luke said as she lowered herself beside him.

'And you're getting a beer belly.'

He laughed and turned his head to look at her.

'Are you stoned?' she asked.

'Nuh, but I wish I was.'

Rebecca relaxed into a laugh.

'Nothing ever changes, does it? Overcooked turkey, limp beans and Neil Diamond on the turntable.'

The wind picked up and the clothes line wheeled more frantically. Rebecca hugged her knees in her arms, squelching her toes into the freshly-mown grass. Dad always mowed on Christmas Eve, leaving at least an inch of turf in summer to guard against scorching. She breathed in, hoping to catch the lingering scent of green.

'Mum said you're living with someone.' Luke sat up, assuming her posture. 'He's ten years older, she said.'

'Fifteen, actually. Mum would freak if she knew the whole truth.'

'Wouldn't they let him out of the nursing home for Christmas?' Luke chuckled quietly and Rebecca was surprised when she found herself laughing as well.

He never judged. Luke viewed all people through the same spectrum. Individuals were just coloured a little differently, that was all, living their lives in slightly different contexts.

'He's in Belfast until New Year. Besides, he's not too fond of the ocean. He can't swim.'

Luke turned to her. 'What?'

'Never learnt. Not much call for it in Ireland.'

'S'pose there's not'.

'But I love him.' Rebecca regretted the words the moment they were let loose.

They sat on the lawn together for some time in silence, their backs rounded against the wind and their hair blowing like banners.

'Do you still feel me, Becca?' Luke asked, staring into the ever-darkening sky.

Rebecca didn't know how to answer and she didn't for a long time. Not until the first fat raindrops that preceded all storms began to fall. To admit the truth felt like a betrayal of her decision two years ago to sever herself from her brother. But Luke would know she was lying.

'Sometimes.' She turned to him. 'I know you're sad. What about me? Do you still feel me?'

'Sometimes, Becca, you're the only thing I feel.' He lifted her hand and pressed his lips so firmly against her knuckles that she thought her fingers would break.

24

———

ON BOXING DAY Rebecca agreed to go for a surf with him. By ten in the morning, the storm of the night before had given way to crystal clear skies and a dry, stinging heat. Luke took to the waves immediately, but Rebecca waited on the sand, sitting on her board that had been housed in a bag in her parent's garage while she'd been gone. It felt good being there, sensing the heat on her face and her pale skin growing tanned.

The sand was becoming congested around her. A beach picnic was a post-Christmas ritual for local families. Neighbours and old friends stopped and welcomed her home when they noticed her sitting in Luke's usual spot at the southern end of the beach. Her parents had told them she would be home in December. She'd see them at the Boxing Day get-together at the Bowlo that night. Another ritual.

Rebecca kept a cautious eye out for Heimo, rehearsing conversations in her mind. He was home for Christmas too; her mother had told her. But mostly she was watching her brother's effortless, graceful movement over and through the waves. He was a god out there.

During the time she'd been gone, Rebecca had come to think of her relationship with Luke as estranged. It was a word she read frequently in the British tabloids. She first came across it on a Daily Star advertisement at a tube station. It was so popular with the media that she had even looked it up in the dictionary, attempting to understand its mystique. It came from the Latin extraneare or to 'treat as a stranger'.

By choice, she and Luke hadn't communicated since she'd left Gerringong, almost eighteen months before. Surely that qualified them as estranged siblings? But now, as she lost sight of him for a moment behind the swell, she realised they could never be estranged. How was it possible to be alienated from a part of yourself? Luke was at her very core. That fact was as irrefutable as the motion of the tides.

She rose, hoisted her board under an arm and began walking to the shoreline.

THEY ARRIVED *at the Bowlo at seven. Her mother insisted they eat dinner out 'as a family' once more before she left. Luke spoke endlessly on the short walk there. He jabbered on and on, complimenting her on her skill. It was amazing, he said, that she hadn't lost her touch after so long. His mood, like the storm of the day before, had dissipated, his sadness slowly melting away over the course of four hours surfing the same waves as his sister. She wondered if he was high. Did it matter? Luke's happiness was contagious.*

Aware of her hair trailing down her back and shoulders, Rebecca felt younger and sun-kissed, pretty in the strappy summer dress her mother had bought her for Christmas. It was as though she had never fractured her neck, as though she had never left. They were fifteen again.

But she wasn't entirely carefree. Before they entered, she took his arm and drew him back.

'Will Heimo be here?' she asked, nervous and hopeful. Rebecca wasn't sure from where the hope had sprung. There was no reason for it. She had left Australia without saying goodbye. And she was in a relationship with someone else.

Luke shrugged. 'I s'pose. Don't worry. I'll run interference.'

Rebecca looked at him and they laughed together. Luke had never used the expression before.

Most of their year from school had already arrived when they reached the bar. Only a few of them had left Gerringong — Rebecca and Heimo and a couple of others who lived on campus at Wollongong. Mostly, the kids in her year had stayed in town, getting trades, finding jobs in local shops or working on family properties. There were a few on the dole, like Luke.

Luke bought them both a beer and soon her nerves eased. He drew her to the jukebox and together they chose a selection of songs, mocking one another's choices. She forgot about Heimo as she and Luke teased one another then talked to her friends about university, the shabby flat she rented in Camden Town and her part-time job at the university bookstore where she earned just twenty-five pounds a week. They seemed astonished at her achievements, amazed at successes that Rebecca didn't consider that momentous.

She studied and worked, had been to Paris and Amsterdam once and Oxford twice. Life with Joe was mere survival. They scraped together pennies for chips that they ate for dinner on the bus. Their flat was cramped and cold. Neither writers nor students earned much money. Even with her scholarship, ends were difficult to meet. But with struggle came excitement and spontaneity. Joe was forging new paths in the literary world and she was writing so hard that she would fall asleep depleted, wrung dry, only to wake in the morning full to the brim.

She couldn't explain this to her friends, the thrill of living on a knife's edge with a passionate man. To those who'd never been further than Surfers Paradise, she might as well have been surviving on Mars.

When she felt a warm hand on her shoulder, she knew it was Heimo. The long, nimble fingers curling close to her neck were unmistakable. Her heart, which had been pounding idly in her chest, now thumped frantically, rising into her throat then plummeting into the depths of her abdomen.

'Hello,' he said when she turned. 'Long time no see.'

She smiled. He looked at her fondly, taking in her appearance, assessing changes, measuring similarities.

'Hello.'

Rebecca moved away from the huddle of girls she was standing with. They looked at one another with wide eyes.

'It's good to see you, Rebecca.'

She was instantly self-conscious. Heimo's face had matured, the angles of his jaw sharper. He seemed taller, broader, and he'd let his hair grow. It fell in soft waves to his jawline. But his eyes were just as blue and curious.

'How long are you back?' he asked as 'Janie's Got a Gun' started to play.

'Just 'til New Year. I head back on the second. Lectures start that week.' Rebecca rolled her empty beer glass between her palms.

He leant closer to be heard over the music. 'Can I get you another one?'

'Yes, please. Maybe we can go outside and talk. It's difficult to compete with Aerosmith.'

Rebecca waited for him on the balcony overlooking the carpet of greens. They were deserted under the moonlight and appeared more pristine than they did in the light. Rebecca imagined lying down on the grass. She imagined it cool and merciful, like the fresh part of a bedsheet on a hot night. When Heimo closed the door behind him, the only sounds evident were the chirp of unseen cicadas in the darkened trees and the muffled music, laughter and conversation from inside.

Awkwardly, the couple discussed safe, neutral topics — 'Have you been to the new cafe yet?' 'They do really good coffee' — barely locking eyes. They sat on opposite sides of a plastic table, navigating the conversational terrain carefully. There was too much to say, too much required in order to clear the air that had become polluted between them. Time and distance sometimes did that, Rebecca figured as she watched Heimo sip his beer and consider his thoughts. Occasionally, time made small wounds gape and fester. She hated the tension between them now. They could never be friends again until they were honest. He was the same person; she could tell that easily.

Her breathing grew faster as she prepared to speak. Heimo glanced at her, anticipating.

'Why didn't you ask me to the formal?' she said.

He sighed and leant back in his chair but didn't answer.

'I ... It's bothered me for a long time. I know it's dumb to be obsessing about something so trivial that happened when we were in Year Twelve. You've probably never given it a thought, but the truth is, I think about it often ... and what might have been.'

Rebecca was aware she was saying too much, perhaps being too honest, but the floodgates were finally open and the release was exhilarating, like the first breath of air after reaching the surface. 'Perhaps I wouldn't have gone to London, I don't know ... but I really liked you and it hurt. Everything might have been different.'

'I'm sorry. I know all that. I know I hurt you. I'm sorry.'

Rebecca waited for more. 'Please tell me the truth. Just be honest.'

'I was going to ask you,' he said. 'But that night on the beach when Rooney and the others beat me up ... you saw it all. You and Luke saved me. I was humiliated.'

'But you asked Kathy Leary. She was there that night, too.'

'I didn't care how Kathy Leary looked at me. That's why I asked her. But I cared about how you saw me.' He ran his fingers through his hair.

'Later, the day after the formal, Luke came to my house. I answered the door and he pushed me up against the wall. He threatened to kill me if I ever came near you again. He said I'd broken your heart.'

Tears sprang to her eyes. 'Luke did that?' she said. What gave him the right? Rebecca asked herself.

'But he knew how much I...' Her thoughts blurred as she struggled to recall the details of those pivotal few days.

'I wanted to talk to you. But then you just sort of disappeared. Your mum told me you were working.'

That summer, Rebecca couldn't be around home. There was too much to avoid. So when a friend of her mother's mentioned a waitress position in Nowra, she jumped at it.

When the other waitress, Cheryl, offered to put her up during the week so she didn't have to take the train home every day, she jumped at that too. Until June, her time was spent at the café or in Cheryl's tiny flat, curled in the corner of a fraying, second-hand sofa, writing and reading. She had cried, too. Sometimes she'd cry for hours, on and off, eventually forcing great gulps of air into her lungs to stop. When the weekends came, she went back to Gerringong with reluctance. Sometimes she didn't go at all, explaining to her mother that she was working extra shifts, trying to save as much money as possible before she left.

Her mother had said, 'Well, at least one of you has a work ethic. We're proud of you, honey,' before she hung up the phone. Rebecca realised she remembered only the scantest of details from *that time. The pink frilly aprons the manager liked 'his girls' to wear; Cheryl's cat, a mottled tabby named Cleo; her estrangement from Heimo and Luke. They were the memories that clung like limpets.*

Heimo took her hand across the plastic table. 'I should have found you and apologised and tried to explain.'

'You were just a kid. We were all just kids, I suppose.' With that admittance, her anger with Luke dissolved.

'Can we be friends?'

'Of course. Always.'

They exhaled together.

When they talked again it was more naturally, of simple things – their studies, the books they were reading, the differences between university and high school – and quickly fell back into their old rhythm. Rebecca didn't mention Joe. Heimo could be nothing more than a friend. She was leaving in a week, anyway. Why add an unnecessary element of strain, she thought, when they were so at ease?

The crowd began to dwindle inside and the remainders joined them on the balcony. Luke wasn't among them.

'Have you seen Luke?' Rebecca asked a few people as they drifted outside.

'Not in a while,' they replied, looking behind them, hoping to be of more assistance.

'Why do you worry about him so much?' Heimo asked. 'He's a grown up.'

'Is he?'

Heimo raised an eyebrow.

'It's hard to explain.'

He frowned. 'Try.'

As Rebecca attempted to piece together an explanation for Heimo, something that didn't sound like an excuse, they heard Luke on the green below.

'Becca! Becca! Where are you?'

She rose and went to the railing. Everyone followed. Luke threw a skateboard onto the turf.

'Luke!' Rebecca called. 'You'll mess up the green!'

He put one foot on the board and the other on the grass and propelled himself over the immaculately manicured surface. Tracks were immediately visible in his wake. When he reached the concrete, he skated along to the neighbouring green and ollied over the end ditch, straight onto the closely shorn turf.

Rebecca ran inside and within minutes appeared below, chasing after her brother. When she reached him she grabbed his shirt and he fell to the ground. The skateboard flew high into the air and landed with a thud on its nose, resulting in a further divot. His subsequent laughter prompted his friends on the balcony to laugh along too.

'What are you doing?' Rebecca held out her hand to help him to his feet. He pulled her down on top of him.

'How did you get so pissed?' He reeked of beer and cigarette smoke. She pushed herself upright and moved away.

'It's been hours. You were talking to him for hours. Let's go for a walk, Becca. I've missed you so much,' he said, trying to stand, but failing. This provoked more laughter and Luke raised an appreciative hand. Had it been hours? she wondered and checked her watch in the moonlight. It was past twelve.

'Get up! Doug will call the police.' Doug, the manager of the club, was a local, a mate, but he wasn't going to stand by and see his greens ripped to shreds.

'Remember when we used to skate?' he said. 'Remember, when you tried that grind and you missed then skidded along the ground on your face?' Rising unsteadily, he attempted to touch the inch-long scar on the base of her chin, but she moved away. Rebecca's hand went instinctively to what had faded to a blemish.

She had always been glad of that almost imperceptible puckering of skin. It was physical evidence they were different.

'Hey, Luke,' Heimo said as he stepped onto the green. 'How's it going?'

'Great, mate,' Luke said. 'Just fuckin' fantastic.'

Heimo looked at Rebecca. She shook her head fleetingly.

'Do you need some help getting home?' Heimo asked.

Luke staggered slightly and Rebecca led him to a bench. He slumped into it heavily and his eyes closed.

'It's okay,' Rebecca said. 'He can rest a minute here. Then we'll tackle the walk home.'

'You sure you can manage?'

'It's not the first time.'

'Why do you do it?' he said, quietly, so only she could hear. 'Why do you keep on saving him? A night in the cells might do him good.'

'You sound like our dad. "What he needs is a wake-up call. That'll sort him out. That kid has had it too easy."' Rebecca said in imitation of her father.

Heimo looked at her, concerned. 'I'm sorry. That was a stupid thing to say. I didn't mean ...'

'He's sad, Heimo, really sad and I don't know what to do to help him.' Luke's mire was her own and she was stuck too deep, where there was no light. 'Who've we got if not each other?'

'Me,' he replied. 'You've got me'.

She was startled by his intensity, his insistence.

'Luke's depressed,' Heimo said, 'but there are doctors that can help him. There are therapies ...'

'Is that your medical opinion?'

'Yes, it is,' he said. 'I know his moods, sometimes they go on for days. Now, it's so much worse. He doesn't want to function. Let me help.'

But she and Luke were wound so tightly together, knotted so fiercely that she felt like there was no room for anyone else.

'You should go. It's late.'

'Come on, Rebecca. We should talk about this more. Can I see you tomorrow?'

She pressed his hand. 'No, I don't think that would be a good idea.'

He looked down at the ground, kicking the wire fence he was leaning against lightly with his heel. 'Right. Okay.'

'Good luck with everything.' Rebecca walked towards Luke. When she reached him she sat beside him, shaking him gently to rouse him. Heimo looked at the scene for a moment, then hurdled the fence that led to the carpark.

---

*D*OUG WAS ANGRY, *but not furious. There didn't seem to be any serious damage and Luke was a mate, after all. By the time they began walking towards home it was almost one. Luke had sobered up a little and was able to walk without his sister's aid.*

'I forgot about the skateboard,' Rebecca said as they neared home. 'Whose was it?'

'I dunno. I found it out the front.'

'I'll ring Doug in the morning and try to find the owner.'

Luke chuckled. 'Little Miss Responsible.'

When they reached their back gate, Rebecca stopped.

'Do you feel like throwing up? If you do, then do it out here. You'll never hear the end of it if you wake Dad up.'

'Nah. I'm alright.' He burped and Rebecca stepped back quickly. 'But I might sleep on the beach.'

'That's a good idea.'

'Sit with me for a minute?'

Rebecca hesitated, looking towards the ocean. She could just make out the surf. The moonlight touched the face of the waves gently as it drew them towards land. Luke could explain how tides worked. He could explain the connection between the ocean, the sun and the moon by the time he was six. But Rebecca still didn't grasp the concept. It just seemed like magic to her, something that shouldn't be explained.

They lay on their backs. The sand was cool and it seemed as if every star in the Milky Way shone more brilliantly than they ever had before. She imagined herself under the sea, looking up. Millions of radiating balls of light hurtling down from space, then extinguished in an instant when they hit the water. Rebecca hadn't seen a sight like that since she left. Stars weren't evident in the London sky.

She looked at her brother and stared at his profile. His nose was elegant and his high cheekbones and forehead gave him a regal appearance in the faint light.

'You're lucky, Luke. To live here, to have this and want nothing else. You should be happy.'

'But I'm not. I can't be.'

He rolled towards her and kissed her gently on the mouth.

'Without you.'

She closed her eyes and waited for his touch to fade. Damp sand, music borne in the breeze and her skin stinging like nettles. When she opened her eyes again, tiny flecks danced in her vision like bacteria under a microscope.

'What's up?' he asked.

Rebecca jumped to her feet.

'I'm going back next week. This is fucked up. You have to find something else and you can't do it while I'm around. I love you. More than anything. But this is fucked up.'

'Becca!'

'Enough!' she shouted. 'No more!'

THAT NIGHT on the bowling green was only time she saw Heimo during her stay. When she returned to London, she wrote him a letter. In it she attempted to explain her relationship with Luke. She told Heimo that she and Luke would be forever joined, and that emotionally, they were two halves of one whole. She explained to him that she viewed herself as the stronger twin, the more adept at survival and, while her love for her brother was intense, it was also inextricably tangled with a sense of responsibility.

She finished with a core truth that she had discovered at seventeen: the only way for her to be an individual, free of her duty, was to distance herself, to be far away.

'WHAT MADE you share that memory now?' Eva asked.

'Isn't that why you changed around the office, to unnerve me into a startling revelation?'

Eva's head flew back and she laughed, her bosom rising and falling.

'I know I read a lot of psychological thrillers, but I would never use such cheap tricks,' she said, when she regained control of herself.

Rebecca grinned then rose and moved to the window before answering Eva's question.

'Heimo, I suppose. I miss him. I don't want to have to say goodbye to him again.'

Eva thought for a moment. 'What do you mean?'

'Last time, Luke came between us and I did nothing to stop him. I don't want that to happen again.'

25

———

'WHERE DO YOU CALL HOME, REBECCA?' Eva asked.

'That's a good question.'

Eva could see her patient struggling to find an answer. It was a good question but not an easy one, especially for Rebecca who was displaced physically and emotionally.

'Is it Hungary for you?'

Eva shook her head. 'I speak the language and miss the food sometimes, but my experience has disconnected me from the place of my birth.'

Eva glanced out the window, giving Rebecca a moment to think. She didn't want to make coffee. That would be too much time for her patient to form a measured response. Eva wanted to watch Rebecca's thought process.

'The notion of "home" means different things to different people,' Eva prompted. 'This is my home here.' She circled an arm above her head. 'Not Australia. I don't feel Australian, culturally, I mean. I feel at home in Bondi. The mix of people, the colour, noise ... It makes me happy. But take me five klicks away from here and I'd be lost.'

Rebecca laughed at Eva's turn of phrase.

'Well,' she finally began. 'I lived in London for almost twice as long as I lived in Australia. And I was happy in London, for the most part.'

'London, then?'

'For a time. But without Joe, it seems foreign, as though I've just been passing through for twenty-eight years.'

'Maybe you were. Joe was your anchor.'

'Joe was my home. My port.'

Eva shrugged. 'In a sense.'

Rebecca nodded, thinking.

'Perhaps London was just a stop on your journey,' Eva suggested.

'To find home?'

'Yes.'

FIRST LIGHT. Five o'clock. The sun's initial rays provided a dramatic backlight for the Jura. It was Rebecca's favourite time of day, although she couldn't recall witnessing the hour in so many years. Joe had liked to sleep late. This was the time of the day at which she and Luke had preferred to surf, if the tides and the swell were agreeable. They'd check the surf report in the afternoon paper when their father had finished reading it and make a plan for the following morning. Then the twins would creep out the back door and across the grass to the beach, feeding off one another's anticipation, beckoned by the wash of water against sand.

Joyce Collins enjoyed telling the story of her children's birth. She went full term, which was unusual for a woman expecting twins, and by the time she entered labour on a Saturday night in December, Dr Langton thought it was safer to deliver by caesarean. He put her to sleep then made an incision in her tummy, about six inches in length, the size of a banana. When he gazed inside all he could see was a tangle of arms and legs.

Joyce liked to joke that he closed his eyes, reached into the gap and, like a lucky dip, pulled out a baby. He snipped the cord then handed Luke to the nurse. A minute later he produced Rebecca. 'A pigeon pair', the doctor had called them.

According to hospital records Luke was only one minute and thirty-five seconds older than his sister, yet he claimed all elder-sibling entitlements. He rode in the front passenger seat and called dibs on the drumsticks when their mother served roast chicken. Indignant, Rebecca told her parents and brother that when she had kids, she'd never show favouritism just because one of them was older.

In baby photographs Luke and Rebecca appeared identical, although she was always clothed in pink and he in blue. As they grew older and began to change – Luke's nose lengthened into a perfect ski jump while Rebecca's remained rounded and snubbed – they still shared the same vivid, blue eyes and smooth, prominent foreheads and cheekbones.

When she was scared at night, Rebecca often climbed into bed with her brother and snuggled close to his back. Imagining they were the same person, her fear would be instantly diluted by Luke's fast-flowing self-assurance. Listening to the sound of his slow slumbering breaths, she'd force her own breathing into the same rhythm and fall asleep.

Now the only noise evident to Rebecca was the rise and fall of her own breath and the cadence of her feet hitting the pavement. It was too early for the gulls.

Once she found her tempo, her muscles no longer

groaned in annoyance. Running became easy and everything seemed perfectly tuned – the length of her stride, her arms arcing at her side and the air drawing in and out of her lungs – and she felt light. Rebecca recalled the sense of the undulating swell of the ocean beneath her as she and Luke waited for a set in the hours before school. It was the best time of her day, the best time of her life.

Watching Luke surfing had raised her above the ordinary. He rarely rode the rails of a wave. Luke could always find the sweet spot, that fleshy point of power that drove him towards the shore. His carving and charging made him a legend amongst the local surfers. He reckoned he could read the waves with his feet and Rebecca envied him. She never discovered the confidence, the ease that Luke found out there. Her joy came from his.

The twins knew it was time to come in and go to school once the water had turned a light shade of topaz. An hour later, with the sound of breaking waves still resonating like the ocean in a shell, the twins would arrive at school. Rebecca could taste the salt on her skin all day. She was omnipotent.

She entered the Jardin Anglais and headed towards the Pont du Mont-Blanc. She lowered her head and squinted against the sunlight that had begun to creep over the mountains.

LATER THAT DAY, when Rebecca arrived at the yacht club, she spotted Gerard on the shore of the lake beside the jetty with a student, a learner. Relieved when, with a raised hand, Gerard gestured her to wait, she moved into the shade of the clubhouse, wondering what she was doing at another covert meeting with this teenager, a meeting she didn't want but was helpless to refuse.

As she watched Gerard closely, the answer became obvious. Self-composed and assured, Gerard stood on his board and lifted the boom, assuming the position one would when they were on the water, with the wind trapped in the sail. Rebecca wondered whether she could have been so confident at fifteen. Confident enough to instruct adults. She didn't think so. It was Joe's poise shining through. It was Joe's poise and Joe's eyes, even Joe's razor-sharp smile she was seeing again. That's why she was here.

When the lesson finished, Gerard jogged up the beach and kissed her familiarly on both cheeks.

'I'll just change,' he said. 'Then we'll have lunch, yes?'

'Yes,' she replied. 'I'll wait in the restaurant.'

A few minutes later, Gerard appeared beside her at the table, wearing board shorts and a t-shirt. His thick black hair was still wet and he held a large manila envelope.

'It's quite ... astounding how much you resemble him,' Rebecca uttered quietly as Gerard sat. Her first instincts had been to use the word 'chilling'. As her eyes examined his face, her hand unconsciously moved to his and touched it. Flesh and bone.

'Your eyes are the same colour and your nose ...' Then she halted and drew her hand away quickly.

'It's okay. I know,' Gerard said. 'It must be weird.'

'A little.'

Gerard ordered for them both, in French, and poured them each a glass of water.

'I wanted to show you this,' Gerard said, spilling the contents of his envelope onto the table. 'Dad gave it to me the last time I saw him.' He thought for a second. 'That was in April.'

Rebecca scanned her mind urgently. Where had Joe gone in April? It was just before the operation. Belfast. Feeling well after the side effects of the chemotherapy had faded, Joe had informed her he was going to Belfast.

'Belfast?' she repeated, shocked.

'I know you don't want to believe it,' Joe said. 'But it will be my last chance and it's a trip I have to take alone.'

'But the operation ...'

'How long do you think I'll be able to live unable to speak, mo ghrá?' he joked, hugging her around the waist. 'Now that's a fate worse than death.'

When the chemotherapy had failed, Joe's oncologist had told them gently that a laryngectomy would give Joe another four to six months of life. The patient had been unwilling, but at Rebecca's urging, her insistence, he had reluctantly agreed to the procedure. She needed to wring every drop of life from him.

'I suppose another couple of months with you isn't such a terrible fate,' he had grumbled, giving in.

Belfast, she thought now as Gerard arranged the contents of the envelope on the table. She had booked the ticket for Joe herself. He must have changed his destination at the airport. Although upset she'd been hoodwinked, as she sat before his son, Rebecca accepted the motivation behind Joe's act of deception.

She examined the collection of memorabilia. There were black and white snapshots featuring Joe's parents, grandparents and siblings. Rebecca turned each photo over. Joe had neatly written the subject's name and the year the picture was taken on the back.

Your Uncle Brendan, Joe had written. *Aged 12 or thereabouts.*

Rebecca stared into the face of the child in the picture

then looked at Gerard. Besides the haircut and the modern dress, the family resemblance was staggering.

'Do you know what happened to Brendan?' Gerard asked.

Rebecca nodded, still examining the photo. 'He was blinded and had his hands blown off when he accidentally dropped a cache of gelignite. He died three years later in Long Kesh prison.'

'The Maze,' Gerard added the colloquial name of the prison.

'And my grandmother?' Gerard quizzed. He slid a picture of Joe's mother across the table. It was black and white. The young woman's mouth was wide with amusement, as though she was laughing at something the photographer had said.

'Aoife O'Neill killed herself the day of Brendan's funeral,' she said, examining the photograph. 'An overdose of sleeping pills.'

'Did Joe tell you much about Northern Ireland?' Rebecca asked, studying a photo of Joe when he was a teenager, his tattooed arms folded across his chest and a scowl of defiance besmirching the freshness of youth.

'Not until his last visit,' Gerard replied. 'He told me briefly about The Troubles and the IRA and our family's involvement.' Rebecca glanced at him. 'Writing saved him, he said.'

'He hated the terrorism, the bombings,' she explained. 'Words empowered him. Words for Joe were something far greater than weapons – they offered a means of reconciliation. Joe loathed the English with just as much passion as Brendan, but he saw the futility of it all.'

They were silent for a moment before Gerard spoke again.

'I knew about you, I knew about you before Dad told me.'

'How?'

'The internet,' he answered.

Rebecca frowned. Joe kept his private life extremely private. Initially he was concerned about retaliation from the English or Sinn Féin, then he simply appreciated the anonymity. Joe enjoyed being a mystery and the mystique only added to his renown. Joe didn't even have a Wikipedia page.

'It was a photograph. You were in the background, but I could see his hand reaching back for yours.'

She nodded. 'I'm sorry.'

'There's no need to be,' he replied casually and unfolded a large square of paper.

'How had that knowledge not torn your world apart?' As it did mine, Rebecca wanted to add.

'I knew he loved me. I knew he loved my sister and mother ... And,' he added with a grin, 'he wasn't exactly a conventional father.'

Rebecca nodded. Joe hadn't been a conventional partner either.

'He made me this,' Gerard said, sliding the page across the table to her.

Joe had carefully constructed the O'Neill family tree. He had been working on this in the months leading up to his death, but Rebecca hadn't understood the purpose until now. It was his legacy, she supposed.

The first date, at the crown of the tree, was 1743 – the year his six-times grandfather, Aedan, was born in County Armagh. Rebecca ran her eyes across the bows of the tree, recognising some of the names. So many of the O'Neills had perished in the 1800s during the Great Famine, or *Gorta Mór* as Joe referred to it, that many names were missing during this period. Few records were maintained in that time. Rebecca pressed her fingertips over the nameless limbs.

When she came to the lowest branches, she saw Joe had ruled two offshoots from either side of his name. One read Rebecca Collins and the other, Karina Bonnay. Rebecca's stomach twisted.

Under Karina's name, Gerard and Marie were listed on separate boughs. Below Rebecca's name, there darted a short vertical limb that hung upon the crisp white page, leafless.

THE REMAINDER of the afternoon with Gerard was a blur. The young man seemed to be speaking from a distance, from the middle of the lake, his voice weakened and muffled into foreignness. She pushed her uneaten burger to the side and answered his questions as best she could. As she spoke, Gerard scribbled notes, nodding and probing as he went, searching for clues to his background.

Rebecca told him all she knew and Gerard scribbled on. But escape was all that was on Rebecca's mind. She felt like a maimed animal desperate for release.

When Gerard suggested he move to London for a year and stay with her, she gasped. Dumbfounded, she sat silent as the teenager voiced his plan, giving it momentum and gravitas in the airing of it.

'How better to get to know my father than to live in London? He spent most of his life there,' Gerard asserted, noting her reluctance for the scheme. 'There are many good schools in the area. My education wouldn't suffer. In fact, I think my education would benefit ...'

'Wait!' Rebecca raised her hands. 'I'm not even sure of my own plans ...'

'But you will probably return to London, soon?' he broke in.

'Probably, but I'm not certain.' How could she explain to Joe's son that without Joe, London was no longer home for her?

'But when you do,' he said, 'I'd like to join you.'

Gerard's voice was so emphatic and the solemn creases etched on his brow so reminiscent of Joe that all rational thought was paralysed. Rebecca merely nodded in shocked bemusement, disabled of speech. Perhaps London could be home again, she told herself, with this boy.

INDISTINCT ECHOES of the past and a confused picture of the future fogged her thoughts when Rebecca left the yacht club two hours later. Missing the walk signal at the crossing, she tried to push the image of Joe's family tree from her mind. What was it, if not a slight on her?

She had arranged to meet Heimo at the Natural History Museum at five o'clock, so she headed in that direction. Lunch with Joe's son had left her feeling alone and distressed. Rebecca began to imagine a life for herself with Gerard in the Holland Park home she had shared with Joe. When she finally raised her head, she was standing outside the museum. She checked her watch. It was four forty-five. She wandered inside to wait.

Rebecca found herself in a darkened hall decorated in imitation of a rainforest. A sign at the entrance read 'Butterflies of the Amazon'. Lianas and vines hung from the roof and bird calls as thin as crystal were transmitted from small speakers nestling in the crooks of styrofoam branches. What seemed like hundreds of butterflies were sealed in airtight acrylic frames that rested on stands, guiding the visitor's journey through the exhibition. More of the pretty insects had been placed on the boughs of trees or on the leaf litter covering the forest floor. Others had been mounted on fine rods, their wings outstretched. They floated from the ceiling as though in flight.

Rebecca stopped for a moment. Smiling uneasily at a security guard, she was instantly aware of the lifelessness of the display. Neither the gentle rustlings of nature nor the myriad of species could disguise the fact that everything on display was dead.

Moving hurriedly along the path and into the next hall, she was startled by an animal cry – the trumpet call of an elephant. She surveyed the hall she had fled in to. Rhinoceros, lions, giraffes and gazelles stood crowded on red sand, their existence belied by their glassy eyes. Behind her, chimps and apes hung from trees and colourful, meaty pythons were coiled around branches. Her chest began to tighten and the air became thick. A deafening roar was followed by the chattering and whoops of chimps. The fraudulent noises filled her head, making it spin. Coldness and nausea enveloped her. She ran.

Finally exiting, Rebecca sat on the grass in the gardens of the museum. Closing her eyes, she breathed deeply, waiting for the air to thin. Waiting to settle.

'Are you alright?'

Rebecca looked up, surprised. Her hand moved instinctively to her chest. It was Heimo, gazing at her seriously. But he wasn't in focus.

'I think so,' she began. 'It was just so ... stuffy in there.'

He looked at her, a sparkle evident in his eyes. Rebecca was confused.

'The pun,' he said.

'It wasn't intentional.'

'I know.' He held out his broad hand and she gripped it tightly. A lifeline. He sat next to her.

'I was watching you from the mezzanine. I got here early,' he said. 'That was a panic attack. Have you had them before?'

'My first.' Rebecca paused and lowered her head. 'That's a lie,' she went on. 'I've had them a couple of times since Joe died and once or twice when I was a kid.'

Heimo put his arm around her and she rested her head against his shoulder.

'I'm a mess,' she said and closed her eyes.

26

REBECCA AND HEIMO saw each other every day over the next week. They ran together then ate breakfast. Mornings were spent in each other's company, sightseeing or wandering the city, dropping into museums and galleries or exploring parks.

Rebecca listened avidly as Heimo discussed the most interesting facets of his work, such as the research his team carried out with Holocaust survivors. Heimo was a time detective scouring the unfathomable folds, dark lobes and hidden recesses of the human brain for clues to the subconscious. Occasionally she sensed he was probing her mind (it was an occupational hazard, she supposed), searching for evidence that might help him uncover whatever she was concealing. Heimo knew there was something in there. Rebecca did, too. But she couldn't reach it. It was like a forgotten word on the tip of her tongue – so close but miles away.

In the afternoons they went their separate ways. Heimo had been asked by the Neuroscience Centre at the university to lead a series of tutorials and Rebecca retreated to her suite to write small pieces, like she used to when she was a girl. Writing had become her deep breathing. Like meditation, it focused and relaxed her. One afternoon when she was struggling with a piece about Joe's illness, she closed her eyes, attempting to recall the smell of the hospital room and the squish of the nurses' trainers on the polished floor. When she opened them, Joe was beside her.

'It's good,' he said. 'Morbid but moving.'

Rebecca shrugged.

'I don't know what I'm doing.'

He laughed. 'Who ever does?'

He leant over her shoulder and read on.

'I never considered my illness from your perspective,' he said. 'I'm sorry I put you through that.'

'In sickness and in health ...' Rebecca joked, enjoying Joe's critique of her work.

'I miss this,' she went on after a moment. 'I miss you.'

When the telephone in her room rang, Joe disappeared. The clerk told her Gerard O'Neill was waiting in the salon.

No text messages preceded this visit. Gerard hadn't asked permission. Rebecca left her room and a flurry of concern erupted in her stomach, squalling and howling the closer she came to the salon. She could see he was agitated when she entered the room, his backpack was still attached to his shoulders and he darted from bookshelf to table to bar. When he noticed her in the doorway, the young man began pleading his case immediately.

He was pressing for a definite response to his suggestion that he move to London. She had wavered and stalled, but he was insistent. He needed to know Joe, he argued, and living in London was the only way. Furthermore, it would benefit his education and his experience ...

'Alright,' Rebecca said. 'I'll speak to your mother. If she's in agreement, we can begin to make arrangements.'

This hadn't been her plan, but she didn't have the strength to resist him. How could she not help him?

He hugged her and departed hastily. Rebecca remained in the salon, considering the consequences of her decision, rubbing the fingers of her right hand absentmindedly where callouses had formed. Although Joe always wrote in long hand, Rebecca had used a second-hand typewriter to write her first book, then a computer for her second and third. Over the years she had grown unaccustomed to holding a pen.

'WHAT DO YOU HAVE THERE?' Heimo asked when she met him at the gates of the university.

'I bought a laptop,' she announced, holding a large package aloft. 'I've begun writing again and there are blisters on my fingers.'

He kissed her on the cheek. 'Are you writing your own story?'

'Ha! Who'd believe it?' she said.

Heimo offered her a crooked smile.

'No, it's more a series of thoughts. Sometimes I write about Joe or Luke, sometimes you. Sometimes they're little things I notice about the world or people – just ideas I've got to get out. But there's a sense of desperation, like if I don't get them down on paper, this unique little observation might be hidden from the world forever, and wouldn't that be a catastrophe?'

Heimo took her hand as they walked. 'Like what?'

'Like the way you never laugh, I mean really laugh. I've

never seen you give a great big belly laugh, yet there's often laughter behind your eyes. I noticed it when we were kids. My mother could never tell if you were joking, serious or just being a smart-arse.'

She stopped and considered him now. There it was. The corner of his mouth was slightly curled on the left side and his eyes were brimming with happiness. Rebecca wasn't certain how he contained it. The expression was so familiar, so comforting that it awakened all the desperate longing she had experienced as a seventeen-year-old. Rebecca swallowed hard and her heart began to hammer in her chest. But this wasn't a panic attack.

AS THEY CONTINUED, Rebecca spoke more about her writing and she didn't notice that Heimo had guided them to the farmers' market in Plainpalais.

'I thought we could buy our dinner here and have a picnic ...' Heimo began, running his hand over his brown hair as he surveyed the various stalls.

But Rebecca moved towards a familiar sound – *Krrrrrrrr, snap ... Crack! Krrrrrrrr* – to find a large skate park. It was bigger than any she and Luke had ever skated on the south coast. Free of graffiti, the expanse of light grey cement just didn't seem a good fit in Geneva and she wondered how such an oddity had been born in this city of wealthy bankers, politicians and global power-players. They must all have kids, she thought, kids with a natural craving for freedom, the desire to be at the mercy of forces they can't explain. Rebecca and Heimo sat down together on the edge of a bowl, their legs dangling, and watched a loan skater, a boy of about seventeen, attempting to master a 5-o grind.

'Remember how good Luke was?' she said. The movement of the youth's arms and the quick pop of his shoulders as he took flight were so recognisable. She, Luke and Heimo had spent hours in the skate park together. Rebecca could recall every inch of every bowl, ramp and graffitied wall.

'You were no slouch yourself.'

'Luke was better than me, much better. He was bold ...'

'Graceful,' Heimo added. 'I was always amazed when I watched him. He could do things I didn't think possible.'

Luke had put together his own boards, buying the decks, trucks and wheels that suited him and assembling the pieces in the garage. Rebecca remembered that when he was working on them, he had a level of focus and absorption she wasn't to encounter in another man until Joe. By the time she left home, she reckoned he must have had more than fifteen skateboards. Her dad threatened to throw them out, but he never did. They were works of art, Luke had said. It would be a crime.

'Luke had an amazing combination of talents,' Heimo said. 'He was remarkable. I envied him for a long time.'

Rebecca had never heard Heimo discuss Luke in this way, with such admiration. It was the way of males, she supposed, especially males from a small town. To keep their affection concealed was the safest course of action.

'I miss him, Heimo,' she said, staring at the young skater.

'Me too.'

Luke came to the back door and banged on the fly screen, his guitar slung over his shoulder and across his back. It was late afternoon. He was carrying a six-pack of beer. When Heimo opened the door, Luke threw the butt of his cigarette on the lawn and stubbed it out with his heel. He entered with a nod and reached for Heimo's hand. Not a handshake, exactly, more of a fist bump. They usually jammed at Luke's house, in the garage, but his parents were having a dinner party that evening.

'I've set everything up in the lounge room,' Heimo said. 'Mum and Dad are at the restaurant. We can make as much noise as we like.' He gestured to the beer. 'Do you want one now?'

'Nup. I'll wait 'til we're finished.' Even though he was only sixteen, Luke never had any problem buying beer. No one ever asked him for ID.

They jammed for almost three hours. When Heimo was at a piano rather than a keyboard, he was better at improvising and Luke did well at keeping up. Luke couldn't read music, but he had an excellent ear and could easily create riffs and melodies behind Heimo's improvisational solos.

At six o'clock Luke stopped. 'That's it, man.' He stretched his fingers and ran his hands through his hair. 'It's all sounding a bit Billy Joel.'

Luke didn't converse. There was no chitchat. He didn't joke about teachers or kiss and tell. He asked serious questions then evaded those asked of him. But he was honest, Heimo believed. Genuine. If Luke couldn't tell the truth, he would rather not answer the question at all. He'd offer the faintest of smiles and an almost imperceptible nod; a signal to move on. But he was interested in people. He was always digging.

'What's Rebecca doing tonight?' Heimo stared at the bottle in his hand, hoping his query seemed innocent.

Luke shrugged. 'Dunno.' He drew on his cigarette and carefully ashed it into an empty bottle balanced on the veranda rail. 'You should ask her out, mate.'

'You wouldn't mind?'

He shrugged one shoulder then reached for another beer. He opened it, took a long swig then focused his attention on the stars. It was getting cold. The boys were silent for a long time.

'Tell me something,' Luke said suddenly, 'that you've never told anyone. A secret.'

Heimo had just finished his third beer. 'Like what?' He was feeling reckless enough to answer.

'Well, I don't want to hear that you're in love with my sister. That's no secret.'

Despite the chill, Heimo felt the heat rise in his cheeks and he was glad it was dark. He thought for a while. Should he play Luke's game? He considered how he should respond.

'You go first.'

Luke raised an eyebrow. 'Okay.' He shifted and leaned forwards, elbows on knees.

'Every couple of nights I have the same dream. It's a replay of the accident. Me and Becca are at The Farm and she comes off her board. I try to get to her but it's like I'm being weighed down. Every wave that crashes over me pulls me further away from her. When I finally reach her, she's been washed up on the sand and her arms and legs are splayed out, limp and waxy like a rotten piece of seaweed. Her hair is all matted together with clumps of sand. She's dead. Then I get this feeling, like my guts have been ripped out and I start to cry and I can't stop. And I wake up crying, bawling like a kid, with that same hollow feeling inside me.'

Heimo looked at him. Even in the dim light he could see his eyes were bulbous, glistening with the first sign of tears. Instinctively, he moved closer and placed his hand on Luke's arm, squeezing tight.

'It's okay. You did everything you could and she's fine.' Heimo knew the words were weak. Even at sixteen he could see Luke's sadness wasn't going to be cured by platitudes, but Heimo wasn't equipped yet for anything more.

Luke broke away and rubbed both eyes hard with the heel of his hands. He sniffed loudly and began rolling another cigarette.

'Do you want to talk about ...' Heimo began

'Your turn,' Luke rasped. His throat was still thick with grief.

It took Heimo a minute to gather his thoughts. Luke had set the stakes very high. Heimo had never confronted tragedy or death. As an only child, he'd been cared for by doting parents, pampered even. He searched his mind for a family misfortune or humiliation. There was one thing, but the idea of voicing it terrified him. Leaping into the unknown was not a comfortable move for Heimo. He preferred to plan, take time to weigh up the pros and cons. But he valued Luke's friendship. So he asked himself: could he betray one trust to gain another? The risk was exciting. The prospect of sharing his secret with Luke was too tempting. Once he was ready he cleared his throat.

'My grandfather, my dad's dad, was in the army during World War II. My parents told me never to tell anyone here. We'd most likely be run out of town if I ever did. Dad hasn't even kept any photos of him, as though he never existed.'

'Was he a Nazi?'

'Not exactly. No, he never joined the Party. He was a maths student at a university. He was pretty well known in the field, apparently. When the war began, the Nazis recruited him to crack codes, that sort of stuff ... He never carried a weapon. But he stayed in Berlin.'

Luke drew on his cigarette, thinking.

'Why the secret? He probably didn't have a choice. Is he still alive?'

Heimo nodded. 'Some people are pretty small-minded. We don't talk about him around other people. I understand it, I guess.'

Luke nodded and rose. 'I s'pose.'

He gathered his cigarette papers and tobacco and threw his guitar over his shoulder.

'Thanks for the jam. See ya tomorrow.'

'Yeah, see ya.'

Luke made his way down the back steps and out the gate, softly humming one of the harmonies they'd come up with that afternoon.

Heimo tracked his path over the grass in the moonlight, desperate to call him back and swear him to secrecy. But he didn't have the chance. By the time Heimo had processed Luke's reaction he was gone. Luke's reasonableness made him uneasy. He'd just given him valuable information. Priceless cachet.

After all, what did Luke owe him?

The next morning, when the alcohol had worn off, Heimo hated himself. He couldn't believe how stupid he'd been, telling someone his family secret. He walked to school with a sense of dread so massive that he nearly turned back two or three times, expecting Jamie, Nev and the others to greet him with the Nazi salute or call him Hitler Junior. He thought his family would be run out of town. But nothing happened. Luke didn't tell a soul.

ONCE THEY HAD FINISHED EATING, Rebecca and Heimo lay on their backs on the grass in a park surrounded by tall concrete apartment blocks. Exquisitely manicured gardens skirted the edges of the green space. Staring at the square of faded blue above them, Rebecca could just sense the soft hairs on Heimo's arms against her skin. She should feel trapped, it occurred to her, in this prism. But the sweet, spicy scent of the lilacs was completely unfamiliar, and a wave, a sudden emancipated rush overcame her. In this hollow with Heimo by her side, she could be absolved of anything. She sat up and hugged her knees.

'I can see him,' she began.

Heimo propped himself up on one elbow and looked at her in enquiry.

'I can see Joe. I've spoken to him.'

'In a dream?' he asked.

She shook her head. 'It began with his voice just after the funeral. Then he just materialised. I can't touch him or smell him. But I see him, and he talks to me.'

She breathed in the lilacs once more.

'Do you want me to be a friend or a doctor now?'

She shrugged. 'Both.'

He gazed at the sky for a minute. The sun was just beginning to wane and the oncoming darkness tinged the cloudless expanse with indigo.

'I think you should see someone, probably a psychiatrist. I can't make a diagnosis. I'm too close to you. You've just gone through a massive trauma – Joe's death followed by the news of Karina ... the hallucinations could be a reaction to your grief or the discovery of Joe's double life, I'm not sure. But a doctor would help you find out.'

The idea terrified her.

'I'll think about it.'

***

HEIMO TOOK her hand as they walked back to the hotel. Teenage desires began to resurface, too strong to be dampened by the good sense that comes with adulthood.

'When you were talking about your writing this afternoon, I saw the Rebecca I remembered. There was a glow or a glimmer or ...'

'You told me once I lit up,' she said.

He glanced at her, amazed she recalled that evening when they'd eaten pizza and played records.

'We never got to kiss.'

'But we got close.'

They stopped at the Jet d'Eau and raised their heads, watching the illuminated spurt reach into the sky. They moved closer and their fingers entwined then they laughed together.

HEIMO COULDN'T SLEEP. Restlessness wasn't the culprit. He glanced at his watch – 3:03 am – then rolled towards Rebecca who was sleeping deeply, serenity washing over her face in waves. There was a faint flicker behind her eyelids. Dreaming, he could tell. Sleep analysis played a large role in his research and he was well accustomed to the signs, both peaceful and predatory.

Gilded from the lamplight in the living room, Rebecca's face told no stories. She had insisted that the lamp be left on when he had moved to darken the room. She had been adamant. Heimo found this interesting.

The first time they made love that evening it had been desperate and furious.

'Making up for lost time,' Rebecca had said as she curled into the crook of his arm afterwards.

'That was the result of more than twenty-five years of pent-up teenage lust,' he'd answered. Then they dozed.

When they rolled towards each other again, it was more thoughtful. They took the opportunity to explore, taste and touch one another. Heimo adored the sound she made when she finally came. Soft, low, private moans – the refrain of utter pleasure.

Now he wanted to examine her face as one might that of a sleeping baby, pore over her long, light eyelashes and the delicate curve of her lips. Heimo had done this with his children often, equally amazed at the softness of their downy cheeks as with the power of sleep on an infant – so needed, necessary and relished. Some people call it the sleep of the dead. Although he'd wanted to look at her this way before now, he'd been reluctant while she was awake, worried Rebecca might see the comparisons he was making.

She was beautiful still. She and Luke had been the golden children, sharing the same cat-like eyes and high cheekbones. Their mouths were different, he remembered. Luke's lips were straight and set firm, but it always seemed to Heimo that Rebecca's were fuller and more elastic. She could quirk her mouth in amusing and exciting ways when the mood struck her. She still could. As an adolescent, then a teenager and then, briefly, as a man, Heimo had made Rebecca the source of every sexual fantasy. How many times, he wondered, had he imagined her next to him like this, naked?

Thin lines jutted from the corners of her eyes and mouth now when she smiled and her skin was slightly mottled. The normal signs of aging. Experience had changed and matured her. Even back then, when they were teenagers, there were volumes to read behind her pale blue eyes. Now there was even more. Rebecca remained elusive. Unlike the other girls in town, she had always been slightly guarded. Heimo was certain she was still holding something back. Luke had shared this trait. Both were impossible to define or pin down.

Heimo wondered what Luke would have looked like at forty-seven. Weathered? Certainly. Damaged from drink and drugs? Probably. Cracks and fault lines were beginning to show when they'd last met. But how magnificent he was, once. To be his friend was really something. How pleased he was when Luke had come to his house to jam.

Searching for sleep, Heimo lay on his back and took Rebecca's hand. She stirred slightly, a soft murmuring in her sleep.

REBECCA WOKE in Heimo's bed, a coil of his hair twisted around her finger. While he slept, she admired his handsome face in the stray beam of moonlight stretching through the gap in the curtains.

She kissed him and he opened his eyes. He took her into his arms and held her close. Undressed, they clung to each other tightly beneath the covers, his fingers tracing each vertebra of her spine. Questions didn't surface in her mind. It all seemed so right, so natural. She needed this closeness, to be stripped raw, all pretense lost, every inch of skin tingling with desire.

Rebecca closed her eyes, recalling the bliss and relief of their first connection, then later the feeling of plunging head-first into the foam. Phosphorescent bubbles had skimmed her entire body, eventually swathing and masking mind and body, the sensation bracing and replenishing.

Relaxed, she hovered in the void between wakefulness and sleep.

'Becca! You still there?'

'Yeah.' She stood, peering over the edge of the bluff.

Luke came into view on the rugged path leading up from the surf. He dropped his board and sunk to the grass, lying flat, skinny chest heaving. They were twelve, but he was smaller than her then. Rebecca looked fifteen and Luke ten. She gripped his clammy arm.

'What's wrong?' he asked.

'I was scared, Luke. I mean, really scared.'

She had waited for almost two hours for Luke to appear, her insides churning like the sea below. Shaking wildly in the stiff on-shore wind, she had wrapped his towel around her shoulders. It had made no difference.

He rolled over and wiped his face with the corner of the towel.

'Scared I'd die?'

Luke had been dared by Nev Bramble to surf the Boneyard, a volatile surfing spot only for the experienced or rash. Her father called the Boneyard a 'monster's mouthful'. He reckoned a hungry sea creature had taken a bite off the coastline thousands of years ago, leaving behind a narrow inlet lined with sharp basalt shards. The currents surged in all directions and white spray obscured those on boards from above.

He stood and began peeling off his wetsuit, then threw the soggy heap into her worried face.

'You were just feeling what I was, retard.'

'You were that scared?'

He nodded.

'Then why'd you do it?'

'I didn't have a choice.'

Rebecca felt a hand on her arm.

She opened her eyes, expecting to see Luke. But it was Heimo who'd woken her.

'You were talking in your sleep,' he said.

She rubbed her eyes.

'I was dreaming about Luke. I never dream about him. It was so vivid.'

Rebecca nestled into Heimo again. He stroked her arm softly then she rolled towards him and kissed him on the mouth.

'I like being here with you, like this. I don't want Luke to come between us again.'

She had buried Luke so long ago, so thoroughly. *Full fathom five.* But that didn't mean he wouldn't appear in the same way Joe had.

'He won't. We're not kids any more, Rebecca.'

Rebecca wasn't so sure.

Heimo turned to look at her.

'How do you know Luke killed himself?' he asked.

Rebecca inhaled. 'I felt it.'

She paused for a moment.

'I saw it too.'

She straightened. Heimo sat up next to her.

'I was on the tube going home, late in the evening with Joe. It felt as though a wave crashed over me, upending me, knocking the air from my lungs. My thoughts skipped from one to another to the next like a stone skimming across flat water – I could feel myself squinting into the sun as I paddled towards the horizon. I saw my father's tanned, leathery neck, my mother's hands buried in suds in the kitchen sink, and finally me at fourteen or fifteen on a board squinting into the horizon, as well.'

'Luke's memories?'

'Yeah, I think so. I think I was experiencing what he saw when he died,' she said. 'And he wasn't frightened. He was completely calm.'

Rebecca paused and took a deep breath.

'I heard him say "Enough, no more," then felt him slide from his board into the water.'

She knew that no tears had coincided with this truth. The ocean had been a neutral zone for Luke. It wasn't part of this world or the next. For him, dying didn't seem so strange there.

'He wanted to die. There was simply no way for him to live.'

Rebecca began to cry. She had been sure at the moment Luke had slid into the unknown and infinite indigo, he had finally understood what she had known since they were seventeen.

'It was his choice, but I ached for him. Every part of me ached ...'

Heimo put his arms around her, cradling her gently.

'Why wasn't I there to save him, Heimo? Why?'

27

AT BREAKFAST LATER THAT MORNING, Rebecca felt compelled to make light of her mental state.

'So, what's the diagnosis, doctor?' she asked, placing her coffee cup on the table. 'Am I nuts? Stark raving bonkers?'

But she knew it was serious. She wasn't insane but she was certainly 'troubled', and sometimes that was much worse. The term implied an inner turmoil, a restlessness of soul that was impossible to calm.

Heimo took her hand.

'No, but you should talk to someone. Otherwise the hallucinations could persist for a very long time.'

She frowned and stared at their interlaced fingers. They broke apart when the waitress arrived beside them to remove their breakfast dishes. The café was busy and noisy. Sunlight filtered through shuttered windows and onto their table.

'I have a friend, a psychiatrist, who I can call. She's busy, but I'm sure she will fit you in. Her methods are ... different ... but she's good. You'd like her.'

Rebecca bit her lip.

'Why do you hesitate?'

'I'm terrified of what a psychiatrist will find hidden in here.' She touched her forehead delicately. 'I'm worried I might be like Luke.'

Rebecca looked down at the table. She refrained from adding that sometimes she felt like she was becoming Luke.

Heimo, waiting for eye contact, weighed up his next words.

'Luke suffered from depression and drug addiction.'

Rebecca looked up and nodded. She watched as his straight lips curled slowly in that familiar way.

'You're experiencing an entirely different mental disorder.'

Rebecca grinned and gazed into her coffee. 'Bastard.'

REBECCA HAD JUST LEFT Heimo when her phone rang. It was Gerard. He never rang. He wanted to meet her at two. He was bringing his mother.

She asked Paul the clerk to arrange for tea in the salon. Then she waited for the mother and son to arrive. Scanning the bookshelves, seeking out a distraction, she rose and drew out a copy of *Gulliver's Travels* from the collection. It was a French translation, but in her nervousness she leafed through the book anyway, attempting to pronounce the foreign words in her mind. When a young woman entered with the tea, Rebecca started and snapped the book shut loudly. She thanked the maid then took a deep breath, blowing the air out slowly through tapered lips. When she heard Gerard and Karina in the doorway she returned the book to the shelf and took one final breath before turning to greet the pair.

Gerard dominated the conversation as they sipped hot tea. He was atypically awkward in his movements, tea puddling in his saucer as he presented an argument for moving to London. Rebecca's eyes travelled to Karina. She was poker-faced as she brought her own cup to her lips.

When Gerard had finished, Rebecca smiled at the boy in encouragement then cleared her throat.

'If living in London helps Gerard with his loss then it would be my pleasure to have him in my home. If he can somehow get closer, feel more connected to his father ...'

'He is chasing ghosts,' Karina said. Her voice was calm, but Rebecca could see her chest heaving beneath her fine silk blouse.

'Gerard needs to live in the present and move on. I don't agree with the scheme. I won't allow it. And think of Marie.'

Gerard's teacup landed heavily in the saucer, spilling its contents on the tray. Rebecca's face grew hot. She felt like a chastised schoolgirl.

'Furthermore, I'm stunned you would agree, Rebecca. Gerard may look like a man, but he is still a child. What he needs now is his mother, his family.'

Rebecca licked her lips. 'It would only be for a short time. I only want to help.'

'Gerard, wait outside for me, please.'

The teenager did not budge.

'Gerard,' Karina repeated. There was a steely edge to her tone that impelled Gerard to stand and walk towards the lobby.

Karina watched her son leave the salon.

'Gerard left his phone in the kitchen last night. I read the texts you've been sending each other. Gerard's passion, his drive to know his father, I can understand. But your motivation leaves me baffled.' She paused. 'You had your chance ...'

Karina's gaze dropped to her lap at the realisation she'd gone too far and skirted the boundary of Rebecca's own troubles. But the words had their desired effect. *You had your chance.*

The oxygen drained from Rebecca's body. She was in no man's land.

'I'm sorry. That was uncalled for.' Karina rose and pushed back her hair. She circled the table. 'You've been allowed to grieve. You have been permitted to be public. Joe told me not to go to his funeral. He wanted to protect you.'

She paused, rubbing her forehead.

'His final concerns were of you. His final moments were with you. I wasn't allowed to say goodbye. Yet, I'm the mother of his children. Who is protecting me? Who is watching out for them, if not me? I shared Joe with you for fifteen years. I am not going to share my son as well.'

'You've no right to speak about what you can't possibly understand. Joe and I lived as husband and wife for over a decade before he met you. He was never yours to share.'

Karina reached for her bag and placed it on her shoulder, carefully straightening the strap. All hostility and resentment had seemingly vanished and her usual calm resolve swathed her presence once again.

'Yet, he married me,' Karina said, and left the salon.

Rebecca sat in her suite, unaware of the time. The shock of Karina's revelation had jarred her into senselessness. She turned off her phone. She couldn't face Heimo. She couldn't face anyone. But as she sat in the darkening room, swamped by the truth, a meagre spotlight in her mind gradually shone brighter.

'I'm sorry, *mo ghrá*.'

Rebecca sensed Joe by her side.

'Bastard. You fucking bastard. You married her and you told her everything about me, about us.'

'Karina was the mother of my children.'

'You were never one to adhere to convention.'

'Stop being glib.'

'And what if I ...' Rebecca began, looking at him.

'We had tried for such a long time. I just never believed it would happen again.'

There was a faint knock. Rebecca stood and Joe vanished. She made her way to the door. Heimo stood on the other side.

'You've been crying,' he said, stepping into the room. He took her in his arms. Rebecca buried her face in the soft cool cotton of his t-shirt. Heimo led her to the sitting room. Rebecca sat with his arms around her until the room grew dark.

28

REBECCA STARED at the print on the wall. Eva had hung the roving artwork so that it now hovered just above the psychiatrist's head. *Architectural Structures 1925*. A 'perfect example of constructivism', Rebecca had learnt from Wikipedia. The artist was Hungarian – Lajos Kassák.

'It helps my patients focus,' Eva said. 'My first husband was a protégé of Kassák.'

'He was an artist?'

'No, a communist. My husband didn't have an artistic bone in his body. He was a union leader in Budapest.'

Eva stared at the painting again. 'It has a depth of clarity, a sense of order I find extremely helpful. Yet, when you look at it for a long time, it transforms into images unrelated to the shapes.'

'I know. I see a bird. An ostrich, perhaps. The red triangle is its beak and the circle, an eye.'

Eva turned and glanced at it.

'I always see a pregnant woman.'

Rebecca tilted her head slightly.

'Oh yes, the semi-circle is her belly.'

The women smiled at each other.

'Why do you think Karina told you she and Joe were married? After all, she had kept quiet for so long.'

Rebecca had asked herself the same question in Geneva, on the flight to Australia, and every day since then.

'I guess she was sick of being painted as the other woman when, in fact, it was me who was the lover, the mistress, even though I came first. It was the final straw when I tried to take her child.'

'And did you?' Eva asked.

Rebecca's remark had been offhand, uttered to amuse.

'I suppose I did.'

'What drew you to Gerard?' Eva went on. 'Why did you want to "take him"?'

'She had taken Joe from me. Maybe I wanted something of hers.'

Eva raised an eyebrow at her patient's glib response.

'And he reminded me of Joe, I guess.'

Eva flicked back through her notes.

'You describe Gerard's poise, confidence and his love of the water ...' Eva lifted her head, removed her glasses and waited for a reaction. When Rebecca remained silent, she pushed on.

'A living, breathing young man ... a young man you could save, perhaps? Was Gerard a second chance, Rebecca?'

Rebecca opened her mouth to answer then closed it again. She sighed.

'I didn't make those connections at the time ... well, not consciously.'

Eva paused and placed her glasses on her nose.

'Karina's words ..."You had your chance". What was she

referring to? Had Joe proposed to you at some point in your relationship?'

Rebecca shook her head. Joe had never proposed. Marriage had never been spoken of. Rebecca had never seen herself as a bride or Joe as a husband. They shared the same space, thoughts and dreams for over twenty-eight years. They shared one another's bodies. Wedding rings were negligible. But Geneva was staid in its outlook. He and Karina had married because of the children, she was sure. They married so Gerard and Marie could be baptised and confirmed, so it would be possible to enrol them in Catholic schools, so the children had a real father. This is what Rebecca told herself. She would have wanted the same.

She looked at the Kassák again. Rebecca blinked hard several times.

'I was pregnant once. I lost the baby. That's what Karina was referring to.'

———

REBECCA GIGGLED UNEXPECTEDLY *when the technician, Emma, squeezed a blob of gel onto the base of her abdomen.*

'Sorry. It's cold. I should have warned you.'

Joe took her hand and squeezed it tightly as Emma ran the transducer over her belly. Three pairs of eyes stared at the monitor. Rebecca's heart beat furiously, tiny hammers against her chest. She drew Joe closer and he kissed her softly on her cheek.

Emma pressed the transducer harder, twisting her arm and tilting her head as she concentrated on the screen. 'Hiding are you? You wee devil. I know you're in there.'

Rebecca gripped Joe's hand harder. She wanted to be a mother. But what if it was all a mistake? What if the home test she'd done last month had been faulty? She'd heard of it happening before.

They waited another moment as Emma searched. Joe sang memories from childhood softly in her ear. 'A Fairy Lullaby'. Rebecca didn't know the Gaelic words but they were reassuring.

REBECCA WATCHED two pink lines appear on the stick. Her reaction shocked her. She was elated. Unwilling to share the feeling, she turned off the light and sat in the dark bathroom for a time on the cool porcelain of the toilet lid, relishing her selfishness, waiting for daybreak.

When she heard the sparrows, she rose and walked into the bedroom, the test clutched between her fingers. Her heart was light in her chest. There was no way of anticipating Joe's reaction. She hadn't told him her period was late. There had been no easing into the possibility of becoming parents, no preparation. One day they weren't pregnant and the next they were.

She lay down beside him and shook him gently. When he roused she showed him the stick. He squinted, moving her hand away slightly to focus.

'Two lines means you're pregnant?'

She nodded.

'So you're pregnant.'

She nodded again.

Joe had hugged her tightly then kissed her. Arms and legs entwined, they stayed like that for a while, until the sun rose. They didn't speak. When the shadows in the room changed and they knew it was time to begin the day, Joe moved into the kitchen and she followed him.

'How do you feel?' she asked as they ate the breakfast he had cooked. 'You haven't said a word. Are you happy?'

He stopped eating and looked at her.

'I'm so sorry, mo ghrá. I'm waiting. I'm waiting until I can speak without blathering, without crying like an idiot. There's so much emotion in me, right here,' he placed his hand on his chest, 'that I'm worried it's all going to burst out at once, knock you right through the wall there.

'For your safety and for the safety of others, I'm going to attempt to release it a little at a time, all right?'

She nodded. 'Can you say anything now? I want to talk about it.'

He thought for a moment, hands clenched in front of his mouth.

'For want of something more original, you've made me the happiest man in the world.'

'AH, THERE YOU ARE.' Emma dug the instrument in hard. Lying right at the bottom of the uterus was a shadowy kidney-shaped figure.

'There's baby.'

'There's just one?' Rebecca asked.

'Yes, as far as I can see.'

'I'm a twin, you see. Twins run in my family.'

'I see.' Emma searched a little longer. 'No, just one.'

Rebecca exhaled. She hadn't shared her fear with Joe, the real possibility that she might be carrying twins. She had no way of describing the real and palpable dread. Joe didn't know what that meant, to be one of two, half of a whole, always shackled to the other. Even 10,000 miles apart, twins were forever connected through tissue and sinew, blood and bone. How could she raise children with the knowledge of that inevitable devastation?

'That tiny flicker ...' the technician went on.

'Is his heart' Joe said.

Emma smiled and pressed a button on the machine.

'I'm going to measure your baby now.' Two yellow crosses appeared on the screen at either end of the form.

'Eight millimetres. Exactly where baby should be.'

'Can we hear the heartbeat?' Rebecca asked.

'We can try.' Emma switched a knob on the machine and Rebecca heard the furious beat of her baby's heart. It sounded even more manic than her own.

'Loud and clear. Heart rate is 134.'

'Is that good?' Rebecca asked.

'Perfect.'

'And there's just one heartbeat?'

'Yes, just one.'

'You're certain?'

'She's positive,' Joe said.

Yet despite all assurance, Rebecca was never completely confident that she was carrying just one baby. Even at the twenty-week ultrasound, she had feared another child would be found.

REBECCA LEFT Eva's office immediately, without saying anything more. The doctor hadn't attempted to stop her. The air choked with heat and fumes from the traffic and restaurants that lined the street. She walked north along the beach until the sand ran into rocks. Climbing the stairs to the headland, she looked around her. Everything was too light. She needed a burrow, a quiet hole, so she continued along a street. She had no recognition of the route she chose. Away from the water she began to sweat.

Then, just ahead, she saw a church. It was dark and cold, beautiful inside. Romanesque. Rebecca wasn't very interested in churches but she lifted her head now and examined the apse. It depicted a mosaic of the Virgin Mary, radiant and regal. What slender light there was inside the church seemed to collect here and cast an incandescent glow on the burnished image.

Eva was right. In Rebecca's mind, Gerard had been a symbol. He represented Joe, Luke and her baby boy. Taking him, protecting him, offered her a means of atonement.

'I've never seen you pray,' Joe said, lowering himself beside her.

Rebecca learnt all she knew about religion from literature. Her family was Catholic, although not particularly dutiful.

'Childless women are seen as lesser, aren't they? Is that how you saw me?'

'You're comparing yourself to Mary now, are you? No woman, childless or otherwise, can compete with somebody who gave birth to the Messiah.'

Joe could always make her smile. Even when she had been paralysed after losing the baby, he had made her smile. This is how he had survived – through words. Finding the absurdity in a situation had helped him find meaning. Twisting and turning and shaking it like a moneybox, until a morsel of truth fell out.

She wanted to touch him now. Lay her head against his chest and say how sorry she was for it all. She longed for his arm to wrap around her and draw her in.

'I never blamed you,' he said. 'But you changed after we lost our boy. You blamed yourself. You immersed yourself in guilt. I wanted to grieve with you but you wouldn't let me.'

'Half of me was lost when Luke died and the other half died when I lost our baby. There didn't seem to be anything left.'

'But there was you, *mo ghrá.*'

The couple sat for a while then, in silence, as the sun sunk lower in the sky. The apse became even more luminous.

'It changed everything, didn't it?' Rebecca said. 'We just weren't on the same journey any more. Why didn't you leave me?'

'Because I never stopped loving you.'

29

———

WHEN SHE LEFT THE CHURCH, Rebecca rang Eva to apologise for walking out on their session. 'I know your time is valuable. It's just that ...'

'Don't concern yourself,' Eva replied, noting the quiver in her patient's voice. 'Are you alright?'

There was silence on the other end of the line. Eva could hear Rebecca's fast, shallow breaths through the receiver. Concerned, she made a decision.

'Would you be up to coming in for a session tomorrow morning? There's still plenty of ground to cover. Nine?'

More silence.

'Sure. See you then,' Rebecca paused. 'Thank you, Eva.'

———

REBECCA ARRIVED at Eva's apartment promptly at nine. Embarrassed that she had departed so hurriedly the day before, she worried Eva would consider her rude. Although she knew she shouldn't be, Rebecca was concerned about Eva's opinion of her. Over the weeks, she had come to rely on this unusual woman's insights. They felt like stepping stones that could eventually lead her home.

Rebecca waited as her doctor made coffee. The sounds of the ritual – the clicks of the gas stove, the spoons jingling, the fridge opening and closing – drifted to her from the kitchen. Eventually the pungent scent of the dark brew came to her as well.

When Eva returned, she placed everything on the coffee table, leaned back and sighed. 'It's an effort, but so worth it.'

Rebecca smiled and Eva lifted her notepad and pen. She scanned her notes from the day before.

'When did you first realise that Luke needed help?'

Thinking back, Rebecca could recall so many instances where Luke's behaviour should have signalled to her something was wrong. But at the time, in the moment, they had just appeared to be quirks of Luke's character – just the way he was. He had needed help for a long time but, as she sat sipping her coffee, she realised her understanding of that now was hindsight at work.

'I went home in the winter of '96. I was completing my PhD – writing my thesis – and I was having trouble. Not writers' block exactly but ... I had an idea that being home, by the beach would help me. Inspire me.'

Eva nodded.

'And it'd been some time since I'd seen my family ... seen Luke. I realised I missed him. We'd had a few conversations that year that made me think we might be friends again. It felt right to go home and see if that was true.

Rebecca saw Luke through the window as the train arrived at the station. Wearing board shorts and thongs, his only concession to winter was a light-blue track top. The hood was pulled over his head. She'd been sleepy during the journey from Central, sleepy and apprehensive, but on seeing him there waiting for her, she was instantly enlivened. She surprised herself by being glad to see him.

After the debacle of her first visit home, she hadn't spoken to Luke for months. Finally, her mother had insisted they try to make peace, 'for her sake'. Since then, they'd talked a bit by phone. There were times when Luke made little effort, but there were other times when things were easier between them. She felt as though they were making a little progress together. She'd been back once or twice, but had kept it short and had avoided Christmas. It seemed to work better that way.

She'd been focused on her thesis this year but she'd come to a point where things had stalled. She needed a break. Joe was busy with his writing, so she thought maybe a change of scenery – a trip home – might be the thing to kick-start her brain again.

Stepping off the train, she walked along the platform towards Luke. He rose from his seat and approached. When they embraced, Rebecca felt a charge, a heady rush of love and regret, hatred and yearning – the desire to go back and change it all. They held tight until it hurt, a broken bone knitting together. When they parted they wiped their eyes.

Once they were in Luke's car, a battered green Valiant, a necessity gripped her to see him completely and Rebecca stripped the hood from his head.

'What are these about?' she said touching his dreadlocks, massaging the coils and knots between her fingertips. They were the same texture as sheep's wool.

'They just happened.'

She laughed and nestled her body into the warm worn leather of the car seat. Luke didn't ask her about the flight or the movies she had watched. He never wasted words. Rebecca closed her eyes, listening to the rumble of the tyres on the bitumen.

'Why doesn't Joe ever come with you?' he asked after a few minutes.

She opened her eyes and stared at the road ahead.

'He's busy. He can't afford the time off.'

From the corner of her eye Rebecca noticed Luke's mouth twitch. She could almost read his thoughts – how could a poet not afford to take time off?

'He's busy teaching and writing – earning money.'

Rebecca immediately regretted her final statement. Still twenty kilometres from home and she was already building defences. Luke was silent for a minute.

'Do you ask him?'

A flurry of lies swept across her thoughts like litter across a deserted street. Then Rebecca turned her body in the seat until she faced him.

'No, I don't. The truth is, I don't want him to come.'

Luke nodded and looked in his rear-view mirror.

'Mum's telling everyone you're going to be a doctor.'

'I'm doing my PhD. I'll be a Doctor of Philosophy.'

'Someone oughta tell her.' His smile cut the tension.

'You've got to write a thesis, yeah?' Luke asked after some thought.

Rebecca raised an eyebrow.

'I saw Heimo last year. He came home for Christmas. He's doing one too, something about the brain.'

She looked out the side window, working hard to stifle her interest.

'What are you doing yours on?'

'Weather and symbol in literature.'

'Like in The Tempest.'

She glanced at him in wonder.

'Yeah. Exactly like that.'

Her brother was a living contradiction. She couldn't remember Luke being present in any of Mr McDermott's English classes. Skiving off was the only subject he excelled in at high *school. But he must have been there sometimes, slouching in the back row between Nev and Stevo. Knowledge had leached in, despite his best efforts.*

'Fuck. How'd you get so smart?' he asked.

'Same way you did, I suppose. It's in our genes.'

Luke slid a tape into the deck. Bon Jovi. When 'Living on a Prayer' came on, they wound down the windows and sang out loud until their throats were hoarse, all the way to their parents' house, their hair streaming around their heads.

---

*R*EBECCA *GLANCED up from her meal at the woman seated next to Luke. She knew her from town. She was a local but she hadn't known her name until tonight. Holly.*

Holly looked at Luke continually throughout the evening with the concentrated gaze of a true believer. She was older than him, in her late twenties, Rebecca guessed. She didn't seem like a Holly, with her dreadlocks bunched together at the crown of her head like a whale's spout and her heavy breasts hanging low under a 'Free Tibet' t-shirt. Rebecca imagined all Hollys to be petite and glamorous, like Holly Golightly with sleek black hair and little black dresses. This Holly had placed her two children at a card table in the corner.

'How's your tea, kids?' Holly said, over her shoulder. 'Isn't Nanna's meatloaf yummy?'

Rebecca shot a look to her mother who raised her eyebrows in grim resignation. Kai, who was ten, looked at his mother through a tangled fringe without expression. His little sister, Sasha, didn't respond at all. Tomato sauce stained her face and the tie-dyed dress she wore.

Rebecca's father remained silent, focused on his dinner, attempting to shut the scene out.

'Luke and I hated it when Mum sat us at that table when grown-ups came for dinner,' Rebecca said.

Kai shrugged. 'It's alright.'

'What do you do, Holly?' Rebecca asked. She had been back in Gerringong a fortnight. This was the first time she'd met Luke's latest girlfriend.

'Nothing much. I'm on the single mother's pension,' she said, as though that was all the explanation required. But Rebecca nodded, waiting for more.

'I take care of the kids, of course, and your brother needs a lot of taking care of.' Holly laughed, glancing at Luke. His eyes were heavy and his food untouched.

Finishing his dinner, her father scraped up the final remnants of sauce, gravy and mashed potatoes with a dinner roll. He rose and pushed back his chair.

'Come on, kids. Let's check on Sharky.'

Sharky was Luke's dog, a Kelpie puppy, currently confined to the garage. The children leapt to their feet.

'Put your shoes on,' he said.

'They didn't wear any,' her mother said quickly to forestall embarrassment, forcing a carefree smile, attempting to pretend that going barefoot in July was the most normal thing in the world.

Her father shook his head. 'Right then. Come on.'

They followed him from the room. Rebecca began to clear the table with her mother, stacking plates and pinning glasses between her fingers. When she entered the kitchen, her mother was filling the sink. She turned, wiping her hands on a tea towel.

'Don't criticise, Bec,' she said quietly. 'She's streaks ahead of the others he's been with. Holly's had it rough and it shows, but she really cares about him.'

Rebecca sighed, disappointed with herself. She had been about to criticise.

When she returned to the dining room, Luke and Holly were huddled together. It was a lovers' pose. Rebecca stopped in the doorway and looked at her feet. Holly stood, grabbing her plate.

'I'll help your Mum. I love washing up.'

Rebecca laughed too loudly. 'Nobody loves washing up!'

'I do,' Holly said, exiting the room.

HOLLY LEFT AFTER DINNER, not waiting for dessert. She hurried the children out the door and into Luke's car. Rebecca believed she was responsible; she shouldn't have laughed at Holly, it was arrogant. The sight of them together made her react ... but why? Who was she to judge, or to think that Luke could do better? After Holly had driven off, Mum served lemon delicious. It was the twins' favourite pudding.

Rebecca had just gotten into bed when there was a knock at her door. Luke pushed it open and leant against the doorframe. He was holding Sharky in his arms.

'Holly was nervous about coming tonight.'

Rebecca closed her book and held her arms open for the puppy.

'She's worried she wouldn't measure up,' he explained, passing the tiny package to his sister.

The dog's coat was so fluffy it seemed electrified and his erect triangular ears appeared too big for his head. He was perfect. Even the large tan patch over Sharky's right eye was skillfully executed. An artist couldn't have conceived of a more picture-perfect puppy. Rebecca let Sharky lick her face, laughing as she struggled to push him off.

'She's got nothing to measure up to. I'm not competition.'

Luke shrugged and sat on the end of her bed, the same single bed she'd slept in since she was ten. She and Luke could fit together in it then, front to back, locked together like puzzle pieces.

'She thought you were making fun of her. That's why she took off.'

'I wasn't,' Rebecca said. 'I really wasn't. I was nervous too, I suppose.'

Rebecca sat up and crossed her legs. Sharky curled up in the diamond between her thighs and nestled into the snug hollow.

'Do you love her?'

Although it was unintentional, Rebecca felt terrible about her treatment of Holly. She suddenly wanted Luke to love her.

'No. But she's nice and doesn't make demands. And the kids are fun to have around. I'm teaching Kai to surf.'

Rebecca frowned, dissatisfied with his answer. Is that all he hopes for? she wondered. Doesn't he want real love? Surely it was a basic element of survival. In her mind, it was as fundamental as food and shelter.

Joyce walked down the hall outside the bedroom and Sharky's ears pointed. The puppy leapt from the bed and onto the wooden floor, his legs splaying out, belly flat to the floorboards for an instant. Then he found his feet on the slippery surface and bolted through the crack in the doorway.

The twins laughed. Luke glanced at Rebecca's bare legs.

'What are they?' he asked, pointing to the eight-inch-long scars on her inner thighs. Four on each leg, a centimetre apart.

Rebecca slipped her legs beneath the sheet. 'Nothing.'

'Show me.'

'No.'

'Show me.'

Rebecca slid the sheet off her legs, opening them slightly. Luke examined the ghostly marks. They were almost translucent now and thin, like thread. She had cut so carefully. He frowned.

'When did you do that?'

'After school. Before I moved to London.'

'Why?'

She shrugged. 'I was sad, I suppose. I could feel you so strongly in those months. It was killing me.'

Luke leant in and went to touch the scars. Rebecca pushed his hand away.

'Let me.'

She nodded. He brushed four fingertips lightly over the neat rows as though strumming a guitar. Then he ran a delicate finger along each scar like a blind man reading braille. Sharp remnants of long ago resurfaced then instantly dulled against the stroke of Luke's fingers. Rebecca closed her eyes. She felt Luke slide closer to her along the bed, so close she could sense the warmth off his skin and the sweet, tangy scent of his breath.

'Do you want me to make up your bed, Luke?' Joyce called from the living room.

Rebecca's eyes shot open and she pulled up the sheet, suddenly ashamed. Luke was staring at her.

'I'll sleep in the swag in the backyard, with Sharky,' he called back, without taking his eyes from his sister's. He offered her an arch smile that quickly disappeared.

'Goodnight,' Rebecca said after a moment. 'I'll see you in the morning.'

He rose to leave.

'I read your book. I liked it. Reading it made you seem close.'

30

____

'THANKS FOR COMING, HOLLY,' Rebecca said. 'What would you like? My shout.'

Holly pulled out her chair and sat.

'Just a coffee.'

'What sort? A cappuccino?'

She had sensed Holly's reluctance to meet down the phone line that morning. It would be difficult to arrange, she'd told Rebecca; Luke would have to watch the kids so Holly could take the car. She'd have to tell him that she was visiting a friend in Wollongong Hospital.

'Yeah, a cappuccino.' Holly hugged her bag, a faded fabric tote, to her chest.

As Rebecca approached the counter, she took stock. Despite their differences, she and Holly could be friends. They could work together to help Luke. In the two weeks she'd been back, Rebecca had seen Luke do nothing except surf and get stoned. He seemed to be living on the edge of survival and he didn't care. Rebecca thought that at twenty-five, he was running out of time.

When Rebecca returned with the drinks, Holly began speaking immediately, before Rebecca had even sat down.

'*You don't remember me, I could see that last night. But I remember you. I was in Year Ten when you and Luke started high school. I left at the end of term one. School wasn't my thing. I worked for a while at the milk bar. You and Luke used to come in while you were waiting for the bus. Luke always bought a coffee Moove and a pack of chicken-flavoured chips. I couldn't believe two people could look so alike. You were something different ... exotic. I looked forward to going to that shitty job because of you two.*

'*Then Luke shot up and filled out and every woman on the south coast wanted him – I even heard my mum and her friends talking once about his "sex appeal" when he was sixteen. They were drooling over a teenager! Christ ... But it wasn't only women. Boys and men wanted him in a different way. They wanted to be like him. His talent in the surf, his sense of humour, the way he could say nothing but still control everybody else – why wouldn't they?*'

Rebecca nodded. Holly was right. Luke had been magnetic then.

'*So when Luke started talking to me at the pub on Christmas Eve, I was a goner, as they say. He was drunk and probably stoned, but I didn't care. It was Luke Collins who was talking to me. It was Luke Collins who had his hand on my bum.*'

Rebecca wasn't certain whether the monologue was intended as a justification or simply a release.

'*I get it,*' *Rebecca said.* '*I know that you care for him. And I'm sorry about last night. I wasn't laughing at you. I didn't want to embarrass you.*'

'*That's alright,*' *she said, placing her bag on the floor.* '*I could tell you were nervous, too. It must be strange meeting your twin brother's de facto.*'

Rebecca hated the term de facto. It was loaded with connotations. Latin was usually such an exact language.

'Luke told me to leave. He said you wanted me to go home. I was upsetting you, he said. That's why I didn't want to come today.'

Rebecca didn't know what to say. She sipped her coffee. It had gone cold, but she drank it anyway, the temperature was of no concern.

'Was he lying?' Holly asked, calmly.

Had she been upset? She was surprised at the intimacy Holly had shared with Luke, certainly. She was unused to seeing him that way.

'It's complicated between Luke and me. We have a hard time letting other people in. That's one of the reasons I moved to the other side of the world. Distance makes everything easier. But Luke is covert. He manipulates and sabotages and I don't think he even knows he does it.'

'He knows. Luke is smart. But, idiot that I am, I love him. I don't want to change him. He wouldn't be Luke Collins if I changed him.'

Rebecca leaned towards her, speaking in a desperate whisper.

'I don't want to change him either, but he needs a job. He needs to curb his smoking and drinking. He should be setting himself up for the future. I was thinking we could join forces ...'

Holly shook her head slowly. 'I was hoping when you came home he might get better. He thinks the light shines out of you. But the other night at your folks' place proved to me that whatever we had is over. We've been together seven months. He's never really opened up to me, but last night he shut me out in an instant.'

Holly smiled in a rueful way like a seasoned gambler who had backed the wrong horse.

'He's good with the kids, but he's fucked up,' she said as she gathered her bag and rose from the table. 'I hope he sorts himself out.'

'Wait,' Rebecca said, placing a hand on Holly's arm. 'I'm sorry if he's made your life difficult, but would you consider sticking around?'

'It's not good for me to be around blokes like Luke. There's been too many.'

Moving away from Rebecca, Holly fixed the strap of her bag across her body, flattening the fabric between her breasts. Then she spoke again.

'You might want to know that a little while ago he saw the GP about his moods. One day he'd be happy as Larry and the next, he couldn't get out of bed. The doc said he was depressed and prescribed antidepressants. But they just made things worse. Side effects. He had night terrors, started sleepwalking. He even began seeing people – "visions", he called them.'

Rebecca's stomach clenched. He hadn't said anything about a doctor or ... he hadn't said anything at all.

'Visions? Of who?'

'You.'

Rebecca looked into her empty cup, feeling sick and confused.

'Like I said, he's fucked up.'

REBECCA WAS in her pyjamas on the back veranda drinking a large mug of tea when Luke came through the gate with Sharky. The sun was rising, its tawny shards just piercing the horizon. She had gone to sleep the night before exhausted after her meeting with Holly and the contemplations that followed, but had woken at two, restless and alert. She couldn't push Luke from her mind. Even now, concentrating on the little pieces of her past that she had missed while living in London, the things she'd hoped would inspire her again – like the pure dewy smell of the *grass and the baleful call of the waking magpies – couldn't distract her from her thoughts.*

'Why do you push everyone away?' she asked as he crossed the lawn.

'What did you say to Holly? She left last night with the kids.'

'I didn't need to say anything. In fact, I tried to get her to stay.'

Sharky jumped into her lap as Luke sat beside her on the back steps and brought her mug to his lips. He finished the cup then tossed the dregs onto the grass.

'They all want more than I can give. They all say, "I want to know you". The expression makes my skin crawl.'

'Luke, that's normal in a relationship.'

'I can't let them in, Becca. I've tried, but how can I explain you and me?' He looked at her, his eyes searching her face. 'Does Joe know?'

Rebecca frowned, hugging Sharky to her cheek.

'Will you tell him about this?' Luke held out his arm, pulled up his sleeve then ripped a plaster off the inside of his forearm.

'Fuck!'

They heard their father in the kitchen making his breakfast. He'd eaten the same breakfast since the twins could remember – strong black tea and four Weetbix with sliced banana. Rebecca lowered her voice.

'What'd you do that for?'

'I wanted to feel what you had.'

Rebecca took his arm and looked at the cut. It was still red and ugly, only just scabbing. Pressing her palm across the wound, she felt the hot, tacky ridge.

'Don't do it again. Promise.'

He nodded.

'Why didn't you tell me you'd been diagnosed with depression?'

'You should have known.' He pulled his arm away from her.

She heard the sarcasm in his tone. Wrong-footing his opponent was what he did best. Rebecca remained silent, waiting for him to peel off his armour.

'We told each other everything once,' she said. 'We shared hundreds of secrets, many of them unspoken. We just understood. Why didn't you tell me?'

She heard his breath quicken.

'Because I don't believe I am depressed.' He screwed his face into a knot. The expression was unfamiliar. It had developed since she'd seen him last.

'Dr Gascoyne checked my ears, took my blood pressure and listened to my heart, then he asked me whether I've been sad for more than two weeks. I said I've been sad for ten years, so he wrote a prescription for antidepressants.'

Rebecca's face twisted, mirroring her brother's. Ten years? she thought. She felt a sudden desperation take hold of her.

'Gascoyne's just a GP and he's at least eighty ... You need to see a specialist.'

'The doctor's not the problem, Becca, it's me. I've been cut in half. And I can screw a million girls and take a shitload of drugs and it doesn't make any difference 'cause the only thing that will make me whole again is on the other side of the world.'

Rebecca began to cry. Her chest heaved under the weight of her burden. She lay her head on his shoulder, struggling to quiet her emotions before her father heard. Rebecca could just detect the smell of the sea in Luke's hair. The familiar scent was masked by the pungency of cigarette smoke. Then she heard him crying too and lifted her gaze. His face was contorted in the effort to muffle his pain.

'I wish sometimes ...' she said, wiping her eyes.

'What? Tell me.' Luke stopped sobbing and put his arm around her shoulder.

'Sometimes I wish I'd died when I broke my neck.'

He gripped her tighter. 'So do I. Then I'd be dead too.'

She could feel his heart against her cheek beating through his shirt. It was slow and strong.

'I just want it to be like it was, when we were kids,' he said. 'Come home, Becca. This isn't working.'

Rebecca pulled away and stared into his light blue-eyes, searching for a hint of irony. But he was serious. She tried to swallow but her mouth was dry. She placed the puppy on the ground and watched him bound in zigzags through the grass.

'It's not working for you, Luke. But I've got a life in London. I can't throw everything away because it's not working for my brother!'

'Brother! I'm more than your brother! I'd die for you, Becca. I'd jump under a train for you without a second thought.'

She knew it was true. She breathed in deeply, regretting her tone. She tried to calm herself, taking a little time to phrase what she said next. She took Luke's hand.

'Will you come and see someone with me? We'll go together and talk it out.' She squeezed his fingers. 'It can be our secret?'

He gave her a look of distrust.

'You'll hang around?'

She nodded.

---

*R*EBECCA DELAYED *her flight home for a month, missing the beginning of the semester. She found a psychiatrist in Melbourne who specialised in male depression. Her parents paid for the doctor, the flights to Melbourne and their accommodation. 'The best shrink that money can buy', her father joked, tempering his embarrassment with humour.*

In the doctor's office, inspirational quotes from Bob Marley,

Mahatma Gandhi and Albert Einstein hung on the walls beside numerous degrees. Luke had three sessions a week for a month. Rebecca was required at one of those sessions each week. They discussed their childhood and their connection, the deep-rooted feeling that they felt incomplete without each other. They covered all the bases; Dr Myer was extremely thorough. Luke began to improve.

They stayed together in an inexpensive two-bedroom serviced-apartment in St Kilda with views of the bay. They got pizza or Chinese for dinner every night. They went to pubs and saw bands and drank too much beer. It was too cold to swim, but they walked every morning along the beach and out onto the jetty.

By the second week, she had begun writing her second novel. Knowing there was hope for Luke spurred her into a period of intense productivity. Her fingers ached when she closed her notepad after the sun went down each day; she was astounded at her fecundity. When Luke was at his sessions with Myers, she'd spend the time at the library, typing up her notes. She saved it all to a floppy disc she kept in her handbag, close to her.

When, during the third week, Luke was diagnosed with psychotic depression, she had held him close for hours afterwards. He told her more about his visions. The truth was, he said, he didn't want to be rid of them.

During their last session, Dr Myer gave Luke a referral to a psychologist in Wollongong, another male who specialised in men's issues. Luke appeared enthusiastic and thanked Dr Myer for all that he'd achieved. He was well on the road to recovery, he said as he shook Myer's hand.

On their last evening in Melbourne, they were both quiet. They went to a pub, but there was a shadow over them both. Of the two, Luke was the most upbeat, talking about the future and how he was going to open his own surf school. The south coast was crying out for it, he said.

Rebecca offered him seed money for his business. She wanted to invest in him, in his future. He took her cheque. It wasn't much because she didn't have much, but she was willing to gamble on Luke.

The following morning Rebecca felt wretched. Sitting at a café on Acland Street eating breakfast, Luke placed his knife and fork on the plate and looked at her seriously.

'You've got to go, Bec,' he said. 'I see that now. You've got to go.'

When she got into the cab taking her to the airport, she was torn in two again. She began to cry as it pulled away from the curb. Luke waved to her from the footpath, stoic. Every sinew in her body was being shredded and the pain only increased with distance. She put on her sunglasses and sobbed quietly all the way to Tullamarine. This was Luke's choice, she told herself. This was the best thing for him. She had to be strong.

By the time her plane touched down at Heathrow, she was optimistic Luke would be okay.

'What happened after that?' Eva asked.

'I discovered much later that Luke never made an appointment with the doctor in Wollongong. He never looked into opening a surf school. He never banked my cheque. I realised too, the therapy had all been superficial.'

She took a sip of her coffee.

'Myer hadn't dug down deep enough into the mire. He never got his hands dirty. Once I left Luke, he became lost again. I should have known.'

31

———

Rebecca sat on the stone wall beneath the yacht club, waiting for Gerard to finish the lesson. She hadn't telephoned or texted. He wasn't expecting her. She read his surprise when he first glimpsed her from the lake. He said a hasty goodbye to his client and ran along the sand to her.

Still in his wetsuit, he embraced her. The cool clammy feel of his cheek against hers felt so familiar.

'I brought you this,' she said handing him a package. 'I asked a friend to put together a few of Joe's things you might appreciate. He sent them to me.'

When the parcel arrived at the hotel, she hadn't unwrapped it to check that every item she'd requested was inside. Angus was meticulous. There'd be nothing overlooked.

Gerard stared at the box in his wet hands. Moisture fanned out from his fingertips onto the brown paper.

'There's Joe's watch which was his father's, his original birth certificate – you'll probably need that one day – there's some first editions of his collections, a few drafts of poems in his own hand ... I don't know,' she said, shrugging.

'You want to get to know him. Perhaps these things will help.'

'Thank you, but I thought we might meet again ...'

'No.' Rebecca remembered Angus's description of Karina as a 'mother bear'. Her bite was deadly. 'I'm leaving tomorrow.'

Gerard was only fifteen. He was mature and sensitive, but in this situation he had no words.

'Joe would be proud of you and you shouldn't be a secret. You should tell people who your father is.'

'Was.'

'He'll always be your father.'

HEIMO TRAVELLED with Rebecca to the airport. He had made her an appointment with the psychiatrist he had mentioned. He had worked with Eva in the past. She was a good doctor and he trusted her.

'I love you,' he said, as they stood at the gates.

She drew him close and whispered 'I love you, too.' Traces of the coffee they had drunk together at the airport café lingered on her breath.

Then they kissed in public, deeply and passionately.

'Goodbye,' he said.

She kissed him again and walked away and onto the plane.

ONCE HIS WORK at the university was finished, Heimo planned to fly to Melbourne to see his kids then travel on to Gerringong. He wanted to spend a few months with his parents. They were in their eighties now. Rebecca had encouraged him to take some time for himself.

Although he had wanted to be with her, support her, she'd insisted on flying to Australia without him.

'Stay and finish up at the university. It's best if I face this by myself,' she'd said, as though heading into battle. 'I know it's going to be big and bloody.'

'That's not necessarily the case,' Heimo had responded matter-of-factly, attempting to reassure her, using the soothing tones of a doctor delivering a terminal diagnosis.

Then she cast him a glance that had made him feel ignorant, as though he knew nothing about her or the human mind. A flaming glint in her eyes said 'this has nothing to do with science'.

He had eventually agreed to let her go.

Although her fear remained unspoken in the days before her departure, Heimo would watch her thinking, watch her dreaming. She didn't mention Joe or Luke during that time. She must have been pushing thoughts of them away, as though harnessing her courage in preparation for what was to come.

She'd always been brave, he thought, as his taxi drove away from the airport. Her ferocity at that long-ago beach party; moving to the opposite side of the world at eighteen; her action in coming to Geneva to face Karina; they all proved she was fearless.

It was only Luke and the memory of him that she was incapable of fighting.

'Do you have a picture?' Luke asked, leaning forward and ashing his cigarette in an empty cup on the coffee table. When he

sat back he placed a hand on Sharky's head, absently stroking the dozing Kelpie behind the ear.

Heimo searched his pocket for his wallet and produced a photograph of his daughter.

'That was taken just minutes after she was born. She looks a bit different now.'

'Three months is a long time when you're a baby,' Luke murmured, examining the image closely. 'Anna.'

Heimo, who spent most of his days in the company of professors, doctors and medical students, found himself relaxed in Luke's presence as they sat amongst the detritus of his friend's ramshackle life. Luke was still handsome, blond and bronzed, still funny and sharp, but Heimo now noticed a weariness about him that had nothing to do with the drugs.

'Yeah, we named her Anna.'

'German, right?'

Heimo smiled. Luke was still switched on despite the cannabis and meth. Each time Heimo saw Luke, he questioned whether he should play the doctor. If nothing else, he could counsel him on his addiction and his mental health. He'd tried a couple of times in the past by suggesting doctors and clinics, but Luke had simply smiled a smile that said 'don't waste your time'.

Anyway, that wasn't his function, he reasoned. He wasn't Luke's doctor; he was his mate. It was a role he still valued, had cherished once. Attempting to play anyone else would only destroy it.

'What's your wife's name?'

'Michelle.'

'Michelle,' Luke repeated, nodding. He adjusted the strings of his guitar, fingers plucking and twisting until it sounded just right. Heimo watched the muscles in his forearms and chest twitch.

'It must be years since you've seen Becca.'

'Eleven.'

'But who's counting, right?'

Heimo resented Luke's reminders of Rebecca. He was happily married. He was a father.

'Surfing much?'

'Every day.'

Heimo rose from the stained sofa and moved to the upright crowding the room, catching a glimpse of Luke's girlfriend sitting in the kitchen on the way. Too thin. Too blonde. Kelly or Carly? Heimo hadn't heard her mumbled introduction. Luke's girlfriends had grown increasingly shabby in the last decade. When he reached the piano, he lifted the fallboard and ran his hand across the keys.

'Has it been tuned?'

Luke nodded and Heimo wondered why Luke – jobless and addicted – would salvage a piano. He didn't even play. It was a battered old Yamaha. The mahogany had lost its gloss, was dented in places and some of the ivories needed replacing, but when Heimo began on the opening chords of 'Bennie and the Jets', he found that it played adequately. He looked at Luke.

'Where did you get it?'

'A mate.'

'Shall we get started?'

'Do you regret not asking her out?' Luke placed a beer on the top of the piano for him.

Heimo loved Luke but he lived in the past. 'Moving on' was a term the doctor in Heimo detested. Until now he could never see its medical relevance.

'I did ask her out. She said no.' Heimo responded clinically, *not looking up from the keys. He had begun playing 'King of Pain' softly, fingering each key with purpose.*

Luke was silent until the second chorus.

'I didn't know that.'

Heimo stopped playing and swivelled on his chair.

'The reason she gave me was bullshit. It was because of you. She always felt responsible for you.'

The moment the words were loose, Heimo regretted them.

'She never told me ...' A strange, unexpected sadness washed over Luke's face. Heimo had never seen his friend look that way before.

'I'm sorry. I shouldn't have said anything. It was a long time ago. Christ,' Heimo continued more jocularly, 'I'm a dad now!'

Luke skulled the last of his beer and placed his hand on Heimo's shoulder.

'Thanks, mate. Thanks for being honest. I owe you. You'll make a great dad.'

Why had he said that? Heimo asked himself now as the taxi merged onto the motorway to take him back to Geneva city. He stared past the driver's head and onto the road and thought of Luke's last moments as Rebecca had seen them. Luke had been tortured. His pain had been so immense he had killed himself, without hesitation.

Heimo's visit had been only months before Luke's suicide. Why hadn't he – a doctor, a neuroscientist – recognised the enormity of his friend's suffering?

Why hadn't he been braver?

32

———————

WHEN THE PHONE *rang at three in the morning, Rebecca knew it was Luke. She opened her eyes and clutched at the receiver, desperate to pick up before the answering machine sprang into action.*

'Wait a minute,' she whispered into the receiver.

Joe slept beside her. She tiptoed out of the bedroom and down the stairs to the living room.

'What's up?' she said, through a yawn.

'How are you?'

Rebecca could tell from his tone that he was holding back. Their last few telephone conversations had ended in an argument because Luke had launched into a paranoid attack on someone he knew before she'd even uttered hello. He was trying to behave.

'Okay.'

She hoped his restraint was a sign of improvement. She wanted to talk to him, tell him her news. It was the right time — out of the danger period, her doctor had told her she was thriving and she should begin telling people. She wanted to tell her brother she was pregnant. Yet, she hesitated; Luke was unpredictable. She didn't know how he'd react. She didn't want to upset him or have him sabotaging her happiness. Not now, when she and Joe were so elated. She'd have to wait.

'How's it going there?'

'I'm having some problems with this woman up the street. She reckons Sharky's killing her rabbits. She reckons she's going to call the RSPCA to have him taken away.'

'Has Sharky been killing her rabbits?'

'I don't know.'

'You need to keep him fenced in,' Rebecca said. 'You can't just let him wander about.'

'Now she's telling anyone who'll listen that Sharky is danger- ous. He's not, Becca.'

'I know, Luke. He's a nice dog.'

She walked into the kitchen, shook the kettle and placed it on the stove. She wished she had put on her slippers before hurrying downstairs.

'Does your place have fences?'

'Yeah. But he digs under them.'

'You need to fix that, Luke. Dad will help you.'

'But what if they take him away?' She could hear the sadness in his voice and her stomach hollowed out.

'I'll ring the woman with the rabbits. I'll explain and tell her that I'll arrange to fix the fences and you'll keep an eye on Sharky until then. What's her name?'

'I don't know,' Luke said.

Rebecca thought for a moment. Sharky was such a gentle dog and always by Luke's side. Rebecca had seen him sit patiently for hours on the beach, watching his master, waiting for the tide to lower. It just didn't fit.

'Is she real, Luke? Is the woman with the rabbits real?'

'Come home, Becca. I need to see you. I haven't seen you in so long.' He paused, but Rebecca could hear his breath, low and deep, through the mouthpiece.

'There's something different about you. I feel it. What's changed?'

She attempted to swallow. He knew.

'Nothing's changed,' she said instinctively. She couldn't tell him over the phone while he was so dark.

'I've just got too much going on here at the moment. I'll be home at Christmas.'

Immediately she began to make plans. The baby would be two months old. She'd take the baby home for Christmas to meet her family. Perfect timing.

'Are you still with Tracey?'

'She left a few weeks ago.'

Rebecca didn't need to ask why. Luke was hard work. Demanding and moody, he gave women nothing in return.

'Christmas is too long away. I'm drowning, Becca. I need you.'

She heard him sobbing.

'Don't cry. I'll be back at Christmas, I promise.'

Rebecca began to cry as well. She touched the mouthpiece. She was so far away but she could still feel him, stronger than ever. Luke hung up the phone first. Rebecca groaned from the pain then sank down onto the floor in the kitchen, still holding the receiver. Joe entered and turned off the gas. The kettle was whistling.

33

EVA LOOKED at Rebecca for some time, wanting her patient to begin. Rebecca ran her eyes over the room, uncertain how to continue. She wasn't being evasive; she was simply stuck. But she knew she had to speak about that time. She'd told Eva she was ready. Very little memory of the birth remained. She had so carefully erased it over the last seventeen years, scrubbed away all traces of her son. One day she was twenty-six weeks pregnant and the next she wasn't.

'I feel as though I've hit a roadblock,' she said. Eva lifted her notebook and replaced her glasses.

'Roadblock,' Eva repeated, writing the word in large block capitals in the middle of her page. 'The term implies there is more ground to cover. Confronting the loss of your child is just the first obstacle.'

Rebecca inhaled deeply, dreading the long journey ahead.

Eva rose and moved to her, taking Rebecca's hand. Apart from the handshake on their first meeting, it was the first physical contact she'd had with her psychiatrist. Her fingers were feathery, with perfect oval nails painted coral pink.

'Your conscious mind, Rebecca, is like a bolted door. I must get past it and into your subconscious. That's where the memories live. Do you understand?'

Rebecca nodded. 'Of course.'

'I believe you've repressed something,' she said, as though it were obvious, 'concerning your pregnancy and your baby's death. It could be an emotion or a specific memory, an incident that was exceptionally painful. As your mind is working to process Joe's death and your discovery of Karina, it has shaken everything up, attempting to slot these recent experiences into the appropriate places. Joe might be helping you repress it or he might be your unconscious trying to uncover it, bring it to the surface.'

Rebecca nodded in understanding.

'I can sense whatever it is stalking me, looming in the shadows. But when I turn to catch a glimpse, it disappears. I can only ever seen the faintest outline. It darts and dodges then hides.'

'Some people describe it as an itch they can't scratch.'

'It's so much worse.'

'I would like to try hypnotherapy,' Eva continued. 'I believe it's the only way your conscious mind will ever let your guard down. We have to sneak in the back door.'

Meredith had used hypnotherapy to stop smoking. She had described the process as meditative, as though she were 'floating in the warm waters of the Caribbean, unaware and unconcerned with the here and now'. The therapy seemed to have no lasting negative effects and Meredith had stopped smoking. Joe had shaken his head in disbelief and muttered, 'That daft cow. Now, why would she want to stop smoking?'

Rebecca smiled at the memory.

'FOCUS ON THE PAINTING – the colours and the patterns. Take slow deep breaths. As you exhale, close your eyes.'

Rebecca surrendered, wrapping herself in the warm and tender lilt of Eva's voice.

The bold geometric shapes and strong lines of the Kassák had grown familiar over the last seven weeks. Now the colours began to blur, and the vivid red triangle and circle began to bleed into each other.

'Close your eyes.'

Rebecca did.

'Now start to relax your body. Begin with your toes and imagine the muscles in each toe switching off, as though a light is slowly dimming.'

Rebecca's mind's eye followed the psychiatrist's deliberate path from her feet to her ankles, knees, thighs and pelvis. Her body relaxed as everything gradually fell away. Soon Eva's voice faded too, and Rebecca was only conscious of the gentle rise and fall of her own breath and the wash of waves against a beach.

'Now you've arrived, explore,' Eva said.

The sand was cool under Rebecca's feet as she took in the extent of everything she had abandoned. The caravan park and the Bowlo behind her were lifeless and grim at first light. Even the mossy rocks at the southern end of the beach, the castles and citadels that she and Luke had imagined once, seemed solemn in the still, purple water.

'Stay where you are but go deeper ... go further.'

Rebecca breathed in the thick, briny air and squinted at the horizon, into a sunrise she had seen thousands of times. Her breathing accelerated as she stared harder into the distance, into herself.

She felt a pull, an uncontrollable force eroding her insides. A cramp, a vast hand clutching at her organs. She grasped her abdomen. Her whole body began to shake.

'Don't leave now, Rebecca.'

Then her vision cleared and everything came into sharp focus – penny-sized crabs darting in and out of holes, a seagull lifted by the swell, a crescent of mourners, a surfboard strewn with bull bay magnolia, her own growing belly, blood on sand. The warmth of it against her thighs made her groan.

Her eyes opened on the artwork and she gasped, as though she'd been holding her breath.

Eva waited a moment.

'Where did you go?'

Rebecca swallowed, frowned then licked dry lips.

'Luke's funeral.'

Her voice was measured, calm even, but her hands trembled.

'A while before, he'd rung and asked me to come home. I was the only person he could talk to, he said. He was so bleak and I was so happy. So I said no. I let him down.

'It was three months later that I got the call from Mum. She told me he had disappeared and was presumed dead. I knew straight away he'd killed himself. I knew I had to go home. I couldn't let him down again, despite the warning from my doctor.'

'What warning?'

Rebecca still gazed at the Kassák, the structures taking form.

'She recommended against flying to Australia.' Rebecca inhaled and blew the breath out slowly. 'I'd developed placenta previa early in my second trimester. I haemorrhaged on the beach and my son died.'

It was then that the tears came, followed by an ache so great she groaned and wrapped her arms around her belly. The agony was as insidious as it had been that morning on the beach.

'Oh, Joe, I'm sorry,' Rebecca murmured through the sobs. 'I'm so sorry…'

***

EVA MADE TEA. Peppermint. She served it from a teapot covered with a cosy.

'I haven't seen one of those in years.'

'My mother crocheted it. It's all of her that I have.'

Rebecca possessed nothing of her son. There were no finger paintings or romper suits or ill-shaped clay vases. All that remained was her memory of those twenty-six weeks when he lived inside her.

'How do you feel?' Eva asked.

'I'm not sure. Like I've run a marathon, I suppose.'

Rebecca took a cup and breathed in the steam. The grassy scent tickled the back of her nostrils.

'What will happen now?'

'There's an expression in Hungary,' Eva said, loading her cup with sugar. '"The black soup is yet to come."'

Rebecca raised her eyes.

'This is where the hard work begins,' Eva explained. 'This is just the start. You have to learn to forgive yourself – for Luke's suicide, for the loss of your son, and for pushing Joe away instead of allowing him to grieve with you.'

Rebecca nodded slowly, wondering if she was up to the task. It seemed monumental.

'Tell me,' Eva said. 'Why didn't you try again for a child?'

'We did, but it never happened. The doctor gave me a

load of medical reasons why it might not be possible to conceive after the event. But I always thought that a second chance for Joe and me just wasn't in the cards.'

'Karma?'

'Something like that.'

'And your relationship with Joe after you lost your baby. How was that?'

'Strained, initially, for a little while. Then we seemed to get past it. But now that I know about Karina and her children ... When I lost our son, I too became lost, so lost. Joe flew to Australia to be with me, to grieve with me but I couldn't comfort him. I was selfish and, I don't know ... stupid. I was selfish and stupid. I pushed Joe away.'

Despite the stuffiness of Eva's office, Rebecca wrapped her fingers around the hot mug and held it against her belly. Her uterus was still throbbing, sending cramps into her lower back.

'Karina was Joe's choice. Suicide was Luke's choice.' Eva said. Her voice was even but her wide hazel eyes were awash with kindness.

'Is that why you stopped writing?' Eva asked then. 'Was it your penance?'

Rebecca sipped her tea slowly before answering. Although it happened gradually, it *had* been a conscious decision, she supposed. It seemed selfish to engage in the task that made her the happiest when her actions, her disastrous choices, had stolen Joe's child from him and forced her brother to take his life.

Rebecca slid her cup across the table and Eva refilled her cup.

'Yes, it was.'

REBECCA WENT to a bar overlooking a car park near the beach, the water visible beyond. She ordered a glass of wine. Sitting alone outside, she watched as a garbage truck cleared away all trace of beachgoers. Bins were emptied and any overflow was swept into a pile by the expert swish of broom-wielding men in orange overalls. It was so easy for them. So final.

She thought of the expression Eva had used – black soup. What was her black soup? she wondered. She could feel it inside her now, simmering and thickening. It was making her insides churn with distaste. As Rebecca swallowed her final sip of wine, the men hung their brooms on the sides of their truck and moved out of the car park. The hoarse drone of the engine cleared a path through the pedestrians. When the waiter approached her table, Rebecca ordered a second glass.

SLIDING INTO BED, exhausted and slightly drunk, Rebecca could find no stillness in sleep. Her mind returned again and again to the day on the beach and the loss of her son, Joe's son. They had wanted to call him Patrick, after his father.

When sleep finally came, she dreamt of Luke. Images darted around her mind, inviting her to follow. Staggering through a maze of repeating memories – running into the waves as nippers, Luke's fingers plucking the strings of his guitar, his cocksure grin and snow-white eyelashes – she'd loop back on herself around corners and into shadows, only ever reaching dead ends. Then she saw him on the beach at night, still and peaceful.

It was an image of her brother so stark that she woke, struggling for air.

34

Eva was dressed in a floral sundress when Rebecca arrived at six that morning. But her stiff curls were askew and her lips pale, her feet bare.

'Thank you for seeing me so early.'

Without offering a reply, Eva led Rebecca down the hallway. There was an urgency in her usual shuffle. She sat and rubbed her eyes underneath her glasses.

'Okay,' she said readying herself with notepad and pen. 'What did you dream?'

Rebecca inhaled. 'It began as a dream but then it wasn't any more. It was a memory.'

'Okay. Go on.'

'I found Luke on the beach. It was the night of the formal. The music from the Bowlo came to us over the sand. I looked towards the lights and the bodies on the balcony. I was trying to make out Heimo. He hadn't asked me, although I was certain he would. Even that afternoon as I walked past the hairdresser and watched my friends getting their hair and make-up done through the salon's window, I thought he might still ask me. But he didn't. He asked Kathy Leary. Mum told me I should still go, but I couldn't go alone. And Luke? Luke said the formal was lame ...'

Rebecca paused and rubbed her temples, searching her mind.

'"Every Breath You Take" ... That was the song the band was playing when I found him. The water was flat. I hadn't seen it so still in a long time. Mum told me that night that I had to let Luke know I was going to London. I couldn't put it off any longer, she said. So I found him on the beach.

'I showed him the letter from the university and he read it. It was only a page. Two brief paragraphs, but it seemed like forever before he finished. Then he folded it carefully and handed it back to me. I remember he kept running his nails along the fold until the edge was honed.

'Heimo didn't ask you, then?' he said.

I shook my head and my eyes filled with tears. Luke placed his arm around my shoulders. 'He's a fuckwit.'

'We sat there together for a long time, with me crying quietly and Luke softly humming each new song that came to us across the sand. I'm not sure how long we sat there like that. Seconds, minutes ... it might have been hours. But soon Luke began to cry as well. I heard him sniff and I turned to him. A big fat tear rested on his cheekbone, on a precipice, and glistened in the moonlight. What were we crying about? The past and the future. It was the end of everything we knew. We were scared and lonely. Luke especially; I realised that even then.

'He still hadn't said anything about the letter and I didn't want him to. I felt terrible about going – miserable with guilt – and I knew he could convince me to turn down the scholarship and stay in Gerringong. It wouldn't have taken much. It already seemed like a small part of me was disappearing each day and I hated it. I couldn't think about what would happen when I left … I hated knowing I was losing him.

'So I let him kiss me. It was my first kiss.

'I was wearing a hot pink singlet. I'd bought it at an op-shop in Sydney when I was there being interviewed by the City University people. The interview had gone so well; I'd bought myself a present. It had that famous Rolling Stones cover on it, you know, the big red lips and tongue. *Sucking in the Seventies* was the album. Anyway, I let him kiss me and I remember feeling his hand slide under the strap of the singlet. Hands are so distinctive and I'll never forget the feel of Luke's on that night – warm and firm.

'We were sitting on his towel, a large blue beach towel with white fringing. We lay back on it together. I wasn't surprised when he unzipped my shorts and moved them down my legs. But I knew what it meant. I wasn't afraid but I froze. I couldn't have stopped him even if I'd wanted to.'

'Did you want to?' Eva said.

It was a question Rebecca had asked herself at the time.

'Something had begun years before, something unstoppable like a stellar collision. It seemed to me at that moment that it would be worse to stop. He was very gentle. Very tender. His care reminded me that I loved him. His breath was warm too, like his hands, and sweet smelling. I can't recall exactly. Licorice or peppermint. I think it was licorice.

'He said, "It'll hurt at first, but just a bit." That made me love him even more. And then he was inside me. And it did hurt. I cried out. Not a scream, more of a gasp, I suppose, and I lost my breath for an instant. But then the sting dulled and I let my hips move in rhythm with his, let my breathing align with his. We were one body, one organism. Our eyes never parted. I hadn't seen him so close in years. The pores in his skin, the sandy whiskers on his jawline and the freckles on his cheeks; everything seemed enhanced. Every part of me could feel him.

'I knew it was wrong, but I had to give him that piece of me that nobody else would ever have. I wanted to. It was my guarantee to him.'

'What do you mean?'

'That I would always be his. Because by doing what we did, we shared a secret, something so immense that we'd be locked to each other forever because of it, no matter where in the world I was.'

Eva nodded. 'Go on.'

'We climaxed together and we felt each other so intensely ... every sensation was doubled. It was extraordinary.

'Then I began to shake. Wildly. I don't know why. Nothing was normal. Perhaps that was what happened when a girl first made love. I had no experience. Perhaps the weight of what we had just done hit me. But Luke held me close. He wrapped his arms around me so tightly, I thought I'd snap, but he calmed me eventually. Then we fell asleep.

'When I woke up it was first light. I was still in his arms with my face burrowed into his chest and it took me a few seconds to realise what had happened. You know, like when you wake up from a dream and you don't know whether it was real or not, or even where you are ... it was exactly that feeling. But I hadn't been dreaming.

'A massive sense of dread came over me. I can taste the disgust now. It's still so bitter after thirty years.

'I broke free of his arms, grabbed my clothes and ran. He called out to me, but I kept running to the water. I dived in, swam away until Luke was just a pinprick in the distance. When I eventually came in he was gone. I went home, took a shower and caught the bus to Nowra to see a doctor. It was a woman doctor and I told her that I had unprotected sex with my boyfriend. She wrote me a prescription for the morning after pill. She said I should go back in a month so she could check me for STDs. I never did. I couldn't have gone to our local GP.

'There aren't any excuses for what happened. I wasn't coerced. Luke didn't rape me. I was willing. Luke wanted to own me and I gave myself to him, freely.'

Rebecca stopped. Her chest heaved freely, no longer burdened by the weight of her secret. She lowered her eyes, unable to look at Eva.

'The worst part is, although I knew it was wrong, I liked what I was giving to Luke. I knew as it was happening that there was no way we could ever be closer. Even if I stayed, nothing would compare to what I gave him that night. Knowing that had made me happy.'

Rebecca began to cry, huge shame-filled sobs rolled down her cheeks and onto her lap. Disbelief made her shudder. What had she done? If she hadn't chosen to give herself to Luke, if he had let her be, she might have saved him and her son. Her ultimate act of sacrifice destroyed them both.

When Rebecca calmed enough to speak, Eva placed her notepad and pen on her lap then removed her glasses.

'Did you ever discuss the event with Luke?'

'No. I avoided him. I *fled*. I was so ashamed. I worried that if I stayed it would happen again. So I moved away to Nowra and then to London. I guess I thought that if I didn't see him, we couldn't talk about it. When I did see him, he never mentioned it. I think he was content with knowing he had been my first, that he owned me in that way.'

'Is that when you began self-harming?'

Rebecca nodded.

'It began when I was in Nowra. It started as punishment, then it became much bigger than that. I could feel him so acutely then. Him missing me, him wanting me. The physical pain of cutting myself made everything else seem less painful. Does that make sense?'

'Yes.'

'Then somehow, when I began university and met Joe, the memory of that night faded. In fact, it grew so faint that I no longer thought about it. I never told Joe. He didn't even know I had a brother until we moved in together and he found an old photo album of mine. He asked me once about the scars on my legs. I said I had self-harmed for a while, when I was a 'troubled' teenager. I didn't explain it in detail. After all, it wasn't unheard of then.

'But that night never faded for Luke, did it? I realise that now. He clung to it like a life ring. And I suppose it never disappeared entirely for me. It not only bound us together physically, but it was as though we'd colluded in something criminal. We shared a secret, but it was a horrible secret.'

Rebecca drew in a deep breath, but it didn't help. She began to sweat then cry, and then she grew cold, so cold she began to shiver and her voice rose to a helpless, frantic pitch.

'I just feel if that night had never happened, everything would be different. Luke would be alive, my baby would be alive and I would have been enough for Joe. I gave part of myself to Luke on the beach that night and I was never whole again. I loved Luke with everything I am, and it still wasn't enough.'

Rebecca could barely sit still. She felt as though her mind was breaking apart from the pain.

'And there we have it,' Eva said.

Rebecca tried to focus on her.

'The answer to my very first question: *how* did you love your brother? With everything you had, with all that you were. You left yourself with nothing, Rebecca. That's where your sadness and your frustration lie.'

Eroded by all she had uttered, by Eva's words, Rebecca felt bile rise into her throat. She hurried to the bathroom. When she returned, she drew a tissue from the box next to her and wiped her mouth.

'Are you alright?' Eva said, handing Rebecca a glass of water.

She nodded and sipped the cool liquid. While speaking to Eva, she had stood outside herself. It was the only way she could draw the memory to the surface. Now that she was present again, she felt raw. With the truth finally out and all pretence stripped away, what was left?

'Shame, guilt and regret are horrible emotions, destructive emotions,' Eva said. 'But you are whole without Luke, without your baby and without Joe. You're a complete person, slightly shattered, but all the pieces are there. You just need to rebuild. There is immense scope for growth after tragedy and loss.'

Rebecca rose and moved to the window. She watched a trio of teenagers make their way down the laneway, heading home after a big night out. To pull herself together, tighten all the threads, seemed like a herculean task. She was not only shattered, but scattered as well: there were parts of her on Werri Beach, on the steps of St Paul's Cathedral and in Geneva. What would she leave in Bondi? she wondered.

'I can help you to achieve that – a rebuilt self,' Eva said. 'But I think it would be better if you went home for a while.

Rebecca faced her.

'To London?'

'To Gerringong.'

Rebecca worried she would crumble even further if she returned to face her greatest fears. There was a certain comfort in evasion. As she stood at the window assessing her options, she heard Eva flicking through her notes.

'"Shit-scared but fucking fearless",' the psychiatrist read carefully, pronouncing Luke's words in her throaty Hungarian accent. Rebecca smiled.

'And Heimo?' Rebecca asked. 'It should have been him. How can I tell him?'

'Secrets are never good in a relationship.'

She frowned. How *could* she tell him? How could she ever find the right words to explain to Heimo what she barely understood herself?

'Thank you, Eva,' Rebecca said, finally. 'Thank you for your time, your coffee and your tea. Thank you for your patience and understanding and for not judging me.'

She paused for a moment then looked directly at Eva.

'Thank you for getting your hands dirty.'

REBECCA CRAWLED into bed fully clothed. It was early morning, but she was drained, entirely depleted. Without dreaming or movement, she slept until four. When she woke she made a sandwich and brought it to her table, opened her laptop and began to write. By eight she began reading over her words, editing and rewriting as she went. Each time a new detail sprang into the light – the colour of Luke's t-shirt or the rustle of the spinifex in the breeze – she added in particulars. Heimo would never understand, but he might come close. Rebecca needed to paint an accurate picture for him and for herself. It was the most difficult writing task she had ever undertaken.

By nine she had moved it and a few other smaller pieces she'd been working on into a folder and attached it to an email addressed to Heimo. Her fingers hovered over the keys for another thirty minutes as she struggled to write a message. How could she prepare him for what he was going to read? By ten she decided that she couldn't.

With love. R. X

35

———————

Rebecca held up her open laptop to the window of her apartment and panned it slowly across the view. It was a gorgeous spring day – the sky and the ocean were the identical shade of brilliant azure and the waves rolled lazily, unthreateningly onto the beach where taut, tanned bodies lay glistening under a cloudless sky. Turning the device around, she sat down on the sofa.

'So that's Bondi?' Angus remarked through the screen. 'What's all the fuss about then?'

Rebecca laughed. 'Raining there?'

'Bucketing.'

He grinned, lifting his teacup to his mouth. She heard the scrape of the porcelain against the saucer.

'Oh, I miss you, Rebecca. How's it all going?'

'Good. Very good, in fact. But there is still a lot I need to sort through, issues that will take time. I'm not quite sure what's next, but I'm optimistic,' she finished, glancing fleetingly at the mail icon in the dock of her screen. No new emails.

'Are you happy?'

'I am. I miss Joe, but I'm happy.'

Angus sighed and smiled at her. He was seated at his desk, in his office. He leant back in his chair and loosened his tie.

'I walked past Foyles the other day,' he began. 'I remembered when *Breathless* was released.'

Rebecca nodded.

'Joe and I were with you on the footpath, standing on either side when you saw your books in the window. They were displayed among yards and yards of blue fabric. Remember?' She nodded again. 'It was quite a unique display for its time, but the manager had gone all out. You slung an arm around each of us and threw your legs into the air. You were so happy, so light and free, as though nothing could every touch you again. Do you remember?'

'Of course.'

'I see a little of that now.'

'I've shaken off a lot of things, I suppose, since I saw you last. But I've still some way to go.'

Angus rubbed his eyes. Rebecca stayed quiet waiting for him to speak.

'Is there any hope for us, do you think?'

Rebecca smiled.

'Hope? You are my hope, Angus. We are hope. Our friendship has held strong through it all.'

He nodded, then scratched his forehead, thinking, a little rueful.

'You're not going to wander in the desert, are you, and embark upon a weird Shamanic journey?'

She laughed.

'I think I've done that already, but my Shaman was an elderly, plump Hungarian woman who made excellent coffee.

REBECCA RENTED a surfboard and a wetsuit from a shop on Campbell Parade. She spent the afternoon on the waves. Eva had suggested it as 'part of her rebuild'. She was rusty, for sure. However, she sensed her confidence and sure-footedness gradually returning. When she got back to her apartment, it was growing dark and her shoulders ached with promise. She licked her arm then closed her eyes, relishing the taste and the memory. After a shower, she slumped onto the sofa in her pyjamas and curled into a ball. Her funeral hat, the Swan Darla, sat on the armchair opposite. Hugh had posted it to her at his mother's suggestion. As hideous as it was, she'd decided to keep it.

Rebecca closed her eyes.

She thought on when she had been happiest in her life. Was it surfing alongside her brother on a November morning, giving herself over to Joe outside The Well, seeing her first book on display in the window of Foyles ... or was it standing in a cramped bathroom and witnessing two pink lines form in the window of a home pregnancy test? She supposed that happiness wasn't created by just one experience. It was the result of many.

'You've been on quite a journey, *mo ghrá*. It's no surprising you're tired.'

Rebecca opened her eyes and looked to her left.

'Hello. I thought you might have gone.'

'You've always been in charge of my schedule.' Joe said.

He still wore the Stranglers t-shirt and his thick black hair fell across his forehead, the first sign of grey at his temples. Is this when she and Joe were happiest? Living in a tiny flat in Camden, writing until they were drained, then making love with just as much ferocity? That perfect time had disappeared in a heartbeat. She sensed a sting behind her eyes.

'I understand it now and I'm sorry for what I did. I was reckless, thoughtless.'

'You're not to blame. Going home for Luke was something you needed to do. We discussed it and we agreed. There were risks, but they weren't overwhelming ...'

'But any risk. I shouldn't have travelled that far.'

'Shhhh. I know you blamed yourself, but I never did. Yours was a high-risk pregnancy. We might have lost Patrick even if you were curled up warm and cozy at home, in front of the fire.'

Refusing to be forgiven, she shook her head. She wanted to wail. She wanted Joe to hate her.

'We all make choices. Some of them turn out bad. But we have to rise over them. Humans have to be more than the sum of their bad decisions. Christ, we'd all be mental cases if we weren't!'

She glanced at him; he was grinning. It was a playful grin she had seen a million times before. She felt the tears on her cheeks and wiped her eyes with the heels of her hands, but it was too late. The door had been opened and they wouldn't stop coming. She cried out, angry with herself, desperate to be held. Then she looked at him, miserably, blowing her nose on a tissue. She took a few controlling breaths.

'Then what about Karina? If you didn't blame me, how do I explain her?'

'Perhaps you can't. Perhaps Karina would have happened anyway. You lived with me for almost thirty years. Did you ever know me to be a vindictive man?

'I loved you and I never stopped,' Joe said. 'I never will.'

'I love you, too,' she said. 'I'm so sorry. I just wish ...' she began.

'I know. Now hush, *mo ghrá.*'

Rebecca felt his arm wrap around her body and draw her in. She pressed her face into his neck. Her chest heaving, she allowed the tears to flow unhindered.

SHE WOKE, still on the sofa, and looked at her watch, but she couldn't see the face in the dark. Joe was gone and her stomach groaned. Wandering into the kitchen, she flicked on the light and spotted her laptop on the bench. Blinking then yawning, she flipped it open. There were five new messages. One was from Heimo. When she read his name, her heart, beating at a frantic pace, moved into her throat, making her instantly nauseous. Sweat broke out on her upper lip and under her arms. Then she clicked on the message. One line.

Come home. With love. H x

ACKNOWLEDGMENTS

Thank you so much for reading Rebecca's story. I hope you found her journey engaging, moving and surprising.

I'd like to thank a few people who have helped me craft Everything I Am. In its various stages of evolution, the manuscript had passed through many hands. Colleagues and fellow English teachers, Bec Markovic and Catherine Jean Krista, read a very early draft of the novel and offered me invaluable feedback on structure and character. My wonderfully talented editor, Sylvia Balog, conducted a full structural and copy edit that enabled me to draw all the loose threads together into a tight and coherent whole. Finally, my friend, Jo Egan (also an English teacher), who has an eagle's eye for detail, proofread the manuscript for me. And, as always, my husband Chris, who read the story at various stages of its journey, offering me criticism, praise and unending encouragement.

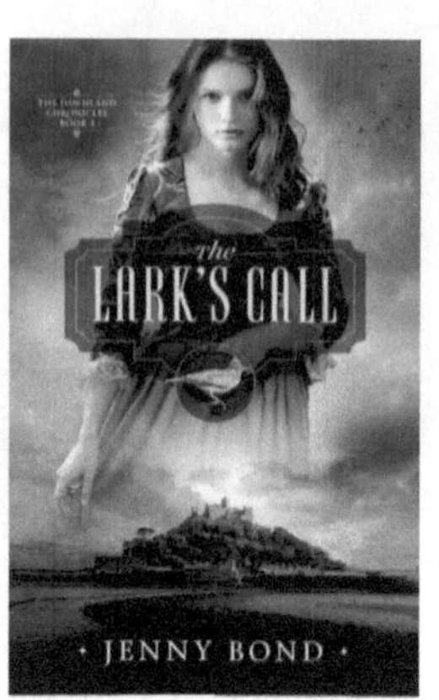
the
LARK'S CALL
JENNY BOND

ENJOYED EVERYTHING I AM?

Thanks for reading *Everything I Am*. If you enjoyed the story, share a review where you bought the book, on Goodreads, or contact me at jennybondbooks.com and share your thoughts.

Get a free copy of the *Everything I Am* short story, *Ocean View* when you sign up for my newsletter via this link: https://BookHip.com/XXGFRLT

You'll also be notified of giveaways, new releases and receive updates of my author journey.

DIVE FURTHER INTO THE WORLD OF EVERYTHING I AM

Check out my *Everything I Am* Pinterest board - images that provided inspiration and information during the writing process.

Listen to the *Everything I Am* Spotify playlist. Music from the novel as well as awesome songs from the 1980s and '90s

---

To access either of the above, on the relevant platform search 'jennybondbooks'.

ABOUT THE AUTHOR

I'm an author of contemporary fiction, historical fiction and non-fiction. I have published my books in Australia, New Zealand, USA and Europe.

I'm also an English teacher and I've been lucky enough to introduce the love of language to many students around the world.

I guess this also planted the seed of an idea that I should give writing a go, myself

Sydney, Australia, is where I was born and raised, but prior to my reinvention as a writer (which had something to do with a friendly argument with my husband!), I held the position of Head of English at Eaton House The Manor in London's Clapham Common. I also taught English and Drama for eight years at a selective high school in Sydney, and for five years at a private girls' college in Canberra.

Whether I've been at home, living and working in another country, or travelling for the sake of adventure, I have never spent a single day without a book by my side. This meant slipping from the act of reading into the act of writing didn't actually seem that much of a change.

I've long been a fan of great historical fiction writers such as Hilary Mantel, but I also spend quality time with books by authors from other genres, such as Margaret Atwood, Kate Atkinson, Tim Winton, Ian McEwan, Jane Austen, John Irving and E. Annie Proulx.

When I'm not writing, I enjoy keeping fit and love to

travel. I live in Canberra, Australia with my husband, two sons, and a lively Staffordshire Bull Terrier named Mick.

I enjoy running, swimming and yoga daily, as I believe staying active is an integral component of a happy writing life. You can visit me at www.jennybondbooks.com.au.

Jenny

Here I am with my lively dog, Mick.